The Turn o

b

Geraint Roberts

First impression 2020

©Geraint Roberts

Cover design: from a painting by Rita Roberts

ISBN:

9781838135812

Foreword

I had just been outsourced to a company. I felt swallowed up, dumped in a corner and forgotten. I needed something else in life.

'Why not write stories?' My wife said. 'After all, your letters made me come over and live with you.'

Somehow, the idea from those words that I could write fiction, gave me mixed thoughts! It did however spur me into the journey I am on now.

I wanted to write about the past and explore aspects of history I had an interest with. Many of which had been forgotten in the way we cherry pick what history to recognize.

This novel was the first project and became the first part of a trilogy; about a family working at the Frongoch lead mine in North Ceredigion. The history of the mine has fascinated me since I studied it at close hand in the 1970s.

Owain is the protagonist and narrator, telling his story, from the day he went underground for the first time. His son, Dafydd featured in my 'railway novels' and there is naturally a degree of overlap with the stories.

The characters are speaking Welsh, but a direct translation would not work, as the two languages differ structurally. I have gone for a Wenglish approach to the dialogue. It's not precise, but it gives a flavour, for the reader to feel the atmosphere.

For this project, I am indebted to Rita Roberts for the cover illustration. It is an artists impression of Frongoch. Some buildings (e.g. the Cornish engine) may not be completely right, however, they are in the right place.

Thanks to Deborah Lea for her editing skills and recommendations.

Thanks to Gareth Jones for another great cover design and Ioan Lord for his support and knowledge. Given his knowledge of the local mines and experience of surveying them, I am encouraged by his enthusiasm for my project. Simon Hughes provided a lot of information and stories in the early days, with his lifelong passion and study of the mining belt.

Jon Guy gives me invaluable support with the website www.geraintroberts.com.

The Leicester Writers Club were so helpful in my fledgling years, setting me on the right path, especially the author Rod Duncan, who also had suffered the snowbound trips to Frongoch and other geology gems thereafter.

I dedicate the book to my late father, Roger Roberts, who looked forward to reading each chapter and threw whatever support he could behind the project.

Frongoch today lies in ruins on a winding road in the hills beyond Aberystwyth. What I studied 40 years ago has crumbled away even more. The site is now private land and residential, so not open to the curious.

Borth

Talybont

River Rheidol

Aberystwyth

CARDIGAN BAY

Devil's Bridge

River Ystwyth Trisant

Frongoch mine

New Row

Cwmystwyth

Pontrhydygroes

Trawscoed Ysbytty Ystwyth

Ffair Rhos

Llanrhystud

Pontrhydfendigaid

Llanon

Aberaeron

Tregaron

Lampeter

Caerdigan/Aberteifi

MAP OF CEREDIGION/CARDIGANSHIRE

10 km

6 mi

© d-maps.com

4

Chapter One

The Beginning

There's a smell down there, you ask any of the boys and they'll tell you. Old ones like Ben Treveglos swear by it. It leads you straight to the lode - if you know how to use it.

There's a taste and all. The dust hangs in the air, from all the blasting. It's like a mouthful of gritty flour. From the moment you step off the ladder it's there in your throat. You'll spend half your life breathing the dust and the rest coughing it back up.

There's a feeling that you're never alone. Something is with you, always. You hope it's watching your back.

There's a bond you have with the others, as solid as the rock you dig. You go through it all together, cold, damp and dust. You make damn sure that you keep your butty alive, for if he goes you may not be far off death yourself. The bond is strong, those who break it live in regret.

There's a struggle to survive and stay whole. You always need to be strong. Keep the ore coming and earn your coin. Each working day, one of toil and dirt and sweat. Of hammer, pick and shovel. Your arms and legs shake with pain as you stagger up the ladders back up top at the end of the shift.

Tuesday the fourth of February 1873 was my first day underground. Dad needed a hand, so down I went. Fourteen year old, I was.

No noise as we all got ready, save the ticking of the clock on the dresser.

Mam put my food in a napkin, Strong woman, my Mam. Dad thought he ran the house, but Mam knew she was in charge for certain. Strong and strict she was, but she knew when to mother and when to crack the whip.

She smiled and kissed my cheek, making my little sister, Myfanwy, snigger.

'What's all that about?' I asked, wiping it off.

'For luck, *cariad*,' came the soft reply. 'So quick it's been. Well, be strong and do your Mam proud.'

'Oh, can I kiss you for luck and all?' Myfanwy said with a giggle. It made me smart.

Dad opened the door and cool, clean air flooded in. The moonlight carved a beam through the faint smoke that was always there in our house.

'What's the matter, *bach*?' Dad said as we all went out and I looked up in the sky.

'It's the stars,' I said. 'Thousands there are, I never seen so many.'

'What you grinning about?' Mam asked, following with Myfanwy.

'Leave him, Rhian,' Dad whispered. 'He thinks he's a man today.'

I tingled with delight and tried to stand tall with my father. He was not a large man, nor a loud one neither, but he spoke with a measured tone and the boys at Frongoch showed him respect.

'Stars are brighter this morning,' I muttered.

'Always bright,' he said. 'Just you never looked proper before.'

We walked on a while then he spoke again.

'They're in groups. Pictures in the sky, the old ones say. See that one straight up? That's the hunter. There's his head, shoulders, belt and legs.'

'Oh yes,' I said, not wanting to miss a moment.

'And them four making a square and three curving off. What do you reckon that is?'

'A *sosban*?' I tried. He laughed and ruffled my hair.

'Not quite, that's his dog.'

'I'm ready Dad, I been waiting years.'

Dad grunted in reply. 'Well, you had to grow a bit. I wouldn't have you a trammer before your back was strong. I seen them that start too young and end up shuffling like old men, when they're your age.'

We had trod this path for years. Me until now in the mill, picking good ore off the tables with Mam and Myfanwy. Today, it was different, I was a man.

Two miles to the mine and the road never flat. Up and down, up and down. We passed Llyn

Frongoch and the reflection of our lamp flickered in the dark waters.

Others were ahead of us for I could see their lamplight dancing in the lake.

Dawn was breaking as we got closer to the mine. When we breasted the final rise, the first rays of sunlight seemed to fall away into a grey wasteland of spoil and buildings. I was getting all nervous by then.

I began to hear voices far off, greetings being hailed. The occasional cough and splutter could be heard, a miner with dust on his lungs.

'Ho! Tomos *Shaneg!* came a shout and my Dad waved the lantern in reply.

'You never told me why Thomas the Spaniard?' I asked and he snorted.

'Well, they know the tale of my Mam and everyone's got to have a name. Besides, I've heard worse. Don't you take no nonsense now, names in friendship is one thing. Anything else and you tell them how it is.'

'Gareth,' Mam chided. 'Don't you be telling him to go off fighting now. Only leads to sin.'

We went on with me wondering how he got to be Spanish, and the mine becoming bigger and bigger before me. My mouth began to go dry with fear.

A small train of lights was bobbing down the path ahead of us, past the great water wheel. Another train in the distance was beyond the giant Cornish engine, the firelight glowing from its door.

A third train of lights could be seen beyond the far side of the mine and the flat wasteland. Past the pool that fed water to neighbouring mines.

Dad pointed to this line. 'The boys will be down there. Ben Treveglos and his son David. Ben said he'd be putting his spare powder in the magazine first. You know David from the mill?'

'Can't remember him. His brother was a nuisance, mind.'

Mam took my sister off to the dressing mill. I started to follow, but she turned me back.

'There's your path now. Besides, I'm just laying my tools ready for when we're done with the *bargenin'*

'Be careful,' said my sister with a kiss that made me scowl.

'Let's go over to Wemyss,' Dad said. 'It's quieter that way.'

The path gained height, so we now looked down on all the buildings. I could hear the rushing of water as the sluices were opened to feed the wheel. As we walked on, it creaked and slowly began to turn, almost in greeting.

We walked above the Cornish engine house, the yellow brick chimney sticking out from its grey walls like a beacon. I could hear the shovelling of coal inside, as they built up steam for pumping the water. For now, it was just adding to the spell that made me tingle with both excitement and fear.

The path dropped sharply and to the left was the smithy. With a quick gaze to the right as we turned, I stopped to take in the dawn scene at the next valley. Falling down the hill ahead of me lay the Wemyss mine, with its massive water wheel that rose above the shadowy figures moving there in the gloom.

The valley ahead was lit up now. On the far side, a circle of grey marked Graig Goch mine. White shapes dotted the hillside, sheep scratching a meal. I was thinking too much of my job to care.

'I love it like this of a morning,' Dad whispered. 'Gives me strength to go down below. Come on, to the counting house.'

'Why do we have to go all the way to the counting house? That's the other side of Pontrhydygroes.'

'It's the last Saturday of the month, *Sadwrn sistans*. So, we get our pay, then set a *bargen* with the Mine for how much we will get per ton of lead. They declare which levels are being worked and we bid for the rights to a pitch. You know this anyhow.'

'Yes, no. I mean why go all the way to the counting house? It's past the village and on the way to Ysbyty.'

'Well my Lord Lisburne has the one place for his business and its not his fault that I chose to live the other side of the mine from it. Got to get there sharp as we can now.'

'Why's that?'

'We got to try and get the best deal when they offer the *bargens*. The best ore isn't always what I want mind.'

'Why not?' I asked.

'The work could be a mile or so down the tunnel. After all the climbing in and out on ladders, you just want the best pitch that will leave you enough strength to get up top at the end of shift.'

'Ben and I have an agreement.' Dad said. 'We like to work together, so with you and Ben's son David, we'll make a pare. Take a few others in when we need, Sion the trammer, Jones wood.'

I looked around as more and more people joined our path as we walked past New Row. Ben must have gone on ahead, I thought. There was less to say for the rest of the journey until we arrived.

I'll go off for the *bargen* now, you stay here and get some sweets or something from the stall. Ho! Ben!'

He went off to stand below a terrace behind the building with the others and I saw a tall dark-haired boy with a hint of a grin approaching. He looked me over. By now, I had got full fright, like being the new boy in school. I was all scowling, stiff as a board and hands balled up.

'Owain Thomas?' he said all serious. 'You wanna fight boy?'

'No.' I stammered.

He broke into a huge smile, all teeth on show, and stuck out his hand.

'Well now, we better be friends then. David Treveglos, man of Cornwall.' He looked around. 'You seen any of the girls yet? I have my eye on some of them lovelies.'

He was nearly sixteen and the first thing he talked to me of was girls. My face screwed up at the thought, which was about the time I felt a nudge in my back. Looking round, I saw a girl walking away, briefly turning to check I was watching her. Long black hair in bunches and mischief in her face.

A boy came over to her and gave me a look of murder. He said something short that the girl ignored as she moved on to the mill.

David made me feel at home. I had thought I would be picked on in my first day, but he talked to me as if I had known him years. Most of his talk was of girls.

'Gwenllian. She's the rose in the garden,' he sighed. 'Should have been Cornish, she's so perfect.'

I had to laugh.

An argument broke out nearby, that quickly turned into a fight. Two miners were giving each other a good belting.

'*Bargen* time is always tense,' David said. 'Especially if you don't get the pitch you wanted. Looks as if one undercut the other. You not been down here before?'

'I was always interested in the sweet stall on *bargen* time.'

'Well, any hint of profit and they all come up from Aber. Like a bloody fair. Here come our fathers - let's see what they got.'

'Well, boys,' said Dad, 'we got a pitch at 78 fathoms.'

Ben grunted. 'It be a mile from the shaft. We do have our work cut out to make a decent return. Too many miners, so the bargen is low.' He sighed. 'Still, we do have a pitch and the lode be fair.'

'Too much quartz for my liking, mind,' muttered Dad. 'Right boy, time to get you kitted out at stores back at Frongoch.'

'I'll take him,' David said. 'I need some bits and all.'

I hadn't the heart to tell him I knew what to do as we walked the miles back up to the mine. He was happy as teacher and I as a willing pupil. Standing with my butty, I began again to feel the strength to face my new work.

'The company sells you kit against future wages.' He said. 'Frongoch is fairer than some, mind. Others charge you for wear and tear on the tram rails and for the pumping of the mine.'

I got a felt cap and tull for my head, candles and hammer, as Dad had told me to. David got a new hand drill, taller than me, and some string. All was marked on account.

That was us done and away back home. We were off the afternoon and, of course, Sunday. Monday was Miner's Day and we were at rest.

If fixing the house and tilling the garden could be called rest. Tuesday morning, we were back at Frongoch, all ready.

We caught up with the others at the shaft.

Dad lit a candle and stuck it on my tull.

'Tie up your trouser legs.'

'Why's that?'

'Rats.'

'Rats!' I squeaked.

'Rats.'

The others looked on amused, though I saw no sign of a tease, as we joined the line of pilgrims waiting to climb down.

'Here,' Dad said, handing me strips of cloth.

'Why?'

'Later.'

The ladder was cold to the touch, as I swung over to start the climb. The wooden rungs muddy and damp. I noticed the shaft sides were all clad in timber. They felt as if they were moving closer in on me the lower I went.

My breathing grew shorter, for the tar-soaked timber gave off a smell. The deeper I went, the dimmer it was and soon my candle became the only light in the darkness surrounding me.

The shaft walls were now rotten wooden panels, green at first then black, then just stone. Slimy wet stone. The rungs were slippery now also, so I needed to slow my pace. I began to worry about falling off.

The ladder ended on a wooden stage stuck in the side of the shaft. A hole in the middle had a chain hanging down it. An opening to the side had another ladder leading down. I could hear faint sounds. A man's voice echoed far below singing gently to himself.

'Who's there?'

There was no answer. Another voice even farther down sang in harmony. It sent a shudder through me.

'Who is it?'

I heard boots, echoing as they hit each rung of the ladder. It sounded like the *tylwyth teg* and I was shaking when Dad's head came into view.

'You coming or what?'

Ladder after ladder, down I went to 78 fathoms. Dad grinned as I swung over to him at the tunnel edge. It was not too high, but I was stooping a little, David was nearing a crouch, as we moved on.

In many places, it opened up into larger caves. Miners were setting up for their work, lighting candles on the walls to help them see more.

We reached our pitch and I stepped up from the tramway and looked up into dark nothing. Gently with the drill I held, I reached to touch the roof I hoped was there. I couldn't find it.

Ben marked spots for us to drill, before coming back.

'Our first job, my boy, is to drill our shot holes. You do hold the drill for us with them tongs and we do hammer it in the rock.'

David grinned. 'You'll get a go with a hammer when we have decided you'll hit the drill not the man holding it.'

'We'll each hit the drill, then you turn it one quarter and we'll do it again.' Dad said. 'Wrap the cloth around your hands to stop you getting cold.' Ben raised his hammer and hit the end of the drill.

Bang!

The shock went through my hands and shook my body. I dropped the drill in surprise and they all laughed.

'Not a problem, young Owain,' said Ben, picking the drill up. 'Your father was no better on his first day.'

Feeling foolish, I picked up the drill and tried again.

By the time we broke off for lunch, my arms were trembling with the shock and the weight. There I sat, water dripping down my neck. Cold, wet, tired and half a day still to go. I looked in my knapsack. There was bread and jam and a bottle of water. It was from heaven to my hungry stomach and was gone quickly. I'd already noticed the dust from the moment we hit the first blow. I seemed to eat it and breathe it. If David was anything to go by, I was wearing it also.

David nudged me. 'Don't you worry Owain, the first few days are hell. After that it's just purgatory.'

16

I looked at David, stripped to the waist, muscles all gleaming with sweat amid streaks of dirt and I felt weak beside him.

After our break, Ben left some crumbs on the rocks. I had no idea why - but didn't ask. They'd had enough foolish questions by then. I took up the hammer and David took the drill. They gave me lots of encouragement as I hit the drill, although I must have not helped much.

On we went, changing around so much that the time holding the drill became a rest.

By the end of the day my hands felt like claws, and only four shot holes had been made.

We made for the shaft and I was done in.

'Don't you worry,' Dad said. 'Just take your time. Have a rest on the stage if you need to.'

'How far down is it?' I asked, feeling the cold air blowing from the opening.

'Not important,' Dad said, while I heard someone say. '117 fathoms.'

I gulped and grabbed the ladder. It was all a blur; I could hear hymn singing from the miners as they climbed. The ladder was clammy, and the breeze made me shiver. My hands did not feel like my own anymore and there was a pain in my muscles that wouldn't go away. Each time my arm moved, I wondered if I would fall. On the third stage, I slipped. The world was suddenly clear again and I cried out in fear as I fell. I hit the stage only a few feet below. Dad picked me up and calmed me.

17

'*Hisht* boy, don't worry. We'll take it slow, climb one stage, let a few miners past us then do the next. I'll be right with you to make sure you're fine.'

It took forever, but I finally made the top and crawled to the surface.

I don't remember anything else until being roused for the morning. I could hear my parents talking in my dreams.

Mam was sharp. 'You drove him too hard.'

'Nonsense girl, he's fine. Just needs to toughen up, that's all.'

'Gareth. I not got many left. I'll not lose another.'

'*Hisht cariad*, he'll be fine. Hardest work today, the next few are not so bad, then we're blasting. I'll rest him when I can, Ben will look after him and David… well, he's like a brother.'

The sound of crockery being placed down was answer enough of Mam's opinion. As I roused and got ready, Myfanwy came and gave me a hug. She'd been listening also. She broke away quick and made a face.

'Best you wash tonight.'

'What you on about?'

'You're wearing dust like a coat.'

'So, just like you in the mill.'

'Worse. I went to tin tub last night. Now you're the big miner, you've forgotten.'

Three days on we had done twelve shot holes. We started priming them with dynamite, capped with clay with the fuses stuck out, all tied back together on a long run. David took me to a safe corner and crouched waiting. Dad lit the fuses and ran like the blazes yelling.

'Fire! Fire!'

I had my hands over my ears, as taught.

David nudged me. 'Mouth open!' he shouted.

'What?'

'Mouth open or the blast will burst your ears.'

Then it came and the noise was like nothing I'd ever heard. The power knocked me back and I banged my head on the wall. Dazed, I sat there coughing and spluttering, rubbing my head even though the tull had saved it from damage. Ben came over and thumped my back with a grin.

'What my boy did not say was you do close your mouth afterwards or you do get a full helping of dust in it!'

The dust settled down overnight and the morning after we started to work on the rubble. We picked at the ore and shovelled the good stuff into chutes, for Sion the trammer boy to drop into his trams below our work and take to the shaft.

Dad put his tag on the tram and shouted to him. 'You make sure they know this one's for us all. It's good ore and I'll have none taking it off us.'

19

'Do it well and it be a jug of ale at the Miners'.' drawled Ben. Sion smiled and pushed hard. The red taillight faded quickly from view.

David stood next to me leaning on a shovel and wiped his brow

'What about when you're ill?' I asked.

'We look out for our own here, as no-one else will. Besides, with all this fresh air and exercise. When we going to get ill?'

Once we had cleared the rubble of good ore, Dad started marking holes on the wall higher up. We had got some stulls, like tree stumps.

We wedged them across our narrow cavern. Then some planking on top and where we could, a bit of rubble packed under. Then we were off again, but all standing on platforms.

Next break, I asked Ben, 'Why we going up, not out? Shaft's no wider than a crack in parts.'

Ben puffed on his pipe and then wiped his moustache. 'Tell you why young Owain, the lode be thin. No wider than you in places, but it also be tall. It goes from here near to surface.'

'We don't take out what we don't need, son,' added Dad. 'For Old Man Taylor don't pay us for it.'

David grinned with mischief. 'And we pack the ore for it to grow again after we gone by.'

'Too true,' nodded Ben, pointing with his pipe. 'The ore be a living thing and we do sow seeds for it to grow, like potatoes.'

I didn't ask no further. David looked a tease, but Ben I reckoned was serious.

20

The air was constantly filled with the 'pick, pick, pick' of hammers, the crash of falling rock and everywhere there was dust. Sometimes it was so thick you could choke

We saw neighbouring teams at some breaks. We would meet at an old stope and sit and talk through the time or just sit and rest, before the work took us back again.

Sometimes Captain Nankivell would come and sit with us. In truth, he was one of the boys – the best men, those who knew the ore and could handle the other miners; they were made the Captains of each level. They ruled like a rod of iron, hard but fair.

Dad and Ben talked of work and the news of the day. David just talked girls with me. Who was with who, who was the prettiest and on he went. I wasn't for wanting to know anyhow, so I shut up.

'You still stiff?' David asked.

'Getting better,' I said, trying to be brave. Failing and all.

'Well, you'll be used to it after a while. We get paid Saturday lunchtime, then it's Miner's Day on Monday. Our day off - you got that every month in the mill didn't you? Then back on a new *bargen* Tuesday. Tell you what. You come down New Row after chapel now and I'll get you to meet some of them girls I was talking about.'

There was always time for girls for my friend.

Chapter Two

On the Roof

I settled in quick-like to the work and Dad was pleased with me. My blisters healed and my body learnt to recover from the daily toil. No flab on the working boys, no time for laziness, neither. My curly dark hair was short, and the look of the Spaniard was upon me. No surprises there, I'm guessing.

Y deulu Sbaneg, the Spanish family, that's who we were, and none ever gone South of Tregaron at that.

I was growing up fast, but I was still learning, and my Mam bore most of it.

'Mam, why do the Treveglos family speak Welsh?' I asked as I cleaned my boots out back, while she scrubbed at the sheets in the tub.

'What would you expect?' Mam replied before gritting her teeth as she scrubbed hard.

'Thought they had their own language,' I said with a shrug.

Mam stopped and looked up at me. 'Well, they do. Leastways the old boys do, like Ben. Them Cornish speak English mostly, but in Frongoch we all speak Welsh. They had to learn our tongue. It's not because we're nasty about it, but you need to be able to talk to one another, else it's dangerous.'

'But David said...' I began.

Mam lifted her finger.

'David's a Welsh boy, same as you. New Row born and brought up.'

'But he said he's Cornish, Mam,' I protested. 'Is he lying?'

'No,' Mam sighed. 'His heart lies with the land of his people. That's alright, to be proud of your folk. Now, them boots getting cleaned by themselves, are they?'

I told David and he nodded. 'I expect she's right,' he said in between chewing his food. 'But I'm Cornish in my mind if that's alright with you.'

We were working the old part of the mine, over by Edward's shaft. There the ore had been mined from the surface down, leaving a lip of rock walled by a crescent of narrow caverns dropping down to dark emptiness. The cliffs rose above you. Hefty stulls seemed to keep them apart at the far end of the cut, tree trunks set like great wedges. David found it a funny place to work.

'It's them sheep, on the banks above. Any who graze too close get scared by it all and forget to walk back. The boys always complain about falling sheep.'

'Bet they never complain about the free meat,' I muttered, sending him off laughing.

'Poor creatures - the sheep, that is. Not too bright and good for a panic. Never would have made good miners.'

'David,' I said a bit nervous. 'Do you have dreams about here?'

'What do you mean?'

'Well there's the same dream I have. Makes me wake up in a cold sweat some nights. In the dream, I feel I am falling off the ladder and down the shaft, slowly like. I fall for ages seeing people clinging to the ladder as I go by. They shout at me words I can't hear, reach for me with their hands, but down I fall until I hit the bottom and my vision becomes hazy as if in a red mist. Like my blood has covered the picture.'

David just gave me a smile and a pat on the shoulder. 'Don't we all get them from time to time, Owain *bach*. I tell you, it's a foolish man who don't respect that drop. Why do you think everyone sings hymns coming up top? Takes their mind off it, scared of falling the lot of them.'

I felt better as we sat there chewing our crusts.

David swallowed a swig of water and then looked over to me. 'Owain boy, why there's only you and Myfanwy?' He said with a twinkle in his eye. 'Don't your Mam and Dad do it?'

'It's not like that, you rascal. Six of us, there were. Two died at birth and two others got the cholera back in '69. Now I just think they try to be careful.' I spoke with confidence, even though I had no idea what I was talking about.

David nodded. 'Too many of us Treveglos around. My Mam and Dad always try to be careful now. Scared of another brat eating us out the house they are. Fair praying I get married and move out. Come on you now, we got trams to load.'

'Don't forget the knockers,' I said. 'Them rock sprites keep us safe according to your Dad.'

'Most times,' said David, tearing a crust and leaving it on the rock, a present to the small creatures.

'All the time,' I said loudly, for fear of offending them.

I would never talk of my dead brothers and sisters, for I feel they should be left in peace. Tragedies all of them and Mam took each death hard like a punishment against her, though she held her grief within.

I was sent up top that day, for Dad had a task for me after the break.

'Owain, you follow the trammer boy and make sure this load gets all the way to the mill untouched. I fear some buggers are taking some of our share.'

Ever was the complaint of the miner that they weren't paid their proper share.

The trammer, Sion Parry, pushed his full tram down to the shaft. I followed a few dozen steps back. He shoved it all the way to the kibble and tipped it in. I got there as they were about to hoist it.

'Away boy, we're busy. Can't it wait?' Sion Parry said with a flick of his head.

'I'm busy too, *boy*,' I said back, making him scowl.

I reached for the ladder in the shaft and Sion grabbed my arm.

'You may think you're something here, but you're not. That was my place. You got taken on because your Dad wanted to make something of you.

You aren't ready yet, never will be. So don't cross me, right?'

I shook off his hand and started climbing. There was a bell and a loud rumble, Sion had signalled the shaft to raise the kibble, making me have to rush up to the platform and throw myself on the floor for safety. As I climbed up after, I thought of how I could take revenge.

The crushing mill was a large shed and noisy with it. Built on steps, so that once one job had been done, they just tipped the rock down to the next one.

Jigging to crushing to the buddles, where the fine ore was separated. They even tipped out the waste into the slime pools at the bottom and tried to squeeze an ounce more silver and a bit more lead from it.

I came in the mill by the picking table, where the ore was tipped down a chute from the tram. The table was a stone circle turning on a cog and children stood around looking for pure ore to pick off. The rest then moved down to the jigger that shook like a demon. Their catches were taken in buckets straight to the crusher, which was where Mam worked. I saw her look at a rock and take out her hammer to cob away some spoil, before throwing the ore into her bucket.

Duw, was Mam in control! She had everyone working away at her commands that she bellowed over the machinery noise. It didn't matter if you were man, woman or child. They all took notice, and you could see the whole mill dancing to her tune.

I was proud there watching my Mam, she knew how to get people off their backsides. I noticed little Myfanwy at the picking table, trying to catch the pure ore in a linen cloth, as other children threw it off the stone slab. Only ten she was and getting muscles from that work and bruises, poor thing.

There was a slight movement beside her and I noticed I was being watched. The girl with the black curls stared back at me. With a slight smile, knowing I had seen her, she was off to work. I caught up with Mam and got a big telling off for being there, as she took the cloth out of her ears.

'I'll have words with that Gareth Thomas, sending you up here when you should be making the *bargen*. It's what puts bread on the table.'

'Dad wanted to know our share was getting through to the mill alright,' I stumbled to reply.

She arched her brow and stuck her hands on her hips. 'Course it is, who would dare make it otherwise? It's not being lost. You boys don't work hard enough, that's why *bargen*'s low. You tell him that and tell him to run his own fool errands in future. Now *Ewch*!' She flicked her hand and was off back to the mill.

On my way out, I nearly walked straight into our Captain Nankivell. I backed off and waited for the barracking, but he was kind, or at least patient.

'Young Owain Thomas, isn't it? Shouldn't you be on 78 with your father?'

'I'm sorry sir,' I blurted back. 'My Dad was worried we was not getting all our work through to the mill.'

Nankivell smiled grimly. 'Tampering, eh? Not while I'm in charge, that's for sure. No, we do all suffer my boy. The lode be not as good as she was, too much quartz there. Returns are down. You be off back down now.'

He ruffled my hair sending up a small cloud of dust. 'Best you check first, they don't normally let men use the shaft while they be lifting ore. Like as not you do end up stuck here. That be your father's fault, so I will have a word with him. We can't have miners running around checking their load all the time, there would be no work done.' He walked off leaving me standing there, putting my dusty hair to right.

Next Miner's Day, I was up on the roof of the house and clinging to the chimney. We had a hole in the thatch over by the fireplace and I was checking the damage.

'Owain *bach*,' my Dad shouted. 'How does it look?'

'I can see it right enough,' I shouted back. 'There's smoke coming through it and it's all green with moss and damp.'

There was a rustle as my Dad came up the ladder, then he pulled himself up on the rope to get to me.

'Well now, a bit of work here and no mistake. Mind you, it's fared well over the years, considering.'

'Is this really a *ty un nos*?' I asked.

'Yes, least it was. We put up the original place overnight to claim it as ours.'

'How do you get it all done in a night?'

'With a lot of help,' he replied. 'We gathered everything and hid them away in a barn, so the spies of the landowners couldn't see us.'

'Why's that?'

'So they wouldn't stop us. When dusk fell, we flattened the mud and built the walls. By dawn the turf roof was coming up fine but there was a worry on getting a fire in the hearth. Finding dry leaves for tinder and all. We were just in time.'

'But it's stone here, stone and thatch,' I protested. Dad nodded.

'A year and a day. That's how long we lived like savages. Then I got a thatch roof done, when I knew no bailiff would knock it down. A year of colds and coughs, but we knew we were free.'

'Why wait?'

'Well, even though it was my land by the old law, the gentry sometimes do not suffer a *ty un nos*. I stood at each wall and threw an axe to mark the boundaries.' He looked at the garden and shook his head. 'Wish I'd practised my throwing first, mind.'

'Why's the roof need them props?'

29

'I put thatch on soon as I could, then when money and time allowed, I rebuilt the walls to clom and stone after. Doing each wall like that pulled the old beams this way and that and later they started to sag in the middle.'

'Why not take the roof away and do it again?'

Dad grunted 'I'm wishing that and all. Too much work for us in one day mind and Mam would give us hell if we left the roof open overnight. Then there's the money.'

'If you ask Ben, I'm sure him and David would help. The four of us could do it in a day'

'I said no, Owain *bach*.'

'Dad.' I knew I was pushing it, but I was young and foolish. 'Why don't we just move to New Row like Ben? It's good housing and dry and warm, with a *ty bach* out back. We'd have less illness then.'

Normally Dad flew into a rage by then, but the moment was broken by a shriek below. We looked down to see little Myfanwy running around. She was supposed to be weeding the vegetable patch, but instead she had found a white butterfly and shouted with glee as she chased it over the garden, the little wings fluttering just out of reach.

Dad shook his head and his anger cooled. He spoke softer.

'Son, here we have claim to the land and at New Row there's rent to pay. Less money to feed and clothe us and the shop won't do us no favours.'

He sighed. '*Tai un nos* do have their problems mind and to have a dry roof and a decent chimney would make it less stuffy.'

He smiled then. 'I'll talk to Mam and we'll count our pennies. Good to see the back of them props - maybe we could use them for a lean-to.

Right, we'll do our best here now and when the weather clears, we'll see. Just stop chopsing me about it, right?'

On the next shift, he approached Ben who was happy to help.

'Just you do tell us the where and when and we'll be there,' he said sucking on his clay pipe. 'Tell you what now, why don't I bring over the family and some food with us? You get a drop of ale too. Then we'll have a bite after.'

'Tell you who would have been good for this,' said Ben slowly, 'Gomer Hughes.'

There was a silence and Dad stiffened slightly. 'That won't be happening.'

'Aye, I do know that,' Ben waved away the thought. 'But his cousin, Iolo, do have the tools and he would be willing to lend them. I'll ask him next time I do see him.'

'That's alright,' Dad replied. 'It's not the family that's bad.'

'I know Gareth. I know.'

'We'll start on payday afternoon, then Owain and I will carry on the Miner's Day. That's settled then.'

Dad had learnt to make and mend roofs while working on Taid's farm. Had to, they were so far away from the village they needed to know what to do. Dad had his own tools from that time, but the others would allow Ben to work with him.

We did not do it that payday, nor the next. We spent our time collecting reeds for drying and branches for fastening rods and battens.

We had some straw for repairs but needed much more. Even a house as small as ours would need a lot of straw, if we were to do it proper.

Our house was not big, one room split by a sheet, that was it. Dad had a mind for making a wall between rooms and to make an upstairs, so he made some floorboards for that. We had all the wood we wanted from a tree that had fallen down in storms. It took months to do, but finally we were ready.

The day arrived and Ben and his family turned up Saturday afternoon. It was July and the days were long, but I still wondered how we would get it finished in time.

'Where's the tools then?' Dad called.

Ben shrugged. 'Said he'd be here by now. Best he be here soon, or we do lose the light before we're done.'

I looked down the road to Frongoch and made out a small figure, walking along with a sack. Someone familiar. Then I knew. The curly dark hair - the girl from the mill.

'Ceridwen Hughes,' I heard David mutter. 'Just started at Frongoch, she have.'

She came up to the house and went straight to Dad.

'Iolo says he's too busy, but I'm to stay and take the tools home,' she said shyly. 'And heaven help me if they are missing or broke.'

Mam came out wiping her hands on her apron. 'You look starving, girl - you hungry?'

Ceridwen nodded, biting her lip.

'Right then,' said Mam, gently. 'You help me, girl, and then you can join us for our meal. Bit of bread to start you off then some work, is it?' Ceridwen nodded again and moved over to Mam.

We quickly took out the old props for cutting and using again. The roof would be tall, to allow the rain to run off. Straw was a good shield from the wet if set right and we lived in a place where rain was never far away, that's for sure.

The old beams were rotting in places, so we laid the new wood and battens. When it was safe, the women went to the fire preparing food clecking away. Not that we were any better, we just called it discussion.

Mam came over to watch our working. 'Aren't you done yet?' She scolded. 'Should be done by now. You're slacking, you are.'

'*Hisht* woman,' Dad grumbled back. 'If I'm doing this, I'll be doing it right and proper.'

I started to worry. Mam was right, this was taking far too long.

'Can we start the floor while you work on the roof?' I said.

'Too dangerous,' Dad replied stiffly. 'And what if I drop something on your head?'

'We can wear our tulls.' I persisted. 'Only we'll do it faster that way.'

'Don't you start,' Dad snapped back.

'They'll be out of our way most times,' Ben said quietly. 'And we can tell them to stop if they do get in the way.'

Dad pulled a face and nodded. He was fed up with all the nagging by then.

David and I began work on the floor. We put up crossbeams to support the floorboards. I was so pleased to see that they all fitted well into the notches cut in the wall. Quickly then we started flooring above the fireplace and worked back.

'That's a lot quieter now,' muttered Dad.

'I heard that Gareth Thomas,' came the muffled reply from beneath the new floor.

'She'd hear a bloody mouse on 117 level from there,' Dad grumbled.

We worked hard to put that wood up all day, stopping only the once for a drink. It was brought to us by Myfanwy and Ceridwen before they ran off giggling, much to my disgust.

As the sun moved ever downwards, Dad and Ben were only putting down the first layer of thatch, but it still wasn't fast enough for me. I was nearly crying with frustration as I hit my thumb and dropped my hammer, giving out a curse.

'Hey, stop that right now,' Dad shouted. 'Language, with women and children around.'

'Alright, alright,' I said in a lather, waving my thumb to take the pain off. I was giving lip, it was dangerous ground for sure.

34

'What's the matter, now?' came Dad's voice. He was still working away, pinning the thatch down, weaving it with rods onto the battens.

'We'll never get this done for tonight and then we'll not see the feast neither.' I sulked. 'I'm hungry and I'm not wanting to sleep under the stars.'

Dad stopped and laughed. 'What? All in one day? Oh, I wish that were true.'

Ben looked over fondly. 'Do take more than one day to do this proper, young Owain. Your Dad be putting on a layer to cover the house. It not be too strong, so you do pray now that the good Lord sends pleasant weather these next few weeks.'

'But Mam said...' I started and Dad's head came into view.

'You're Mam's forever telling me I'm not doing things fast or hard enough. Don't listen, it's just her way. We'll have a cover on for the night. We'll do a lot on Miner's Day, then we'll have to do it when we can after that.'

By evening, the small roof was done. It had been a hot day and I was ready to strip off and swim in Llyn Frongoch, but for modesty. We looked on with relief when the women appeared with bowls of *cawl* and jugs of ale for us. We all sat out to eat, on a ridge of grey rock that stood up by the front. A fire was made of the wood that was past use and we gathered round it. There was mutton in the cawl, a treat that we normally had on a Sunday.

The girls came to give us our ale and Ceridwen handed me one, then stood there watching.

'*Diolch.*' I said, all polite as I had been taught. She didn't move. 'What's the matter?'

She stood still as a stone, then blurted out 'My brother Gwilym reckons he can duff you up a treat.'

'Let him try,' I scoffed. 'That all you got to say then?'

She swayed a bit, back and forth all nervous, then said quietly. 'Do you like kittens? My cousin's seen a cat with kittens. All lovely and black and brown they are.' She looked sideways through her long black eyelashes. 'I could show you if you like?'

I opened my mouth to scoff, but I saw her look. Her eyes showed pain, waiting for me to say what I'd just bit back, waiting for me to say no. I thought a bit and then nodded.

'Tell you what. Next time I go down the village you can show me, alright?'

She smiled and breathed a sigh of relief and nodded.

'You not eating girl? It's good *cawl.*'

She hesitated and I could see she was scared.

'I'll get you a bowl, come along now.'

I moved over and got her a good helping, which she wolfed down greedily and tore at the bread. Strong will with that one and no mistake. After food, we sang some hymns in celebration.

Darkness came and Ben lit a lantern for them to see on the road back. He and his family made ready to go. Ben would see Ceridwen back to the village.

David gripped my arm. 'Don't worry boy, I'll take care of your girlfriend.' He chuckled as I rose in anger and punched my shoulder.

It took Miner's Day and a few weeks after before we were done. Then we could feel proud of our little house once more. We made a screen to fashion a bedroom away from the rest of downstairs. Mam stood looking at it, then gave a stiff nod. Dad beamed and ruffled my hair. Then we were in and eating our supper, listening to Dad's plans for the future.

Chapter Three

Cornish Boys

With work, the garden and chapel, there was not much free time for me. Mind you, sometimes I did get some of Miners' Day to myself.

'You get your work done of a morning and I'll let you off on an afternoon.' Mam would say. 'Come back late or untidy and there'll be hell to play with your father.'

'Only off to New Row to see David,' I said.

'You and New Row. Good houses I grant you, but we're better off in Trisant. One day you'll know why. Now don't get up to no nonsense or I'll hear of it.'

Many families lived in them terraces, built by the mine for miners years back. The children there would be ones for going off adventuring or having the occasional fight with the boys from the village. This was down in the wood on the valley slopes. The village boys worked in the other mines nearby, like Logaulas, Glogfach and Glogfawr.

Big rivalries had sprung up, David's bunch were called the Cornish Boys, though many were not from that ancient land. Fed up with being called the 'Spanish Bastard' by the locals it meant I had no desire to be with home–grown folk, so a Cornish Boy I was and proud.

One Miners' Day was really misty. We were down the woods at the fast running stream that wound its way down through the wooded valley. On its journey, it had formed a sturdy bank with a large amount of mud and there we spied a group of Logaulas boys waiting to ambush us.

Very soon, a huge mud-fight had started, big lumps flying to and from every child. All of us were quickly brown and sticky and laughing with it. I got separated from my boys in the mist and to my despair found that my path had led me into the middle of the other gang. I was right close to five of them. Thank God they had not seen me, but in my panic, I flattened myself on the ground in a hollow, keeping my head low and my breathing as quiet as possible. I just prayed they would go away.

I heard a movement above and I looked up with dread. There she stood, Ceridwen Hughes, with the black curls and that little smile, oh so sly.

'Quick! Down!' I whispered, waving my hand.

She jumped down and sat on a rock close by me with a giggle.

'Trapped now, are you?' The little minx mocked me. She sat up and made a show to be looking around. 'Logaulas boys are nearby, my brother Gwilym there too. They'll duff you up for sure.'

My heart sank at the thought, as she sat there curling her hair between her little fingers. She pulled her hair over her shoulder a bit and looked sideways at me over the strands.

'Unless,' she said slowly, 'I could find you a way out.' Then she sighed sadly. 'Mind you, I could do that Owain Thomas, but I would need something in return.'

'What's that?' I said quickly, feeling the jaws of the trap slowly closing.

She stopped playing with her hair and beamed at me. 'A kiss!' She said.

'What you on about?' I spluttered in a whisper. 'You are thirteen, what would you be wanting with a kiss then?'

I heard voices coming closer, harsh angry shouts. I got the feeling the Logaulas boys were losing. It made me panic.

'Alright then,' I said quickly, 'Once I get free, right?'

'Ooh!' she replied with a grin 'One now and one when you get free then? That way you can't run away after.'

I scowled - was I really that obvious?

Ceridwen looked over the ridge. 'Best be having you now - I can hear Gwilym coming over.'

There she stood, lips ready and eyes closed. I dipped down and pecked her quickly on the cheek. She giggled prettily and grabbed my hand, pulling me down the valley and into the mist. We rushed down through the trees and bushes, slipping down the hill on masses of leaves.

Down and down the valley we went, branches whipping into us. Ceridwen was ahead laughing all the way and as I could not hear any sounds of a chase, I too raised a smile. Ceridwen pointed up to the road.

'There's a gap there now. We can sneak out before someone sees us.'

We carried on moving fast until we reached the bottom of the long winding hill, close where the road forked for Devil's Bridge and the village. We started walking and I tried to listen for the Logaulas boys as my heartbeat was in my ears. All else was quiet, even the Miners *tafarn* at the top of the hill was strangely silent. Like it was Sunday, and all the sinners were repenting at home in their gin cups before attending evening chapel.

I quickly looked around to see that nobody was watching then gasped in surprise. Ceridwen had grabbed hold of my jacket, pulled me down and kissed me full on the lips. Strong girl that one, too many days working at the mill. Before I could think of anything, she was away shouting.

'Now we are sweethearts, Owain Thomas!'

She skipped off laughing before I could answer. Funny thing was, her laughter was like little bells to my ears, but the feeling only made me angrier at how I'd been tricked.

A long walk back up the hill to New Row was now in order. Faced with the choice of that or chasing that nuisance of a girl, there really was no option. I walked up the hill towards the Cornish chapel, taking in the calm of the whole place. The gentle breeze in my face, the running water of the stream, the forest of strangely twisted trees covered in green moss. A bird singing made me stop and listen and I took a deep breath and thought about how beautiful it all was.

The only signs of life were the wisps of smoke coming out of the cottages over the valley, clustered around the chapel. There was a faint sound now of someone chopping wood.

My dream was shattered by a sharp thud against my lower back. It made me cry out in pain and knocked the breath out of me. I touched my back and felt mud on it, as somebody laughed behind me. A voice called out.

'You all right, boy?'

I gave no answer straight off, as I fought for breath.

'Hey, Spanish boy? You all right?'

'Yes,' I gasped and turned to find Gwilym Hughes standing behind me.

'Well, don't want no-one hurt, see,' he said. 'Only a bit of rough and tumble after all, you and us. You want an apple?'

He took out a couple of small apples from his pocket and handed me one. 'Scrumped 'em, I did this morning from *Jones y Bont*.'

He sat down on a patch of earth and I joined him. We crunched our apples in what felt an uneasy silence.

'You Frongoch boys are alright, you know,' he said with a mouth full of apple. 'Hard, but fair, not like them Glog boys over Ysbyty way. Hate them we do. You ever want to team up and thrash them, you let us know.'

He bit more apple and continued; mouth as full as before.

'You know the main adit in Logaulas, the *Lefel Fawr*? We share it with all the other mines, so it doesn't just drain our mine it drains theirs also. Thing is, it goes through us last and those bastard Glog boys know it. They throw everything down that adit and use it as a lav too, so we have to put up with all their piss and crap coming through our mine. Bastards!' He spat and threw his apple core down the hill in disgust.

We sat in silence for a little while then, chewing the last pieces of apple. Then he said.

'So, how are you Spanish then? You don't sound it.'

'I'm not Spanish,' I replied. 'Just my Nain was bad with a Spanish sea Captain once and the baby was my Dad.'

'Your Nain? Like your Mam-gu then?'

'Yes, it's just my Dad is from Barmouth and that's what they call them there.'

'What's your Tad-cu called then?'

'That's my Taid.'

'Nain and Taid,' he said slowly, 'sounds all English really, like number nine and the tide of the sea.' He nodded to himself and then grunted.

'So you're a Gog then,' he grinned. 'Well better a Gog than a Glog innit.' He burst out laughing at his joke and I had to smile.

'So, what you been doing with my sister?' he asked.

'Nothing,' I said with great feeling and told him what had happened. He shook his head.

'She does have her eye set on you then. Best be careful boy, she's stubborn that one. Now, don't you go messing about with her. You know what I mean. If you do, we'll have to stop being friends and fight, see.'

'No way am I going to do that,' I said. 'Girls are a nuisance.'

We sat and talked a bit longer, until I had to make my way home. Gwilym told me that most of his family worked Logaulas, but there was not enough for all of them, so their Mam had gone to work in Frongoch and taken Ceridwen, another sister and two brothers with her.

'Dad used to work there also, but he had to leave. My two brothers Gethin and Iorri, they're Logaulas too.'

I wanted to ask who his Dad was and why he left, but the look on his face made me change my mind. You could tell he didn't want to talk about it, so instead I said.

'What's it like at Logaulas then?'

'Wet,' he grunted. 'Not as good as Frongoch, they say. Same as your place probably, mind. Up and down ladders and hitting your head and back on the tunnel roof all day.'

He took out two more apples. 'Last ones, mind,' he said, and we chewed some more.

'How do you find them Cornish boys, then?' he asked me.

'Fine, same as me, really.' I replied 'They're not real Cornish anyhow, all the children are Cardi born anyway. Their Mams and Dads are the real Cornish ones. Cornish are Celts mind, same as us.'

44

Gwilym nodded slowly. 'Never knew that,' he said. 'Well, maybe I'll give them respect then. If they weren't Celts mind, the valley would go up in smoke, the number of them that have come over here and taken our jobs.'

I meant to say there was plenty of work for us all, for the mines were busy, but again his look stopped me. He threw his apple away and held out his hand with a grin.

'Got to go now, been good to meet you, Owain Thomas. You behave with my sister now.'

I went off back to Trisant, cutting through the mine to get home while no-one was looking. My arrival, all plastered in mud led me to get a tongue-lashing from Mam. My Dad was much more practical; he marched me to the Llyn and threw me in, clothes and all. He would not let me out until both my clothes and my body were clean.

Sopping wet and shivering, I was taken back home. By now, Dad was talking to me and he asked me what happened. When I told him, he grunted out almost a laugh.

'Did you win?' he asked.

'Yes.' I said not knowing or caring by now.

He nodded. 'No use you getting trouble unless you won after all.' He sighed. 'Must be getting to the day I need to teach you how to fight then, right?'

'Can I, Dad?' I begged, all eager. 'I want to be able to stand up to the boys, not skulk in the hollows.'

Well, maybe so, but you must promise only to do it in defence. I'm not having any ruffians in my house. Now then you, back and change, put your clothes out to dry and pray they do so in time for work tomorrow.'

Next day, I met David by the shaft, while Dad went to the *bargen*.

'What you been doing then, matey?' he said with a grin, 'Ceridwen Hughes has been telling everyone you are sweethearts, and her Dad is saying he will bring over the Logaulas boys to kill you!'

I was stunned. My mouth opened and closed like a fish, as I started to splutter.

'No, hang on. What the…? It was a kiss and she just kissed me and no more than a peck on the cheek at that.'

'Yes, yes,' said David. 'We all know you been a saint.'

'Come on Davy boy,' I nearly shouted. 'You know her. You know me. How would I be doing that and you not knowing?'

'True,' he replied. 'Then some girls do have strong ideas. Best be careful, lest you be swallowed up and best we guard you from Logaulas for a while.'

'Bloody Logaulas.' I hissed. 'Bloody nonsense!'

I was seething all through work. I picked up the drill and when I missed the charge hole, I flung it down in disgust.

46

I bashed the rock face like it was at fault. Dad called a break early that day and took me to one side.

'What the hell do you think you're doing, Owain? You'll break the damn tools if you're not careful and yourself in the bargain.'

I was frustrated by it all; the attentions of a girl, the threats and the gossip. 'Logaulas.' I managed to mutter.

'Well, don't take it out on your tools, we can't just go out and get new ones. Forget it man, it's all nonsense anyway - Gomer Hughes wouldn't be seen dead round here. It's all talk, that's all it is.'

By the end of the day, it felt as if I had almost worked the share of two men. I hauled my way up the ladders to the surface with most of the anger worked out of me, in need of a good stretch and a bath in the tin tub back home.

As I reached the top of the ladder, it was if there was a shadow over me and I could sense a gathering of people above. As I walked away from the shaft, I stopped to catch my breath. I heard a call, a warning. Suddenly, the world went white with stars as I collapsed to the floor.

Feeling very groggy, I lay there as my mind spun and I desperately tried to understand what was going on. I saw a large fat miner standing over me. Grey waistcoat bulging out of his jacket, patchy with dirt and rot. A moustache and sideburns hid a large face, blotched red through years of drinking.

'Get up!' he snarled and aimed a kick at my ribs.

47

His swinging leg was blocked. I realised my father had stepped over me and into the kick. As the man tried to regain his balance, my dad fetched him to the floor with a beautiful crosscut that smacked like a hammer to a melon.

'You touch my boy again and I'll cripple you,' he snapped at the man on the ground.

The man tried to gather himself up, fell back and felt his jaw and the blood trickling from the side of his mouth. 'I'll throw you down the bloody shaft, you and your bastard son!' He lurched to get up, but Dad put him down again with the sole of his foot.

'Stay where you are, Gomer,' Dad said coldly, 'or you'll be doing more than holding your jaw when I'm done.'

Masses of people were gathering to watch. Mutters could be heard as they recognised the fat man. A group of miners, all strangers to me, stood behind the man. Some had sticks, all looked ready for a fight as they glared at the crowd. I got to my feet slowly, feeling the side of my face that had developed a lump and was numb. A tooth was loose, and I sucked on it until it broke free and I could spit it out.

There was a fuss to one side and then a shrieking mass of curls hurtled into the fray. Ceridwen, it was.

'Stop it!' she screamed, then screamed even louder as a man yanked her back by the hair and then slapped her silent.

That got to me. She was just a girl at that. The anger that had been with me all day rose up and I was on my feet and running straight at the man. He stood there in surprise, so much I ran through him, my head taking him on the chin. Then he was on the floor and me standing over him, with a throbbing forehead.

Two others made a step towards me, but Ben Treveglos was quickly at my side, holding an iron bar. I heard David mutter, 'Nice and easy, boy,' and saw he had another man by the throat. David's normal good-natured smile was almost demonic, his face white with rage. The man tried to glare back, but was having trouble breathing, clawing at David's vice-like grip as he was held high.

Captain Nankivell burst through the growing ranks of miners. 'Break it up! Now!' he shouted. Everyone stopped in their tracks. 'Right,' he said looking over the scene, 'I want Gareth Thomas' pare and the Logaulas men here. The rest be off about your business.'

The crowd cleared, muttering and throwing dark looks at the outsiders. Nankivell did a quick check of the faces left then looked at old Ben.

'Not like you to be fighting Ben?'

'I'll not have folk be attacked for no reason,' Ben drawled, eyes still fixed firmly on the two he had stopped. 'Even if there be reason, it ought to be declared before. Tis cowardly the way young Owain be attacked without warning at that.'

The mine Captain gave a sharp nod and then he pointed at the fat man.

'Right, Gomer Hughes stay here. You too, young Ceridwen. The rest of you be trespassing on private land and I do politely ask you to leave. Now!'

Nobody moved, though some looked uneasy.

'Perhaps I do make it easier for you with some of my boys who be loitering over there, waiting for my call. Or a visit to Captain Russell at Logaulas might help, as I am sure he do take an interest in the reputation of his workforce. You will be out on you ears by tomorrow.' Nankivell's voice lowered to a growl, 'I do suggest you do not try my patience.'

Gomer looked at his men and nodded curtly. Sullenly, they turned away one by one and withdrew. The one I had knocked over started to speak.

'Do not start anything,' I snarled.

'Iorri, get home,' Gomer said sourly.

Iorri spat at my feet. 'There will be a reckoning, boy,' he muttered and pushed by me.

'Gomer Hughes!' Nankivell shouted. 'Tell me what be happening here. You were dismissed from Frongoch and as such, I could have you thrown to the Aberystwyth constabulary for trespass and assault. So, you do tell me your tale now and it better be good.'

'That bastard's been fooling with my Ceridwen,' said Gomer with hate. 'She's been made a slut by that boy and now I'm going to kill him.'

'That's all lies!' I shouted.

'Silence!' thundered Nankivell, 'or you do walk from Frongoch this day and never return. Ceridwen Hughes. I think we do need your tale and I hope it be truth, for this boy's job doth depend on it.'

Ceridwen had not moved from the floor. She lay there, trembling and sobbing, but lifted her head towards the Captain.

'He never touched me! I swear! It was just a kiss and I tricked him into that...'

Her words began to tumble out, 'I told you that, Dad, and you never listened. Drunk, you was and wanted to fight. He'd never be like that. He couldn't, I don't love him or anything - I'm walking with Tom Griffiths anyhow. Just he's so nice and I'm sorry, I....' She sighed. 'I been teasing his sister he was my sweetheart, that's all. The others started clecking on it. Dad, I been trying to tell you nothing happened, but you just wanted to have it out, with him being a Thomas and all.'

My mind was reeling with her words and I had no idea what to do next. Captain Nankivell though stepped forward and rested his hand on her shoulder.

'It's alright my girl, you have spoke true and I do thank you for that.'

He turned to Gomer and I could see his cheeks had turned red with anger.

'So, have your brain been rotted with drink so much, that you do not tell careless words from the truth? Do you not think to listen before you act? Has your mind been poisoned so much that you would spark this valley to flames with your hate? I dismissed you from this mine and today do prove how right I was to do so. Get from here now - if you do come back, I will have you thrown into jail.'

Gomer got up awkwardly and threw a dark look at everyone. He reached out for his daughter but stayed his hand as the Captain's voice continued.

'Depart now Gomer and do know this, I do see Ceridwen every day. Should I ever notice any marks or bruises, I will know where be the house I do go to exact justice and it shall be as the bible do say; an eye for an eye, a tooth for a tooth.'

The drunkard spat on the ground, muttered something in disgust and then limped away down the path.

Nankivell looked at us all. 'What I see here today do vex me, the way men do stray. I do commend you all to Banc Llety Synod this Sunday after chapel, where I will impart on you the Word of The Lord and perhaps you will all learn some humility. I take it now our business be complete. Until Sunday then.' And he too was gone.

Ceridwen wiped her eyes then ran off towards the mill.

Dad put his hand on my shoulder. 'Leave her boy, she is best alone. Gomer will not touch her now - he fears Captain Nankivell too much.'

'Why is he wanting to attack me?'

'Gomer worked here not so long back, in '69. He was the only one to survive a blast.' Dad answered, looking grim.

'Rumour had it, they was smoking baccy at the magazine and he did put his clay pipe on a powder barrel and went off for a piss,' said Ben,

'Blast did blow his butties up. Gareth here dug him out, and Gomer do hate him for that. Wishes he be dead, does old Gomer.'

'No-one wanted to work with him, so they got rid, because all the mine by then thought he was bad luck.' said Dad. 'And before the men strung him up from the Cornish Engine, as a Jonah.

He only attacked you for who you were. I never thought he had the courage left to do what he has done this day. Be calm, Owain, he won't be back. He knows what awaits him now.'

He clapped his hand on my shoulder. 'Now, you go easy on little Ceridwen, boy. It is not easy to live in the shadow of a man who hates to be alive and finds his only salvation in drink.'

'Besides' said David with a grin 'She's shown you respect by opening up her little heart, you should be honoured. She finds you nice.'

Ben chuckled 'Take note of that one young Owain, she will have men falling over themselves to win her in a few years. Best to keep her sweet for when you be both ready.'

They all laughed, leaving me fuming with shame.

Chapter Four

David's Hat

We were all dressed up in our Sunday best. First up to chapel in Trisant for some hell and damnation. Then Sunday school to read about the error of our ways. Then off back to the mine to hear Nankivell telling us to repent. Some days it was a hard life being a sinner.

Captain Nankivell was a lay preacher. Not a man of the cloth, but a man of God just the same. Banc Llety Synod was the hill at the far end of the mine from us. To escape the crowds of people who often came to these gatherings, we had arranged to meet the Treveglos family at the point where the hill became the mine.

Nankivell must have commended a few to this meeting, or was it commanded, indeed? Miners, farmers, even some of the richer folk from thereabouts. They all came to hear the good Captain speak.

We made our way past the mine to where we could see Ben and his large family waiting for us.

'Good to see the old place quiet for a change,' said Mam.

'Yes, but without it, we would never have our *bargen*,' replied Dad.

Quick as a wink, Mam was back at him. 'More like we'd never see what a bad job you boys do make of it all.'

She got a switch on her backside when Dad thought no-one was looking.

'It be breezy today,' said Ben in greeting. 'Be good to stand wind side of him, lest we do miss his words.'

He was right, for although it was a beautiful autumn day, the wind made it that bit colder, getting right into your bones. My sister Myfanwy was already off playing with little Mary Treveglos. The two were nine years old and full of innocence. Doing a full day's work at the dresser, they looked and acted like young women. Today they were allowed to be children once again as they chatted away and giggled, especially at David.

David stood there, in his Sunday best, with a bowler hat on his head. A bit tattered and too big for him, it was, but it was his pride and joy. He had bought it from a tinker travelling through on the way to Aberystwyth and said it made him look gentrified.

'I'd take your hat off, Davy boy,' I teased. 'This wind will pick it up and take it all the way to Graig Goch.'

'Never!' replied David with his normal grin 'You think the Captain will let me keep it on for prayer?'

'You're hopeless boy,' I sighed. He was so lacking in worry and urgency.

I shook my head in despair and moved to follow our families who were already past the gunpowder stores that sat on the hill slope, out of harm's way.

Below, the pool glistened in the sunlight. Not more than a big pond really, the water used by the pumps and dressers at Frongoch fed it.

Another leat took it around the Banc and away to Wemyss for it to do work with their wheels. They then sent the water to Graig Goch. Never ones to waste, us Cardis, but it would have been black by the time it came down the valley.

We had not gone twenty feet, when a sharp gust of wind took the hat clean off David's head. With a soulful cry, David watched his beloved hat fly off towards the lake It was spring and after a wet winter, water for once was plentiful in reserve. So much there was, that someone had left the sluice gate open to stop flooding. David ran off to get his hat, but the wind seemed to give it a will of its own. It rolled down the hill and into the flowing leat.

I ran after him, with his cries of 'my hat!' making all folk around stare. I caught a glimpse of it gently bobbing around the hill. The water was fast, and we did not look to be gaining on the hat at all.

Round the hill we went like madmen. David's despairing cries were mixed with my laughter. How mad we must have looked. On we went, past the farm on the other side and ever onward. Dogs barked as we ran, hens scattered clucking.

'*Ddrwg gen* I', I shouted out as I ran to catch up with David and his daft hat, even though no-one was to be seen.

We ran for ages, and still could not catch it. It would be in view, and then disappear for a minute, bobbing gently along. We had almost run round the whole of the hill.

'To the road,' gasped David. 'Or we'll lose it in the wheel!'

We left the leat and ran for the road to Trisant that split Frongoch and Wemyss. We were quickly onto Wemyss land, desperate to catch the hat before it got to the lander that fed the fifty-six-foot waterwheel beyond.

'We must have got ahead of it by now.' I panted standing by the wheel and out of puff.

'Yes,' wheezed David. 'Then it must be stuck where the leat goes under the road.'

Back we went there, a bit slower this time, wheezing and coughing. We looked at the tunnel, but there was no sign of the hat, David was heartbroken.

'Gone,' he said sadly, for once the smile not on his face. 'Either stuck on the wheel or it will be halfway to Graig Goch by now.'

It seemed like ages that we waited there and then there came a slight cough from above that made us look up. Ceridwen Hughes stood there holding the hat.

'I tried to call you, but you did not hear.' she said very quietly.

'God be praised!' said David fervently, and then whispered to me, 'You'd better grab that one quick, before I change my mind about Gwen.'

He was up the path, swept a bow to her and took the hat. Then, with a kiss on her cheek and a huge grin to me, he walked away up the hill. Still catching my breath, I followed and when I got to her, by God she looked a picture! Her hair was tied up under a frilled mobcap.

She wore her best blue dress and a red checked shawl around her shoulders. Her shoes had seen better days, but she had cleaned them, and the buckles showed a faint shine. Perhaps she was too young for a steeple crowned beaver hat, but I know she would have worn it with pride, tied with lace under her chin. A Welsh doll she was and beautiful with it.

She would not look me in the eyes, and I could not think of anything to say either. We just stood there and stared at the grass for a while. Finally, I plucked up the courage to say something, although it was blurted out.

'You all right then?'

Oh, so blunt and to the point! I felt like I could talk to kings that day.

She nodded, still looking down, tears on the edges of her eyes.

'Has...? Did... Gomer touch you?' I started.

She shook her head. 'Not me. He wouldn't dare now.' She bit her lip, 'but my brother Gethin did. Slapped me red he did, the brute. Then he threw me into the cow shed. It's where I live for now.'

I looked sadly at her and wished I could go down and slap Gethin about a bit also. Then I knew he was like an ox and me with only a promise of fighting lessons to come.

'Gwilym got it worse,' she continued. 'He argued with them, before they came to Frongoch. Said you wouldn't do that. Told them to listen to me. Dad laid into him with a stick. Gave him a proper good hiding. They had to pull him off poor Gwil in the end.'

She looked at me and nodded her head up. 'He's up the hill now, came with me, but he should be on sticks the way he was beaten.'

More silence. She swallowed hard and took a deep breath. 'It is so sorry I am. I hoped, I mean I just...' She tailed away.

I finally found my voice and stepped forward and patted her arm. 'It's alright girl. It's not that bad. You're a brave one, Ceridwen Hughes'

She raised her eyes up to me, brimming with tears, and tried a smile. 'We can be friends then, can't we? You won't stop talking to me, will you?'

I smiled and shook my head. 'No, we're butties.'

She smiled then, showing her teeth 'You best call me Ceri then. That's what my butties call me'

I chuckled. 'Alright then Ceri. Now, seeing as I am in the presence of such a pretty lady, it is my duty to escort you to this gathering. That's if Tom Griffiths don't mind.'

She laughed and shook her head. Then she curtsied and linked her arm in mine. We started walking up the hill towards the meeting. Me in my waistcoat and jacket and her in her frilly cap and shawl. Proper gentry we were!

As we walked up to the top, the breeze picked up. Ceri shivered and pulled her shawl closer. We could hear singing and as we grew closer. I could make out the end of the beautiful Welsh hymn *Sanctaidd*:

> *Llawn yw'r nefoedd o'th ogoniant*
> *Llawn yw'r ddaear dir a mor*
> *Rhodder iti fythol foliant*
> *Sanctaidd! Sanctaidd! Sanctaidd Ior!*

The voices sang with such strength and beauty, I was so proud. I know it sounds so silly, but we Welsh have never been rich in money. We were always proud though of the rich beauty of the land and the wealth of our music. God was always an excuse to sing and it did bring joy to our hearts.

I felt embarrassed that I had nothing to say to her and I really wanted to tell her that the singing was from heaven, it was good to be with her and I hoped she would enjoy the service.

'You don't smell of cows.' It was the only thing I could think of saying.

She smiled. 'Well, we only have the one anyway and the hay on the other side of the room is dry and clean. Better there than sharing a bed with my sisters and brothers isn't it?

Warmer where I am and the cow does not snore, though I wish she went outside to do her business.'

She talked of the house and it was much like ours. All except they had a cow shed and it shared the same doorway as the house; One room for the family, one for the animals and the children probably asleep in the roof or under the bed.

Ceri and I reached my family near the top of the hill and I noticed Gwilym nearby. His face was a mass of bruises, with two black eyes and a split lip also. I went over to him and took his hand careful not to squeeze it, as he trembled to the touch.

'I know what you did,' I muttered, 'I'll not forget. Friends we are.'

He grinned at that. 'Being your friend isn't always that easy Lloyd *Shaneg*,' he slurred through broken lips. 'Told you to be careful with my Ceri.'

'Are you safe back home now?' I asked and he snorted in reply.

'Sure, doesn't your Dad knock you about every once in a while?'

'No...well once or twice, but I been really bad then and never with a stick.'

'Well blessed you are for that then,' he replied. 'Maybe someday I'll come and live with you.'

'Look, in all serious now, if things get too bad, come over and we'll have you as a lodger.'

He gently touched my arm. 'Thanks butt, but I tell you if I ever go, I'll leave some reminders to my beloved family first.'

The gathering started and all began to sit on the grass around Captain Nankivell, who stood at the crest of the hill. The Captain read from the bible, his words breaking through the breeze as water cascades over a fall. His bass voice boomed out clearly over all assembled, it was incredible to hear.

He prayed for our souls, laughed at the weakness of man, raged at the temptation of drink, and wept for the sinners who were beyond redemption. He played on all our emotions and by the end of his sermon, many were up on their feet in a frenzy, praising the Lord with great Hallelujahs.

Such was the stuff of revival meetings. Me? I liked his words. They all made sense. However, I was more of a liking for the singing and my eyes that day were only for the beauty of the valley and I felt calm with little Ceri by my side. At the end, the Captain spoke gently to us all.

'Remember, my children. Remember well. Our time on earth be short and our lot do be hard. But if you keep to God's laws and do love thy neighbour, there be room in our lives for great joy, Joy of our beautiful land. Joy in having friends, family and children. Joy for us knowing that at the last, we be saved by Lord Jesu and our reward to be the kingdom of heaven. Now let us pray.'

He knelt on one knee and put his hat to his heart. As the folk bowed their heads in prayer, Captain Nankivell spoke the Lord's prayer. Not in Welsh or English, but in Cornish and lovely it was to hear it spoke:

Agan Tas-ny, us yn nef, benygys re bo dha Hanow…

I could see Ben and some of the older Cornish join with him. Ben's face looked proud, as he softly whispered the words like they were magic. His wife was in tears and David looked ready to weep with joy also.

Funny you may think, how language is so important to some folk. You have to understand why. It tells you who you are and where you are from. It gives you pride that money will never buy.

The Captain stood up and dusted his knee.

'Now, let us do sing one more hymn together and then we do part as friends. We do sing in Welsh - but know that us Cornish folk will be there to help you if you are found wanting in voice.'

That brought a laugh from all and a few hearty 'Amens' too.

Nankivell took a deep breath and began:

I bob un sy'n ffyddlon, Dan ei faner ef
Mae gan Iesu goron fry yn nheyrnas nef….

They all sang with great feeling, most were even in tune. They must have heard us in Hafod that day, for the *hwyl* was there with us. At the end, they all fell straight into a chorus of *Bendigedig Ffyddo'r Iesu* and then it was done.

There was much hugging and handshaking as people said farewell to each other. Many made for the Captain to offer their thanks.

We said our good-byes to the Treveglos family and then a nod and a wink to Gwilym and Ceri and we were off back home.

'Dad,' I said. 'When are you going to teach me how to fight?'

'Hisht now!' my father hissed. 'When did that all enter your head? And after such a beautiful sermon just now, about turning the other cheek also?'

'I want to teach Gethin Hughes some manners and stop him from hitting women.' I said solemnly.

Dad tried to hide a grin 'Well now! We had better educate you then. If my son is going to be a knight in shining armour, he had better learn the right way to hold a lance!'

Everyone laughed at that, except me of course.

A few nights later, Dad hung an old sack of wet straw in the lean-to. Our goats looked on, wondering if it was food. They would have it in the end, but for now it was ready for my lesson.

'Right you,' Dad said to me. 'Strip to your waist and I want you to hit this sack until I say stop. Straight punches from the shoulder and punch as if you were going through the bag. Thumbs out of your fist, unless you want them broken. Before you start learning how to hit, you need your hands toughened up. Off you go then.'

Off I went like an express train and it wasn't long before I came to realise you had to pace yourself.

64

Thump! Thump! Thump! He had me at it for days after work, until I was raw and then we stopped for the Sabbath. As the weeks passed, he showed me how to fight. Not just punches, but footwork, breathing, movement, wrestling, kicking, gouging and just about everything he could think of. As time went on, I became good. I'd never be a prize-fighter mind, but I wouldn't be no pushover neither.

Next time I saw Gethin Hughes, it was in the spring and a different story to what I was expecting. It was after a time of heavy rain and, I was down the woods looking for the Cornish boys, Ceri, Gwilym…any friendly face really.

David had been off many times of late, trying to catch the eye of Gwenllian in the village by all accounts. I had been late with all the work around the house and looked as if I had missed everyone. The place was silent, save the rushing water and rustling leaves. I decided to go down to the Ystwyth, to look for trout in some of the pools.

Not that it was legal, but in them days you got whatever food you could as extra. We grew vegetables and had lockups for a goat and a pig. Milk and meat when you could get it. Everyone around had a pig and we were fattening them up to the point when they would keep us in meat. One by one we killed our pigs and shared the meat among the village. Then off to Ffair Rhos to buy another.

Mam tried not to buy at the store. It was never cheap, she said, and we needed the coin for fixing the house, buying tools, births, marriages and deaths.

At the bottom of a steep bank, I saw a movement at the river's edge and heard a cry over the din of the water. There was someone lying there and by the way one shoulder was drooped and the way he held it, he looked in trouble.

Looking at the valley side, I noticed the streak of mud trailing down the bank, ending with a drop to some rocks.

It was Gethin Hughes, he had grabbed at a tree and the branch had given way and now he looked in pain.

I looked at the river and it was fast running. You needed your wits about you to get to him without falling yourself. It was not easy. I had to go back a fair way and wade the river a bit. When I got to him, he was still groaning with pain, but he turned on hearing my approach.

A gash on his head had dripped blood over his face to add to his distress. He needed help to get out of there no question, but by the look he gave me, I think he would have rather been stuck there than use me.

He rolled over a bit and arched his back in pain as his shoulder moved '*Iesu Grist*!' he moaned between gritted teeth. 'What do you want boy?'

'I saw you had fallen and thought you were needing help.'

Gethin groaned and slowly raised himself to a standing position, resisting efforts to help. His right arm dangled almost useless at his side as he panted with the pain. He looked up the bank.

'Slipped down the bastard mud. Grabbed the tree to stop and must have pulled my bastard shoulder out,' he gasped. 'You come to gloat, boy?'

He was beginning to annoy me; cold and wet as I was, I was in no need for this. 'No, I'm here to help. But if you're going to be like that, I'll be off then.'

'Shut your mouth boy! Or I'll knock you down the river, you hear? Would have done it by now, if it wasn't for this bloody shoulder.'

I snapped then. 'That's you all over, isn't it? Fists first and then think later. Fine! You stay here and rot then. I can't see you getting out of here without me anyhow; no bugger's going to hear you over the noise of the river. I'll leave you to the bloody fish or maybe until they get you for poaching them.'

'What bloody fish? Everyone knows there's no fish in the Ystwyth, they've all choked on the lead!' he spat back

Gethin stood there a long while panting, then just as I turned he said.

'Alright, I spoke in haste. I'm sorry. I need your help. I can pull myself up with one hand, but you need to guide me and give me support when I ask it.' He paused. 'You done well coming here, knowing who I am and the bad blood there is.'

'No bad blood with me. Let's get you up and be done with it.'

We backtracked up the river to where it was easier to climb. Gethin started up slowly; he moved like each boot was filled with lead and a sack of coal on his back.

He was making good progress when he slipped. His right foot went down throwing him forward on his injured side. He had to put out his injured arm to stop himself and it made him scream. Losing his footing, he tumbled down to the river again. I quickly made my way down to him.

'The pain. Oh, *Iesu* the pain!' he wheezed all bunched up in agony, before passing out.

Nothing for it then, I picked him up carefully over my shoulders like a bullock. My left hand pulled his left arm over me, right hand between his legs and grabbing the back of his trousers. Not a pretty sight, I can tell you. I started up the bank once more. After a few years of mining I was as strong as an ox, but my knees creaked with every step.

Twice, I slipped and managed to dig my knee in to the ground to stop me falling. The next step after that was hell, as I put all our weight on one knee to raise us back up. Finally, I got us onto the road and down to the bridge below the village. My legs were shaking as we faced the hill up to Pont-Rhyd-y-Groes. Gethin was stirring by then.

'Don't move,' I said. 'You'll regret it.'

'*Iesu Grist!*' he moaned. 'It is bad with me, it is. *Iesu Grist!*' Then as his wits returned, he whispered, 'Do you have to hold me like this? Embarrassing it is.'

'How do you think I feel?' I shot back and he chuckled, although it was strained. 'Put me down boy, I can feel you shaking. Put me down before you collapse.'

I put him down and he was leaning on me for support, as he began to direct me to their house. We limped down the hill to a dark, smoky ruin of a place. Moss covered the roof and smoke seeped out of the straw and walls.

The smell was awful, but I was standing by a pig-pen in need of mucking out. Ceri was outside, stitching some clothes. She looked, dropped her stitching and ran to open the door We shuffled in and I had Gethin laid on the floor.

'What you done to my boy?'

Gomer Hughes rose from his seat, his flagon dropped to smash at the floor and he was up and at me! I stepped back and fell over Gethin. Gomer had me by the throat before I could do anything. I flattened my hand and jabbed him below the breastbone. He went down with a great whoosh, got back up quickly and grabbed a knife.

Gethin cried out, 'Dad, leave him!' and Gomer stopped. From nowhere, hands grabbed me and shoved me to the door. I looked and it was Gwilym. Ceri was at the door, pushing me out.

'Go you!' she said. 'Before he kills you.'

'I didn't do it, I found him lying there.'

'I know. I'll see you at the revival meeting on Sunday. Go you now!'

A roar came from behind her and I ran as fast as my failing legs could carry me.

Chapter Five

Superstitions

We began to be regulars at the revival meetings, Ceri and me. Since that first time, my family decided that chapel was enough for them and with Ceri's family being beyond religion, we were happily free of shepherding. David would not come, but then his eyes were always looking for Gwenllian Lewis.

Ceri was waiting for me at the point where she had found David's hat. Still the Welsh doll and happy with it. The way her smile warmed my heart, it was if the sun had broken from the clouds. Gwilym was there also, his bruises leaving his face a mass of purple and yellow from the pounding his father had given him. He nodded in greeting,

'All right now, *Shaneg Bach*?'

'*Sh'mae* you two, you'd think they'd start meeting indoors on days like this.' I said looking at the clouds brooding above. 'Seems to me that God feels his flock is in need of a wash today.'

We could hear the Captain speak as we moved up the hill to take our places. The sermon flowed with the pace of the gathering wind that was picking up and very soon we felt the falling drops of rain on us.

Nobody moved mind you, partly from duty and partly the hold that Nankivell had on them. He cast a spell with his speeches, but today he was at least merciful on his people.

'My children, I am so pleased to see you here once more, eager that you be to hear the word.' He spread his arms open and above. 'But today, I think he do wish my lesson to be short. Think on my words as you do carry out your daily lives. Remember them well. God's will be done. Now, let us pray, for I do wish to keep your Sunday best from ruin.'

A quick prayer it was, then he bade us all safe journeys and we fair ran down the hill as quick as we could, as we sought shelter from the rain that now fell like a waterfall. Ceri and I found a small group of trees and hid there, shaking the drops from our hair and clothes and giggling about it all.

'How's Gethin?' I managed to ask after a while; the question had burned at me since we had arrived.

'He's fine now, we got the Doctor and he put Geth's shoulder back in. Geth was quite noisy about it all, so it must have hurt, I'm thinking.'

She placed her hand on my arm then. 'You done well there Owain, Dad would have killed you.'

'Why's he so bad with me?'

Ceri just shook her head. 'Not you, bitter he is with the Frongoch men and he hates your Dad like no one else. He feels your Dad is the reason he is still alive. He wanted to die after the blast.

Full of hate for the world, he is now. He poisoned the minds of my kin too, except me and Gwil of course.'

'Well, if he really wants death that bad, he could always cut his wrist. How does he feel now?'

'To want to die is one thing, to kill yourself another. He's more bitter now. Gethin has cooled down, mind you. He respects what you done and has talked Dad down a bit. They don't want to kill you no more.'

'That's nice!' Then I thought a bit and added. 'Does he beat you?'

'Dad wouldn't dare because he is scared of Captain Nankivell. He came down and had a few words bout Gwilym also after the beating. Dad was warned off, so Gwil should be safe now also. Gethin's quiet also, thinking too much of his shoulder, I expect. That or he's found God.'

Ceri laughed; it was like little bells.

'Poor Dad, I do feel sorry for him though. It's sad to see him now drunk and not caring. It broke Mam's heart. That's why she ran off with the gypsies, I reckon.'

'What? When?'

'Last summer. Went with them, poor love. I miss her, but she got a few bruises from Dad when he was in his cups and I can understand why she ran. Couldn't take no more.'

'Can he be saved?'

Ceri shook her head and her lip quivered. 'No, he's past that and I fear he will leave his mark on us all, but...'

She sighed, then smiled sadly. 'We can always pray – that's why we come here for, isn't it?' She laughed again. We stood there watching the rain for a long while until it eased. Ceri looked at me all shy and blushing.

'So perhaps we'll see you here next week?'

The approach of footsteps made us both look up and we saw Gwilym come limping over.

'Best be off Cer,' he said. 'Or we will be missed.' He nodded to me and Ceri took his hand.

'I'll be here.' I said. 'Perhaps we'll have more time to talk then.'

She smiled that smile then and was on her way.

In truth, that's how it was. We started going regular to Captain Nankivell's revival meetings, but really it was to see each other.

After a few months, we didn't go neither, we just met up and went off walking somewhere else; the pools or by the stream, even down the woods. We walked and talked. Only friends mind, Ceri was forever telling me of Tom and what he did.

'He's an ignorant fool sometimes, but his heart's in the right place,' she said with a faint smile. 'Not big on religion mind, the deacons think he's gone to hell already.'

Gwil came along with Ceri, but went to the service, then came back to pick her up and take her home. I never had Gwil as a religious boy, but he always came with Ceri and always made sure they came back together.

73

Good old Gwil always managed to keep out of the way, loved his sister like a father, he did. Leastways as a real father should.

One time we had just met at the Banc. It was many months after my meeting with Gethin and we were chatting over by the stream.

Nant Cwm Newydion they called it, but it was always the stream to us. Gwil had gone off to the meeting, leaving us to sit and admire the valley.

'You miners are so superstitious,' said Ceri all of a sudden.

'What do you mean?' I gasped. 'I only said the robin is bad luck.'

'Poor robin, going about his business and you go off cursing him, only a bird after all.'

'Alright girl,' I said all defensive. 'It's a tradition, not a superstition.'

'Yes, but it's not just that,' she continued, 'It's all those funny things you miners do. Dad nearly killed a black dog the other day. Said he would bring a rock fall at the mine. Gwil got a smack for whistling underground - said he was bringing up the devil.' She had her hands on her hips now. 'If that's the case, why don't you let people make the sign of a cross down there? Should be protection, but it's bad luck, they do say. Strange it is, and that is nothing as to what they said to me when I went underground to find you!'

That was a shock. My mind was scrambling for any idea as to why. She was nearly fifteen by then and beginning to develop those curves that started my mind thinking there was more to life than work, family and chapel.

'What you been doing underground then?'
I managed to splutter.

'Well,' she said all defensive now and biting
her lip. 'It's not long back that women worked
underground. My Mam-gu did until they made a
law.'

'Yes - hang on girl. What you said just
now. You came down looking for me?'

She looked at the stream for a while. 'Well,
I tried to…back when we had the trouble and my
Dad….' She sighed. 'Never said how sorry I am.'

'It's alright girl, we're friends now.'

She perked up a bit at that. 'Yes well, I was
so upset with it by then that I tried to get to see
you to say sorry. One day I found out where you
were. On level 117, so I went over to Vaughan's
shaft and tried to go down it.'

'117? That's over 700 feet, girl! Do you
know how hard it is getting in and out on those
ladders? And what light did you have?'

'Well, I thought the mine was lit up down
there. Don't laugh! I tried to get down, but old
Evans the shaft had me out. Clip round the head
too. Tried walking in an adit also but got chased
out, nearly drowned trying to escape. Women
underground are bad luck, that's what they mostly
said anyhow!'

'What of Tom Griffiths?' I'd not met the
boy, but I guessed he'd be handy.

Ceri snorted. 'What of him? Doesn't own
me. I'll see who I see and talk with who I want. If
it's a problem…well, he can go and sweet talk the
girls at the fair once a year instead.'

She said it so sweetly, but I heard the steel edged in her voice. Had to grow up quick had my friend. Done that and all.

'Look girl. I don't think I'm that superstitious really. I don't believe that doing a cross underground is bad luck. But it would upset others. I don't hold with all that nonsense, like a white rabbit foretelling a death. It's just you've got to respect other people's thoughts. I mean, I always leave a bit of tallow for any snail I pass on the way to work, but that's polite not superstitious!'

'Pah!' She spat, 'you're just as bad as the rest. Then there's them knockers. I mean who's heard of pixies in rocks? *Tylwyth Teg*? Since when?'

'Well you say that, but there are strange things that go on down below. You're working away and you start hearing knocking noises from inside the rock, especially after blasting. What would you think then?

The Cornish lads have it that's knockers who do it. Another thing is we always leave a bit of food for them on the way out and it's gone come morning. Explain that one, Ceri *bach*!'

'You're hopeless Owain Thomas! You blow up the rock and it's like giving it a good old punch. Somebody punch you and you'd make a noise no problem! As for food, you never seen any rats or frogs down there? How do they feed? Or what about your butties? That David Treveglos is always eating. Hopeless, the lot of you!'

'Alright girl, you're the expert. But it's dangerous down below and you can't blame folk for wanting to be lucky. I'll just carry on like the rest, just in case.'

She patted my arm then and smiled. 'You do that Owain *bach*, you stay lucky now.'

I looked up to see Gwilym was walking toward us and Ceri jumped up and smoothed her skirts.

'You carry on with your knockers then,' she said with a gentle mocking smile, 'but don't forget to clear the mine next time a cross-eyed man crosses your path on the way to work!'

'Cross-eyed man,' I snorted. 'What's doing with a cross-eyed man? Never heard that one.'

'Really? Thought it was common. If he's the first you see on your way to work, there'll be an accident. Don't forget now, you keep an eye out for that cross-eyed man,' she shouted over her shoulder with a giggle and they were off.

Mining was dangerous, no doubt of that. To make it worse, the tunnels were hot places. Too often, miners ended up nearly naked working in the heat. Wouldn't have kept their trousers on but for modesty and protection. Dust, dust, always dust. Even rougher after blasting, the quartz bits felt like little sparks on the back of your throat.

I knew it gave us the cough, but what could you do? Some would say we got the cough from the consumption or our damp breezy houses. Others had it due to smoking baccy or the lack of sunlight.

77

Me, I had it down to them little stones that cut me like glass inside. Still, a man's got to live and mining paid well in Ceredigion in them days. The farm labourers were poor compared to us. We ate well, considering. Well, had to really. Only way to get the strength to climb all them ladders and swing all them hammers and picks.

The rock was hard enough, but blasting it still gave us the danger of the roof or sides falling in, which sadly I saw for myself. We were underhand stoping, that is mining the ore as if in a cave, digging the roof away. Charge and blast, clear all the ore, stand on planks on the mess left and drill the next charge. We were down 117 level that time and a fair way in too. The shafts allowed ventilation through the levels, but the further you were from the shaft, the worse the air was. We had to cut our shift from eight hours to six.

The ore was being mined in many places, so we slowly made a cavern through the level and up to the next. Many caverns were now still narrow but long, so you could have more than one team there.

March 1876, I remember it too well, I still dream of it sometimes. We was clearing the loose from a stope for Sion to take away in his tram. Then making the deads secure for us to stand and drill blast holes. A normal job and we were well into it, when we heard a cry. The most awful cry ever, as if a man had been sent to hell. David and I were up on stulls working, but Dad and Ben were not and rushed down the tunnel, tools still in hand.

78

'What shall we do?' I asked.

David shrugged. 'Best we get down and go help. Sounds like trouble.'

As we picked our way down the spoil, someone screamed for the Doctor. Then the rumble of trams came down the tunnel, as a man ran past towards the shaft shouting 'Get Doctor Rowlands!'

The tram burst through the dark, men pushing it as fast as they could. One was beside himself, yelling, 'Quick boys, faster! For God's sake, faster!'

I had a glimpse of the tram as it sped through and the sight will stay with me for ever. A broken body, a boy not much younger than me, looking lifeless and covered in blood. One arm almost hanging out and moving up and down as the tram bumped its way along. Then it disappeared in the shadows.

Dad and Ben came back, breathless and looking so sad. Ben looked white with the running and Dad showed the strain in his eyes. Ben spat phlegm on the floor.

'When a boy do go, it's a bad business.'

Dad bent over to catch his breath, and then he looked at me. 'It's Richard Jones. His Dad was up on a pile knocking away the loose, and he told Richard to stand back down a way. A rock fell and took him full on.'

'He'll be alright won't he?' I asked in a panic.

Dad's winced and Ben muttered, 'Bad business.'

They were silent after that for the rest of the shift. We did not get much work done. I caught up with Sion Parry at the shaft at the end of the day, waiting for our turn up the ladder. He sat smoking on a stub of clay pipe.

'Do you know how Richard is?' I asked.

'Don't know,' he snapped all sullen toward me. 'What you care, anyhow?'

'He's one of us,' I replied. Sion glared at me.

'Wrong boy caught it if you ask me. Don't you bother me anyhow, Spaniard.' He got up to walk from me, then stopped.

'Another thing. You fooling around with that Hughes girl. Who gave you permission?'

'I don't need permission,' I snapped, rising to his tone.

He took the pipe from his mouth to jab in my direction. 'She's someone else's, you remember that. I hear you're still carrying on and there'll be trouble.'

I started to reply, but he had moved away.

'Bad tempered bastard,' chuckled David. 'Don't you worry of him. He's all wind and no sails. Probably shook up by Richard, we all are.'

Back up top we heard the news that Richard had died within an hour. Dad told us in hushed tones.

'Problem when you are 700 feet down is they have to winch you up the ladders to get you to the doctor. He's coming up the few miles from Pont Rhyd-y-Groes.

Only the lucky survive such a long climb. He wasn't one of them. Best you be careful boys.'

He didn't want to talk any more and it left a bad taste. I'd known Richard and he was alright. Novice, he was, bit like me I suppose. It scared me as to how easy it could be for the mine to end it for you. He was only fourteen, not much younger than me and the mine was in deep mourning for his soul as we tried to console his dad. After seeing his son dying in front of him, the man could not stop blaming himself, feeling he sent the boy to his death.

It shook my Dad to the core. He became quiet and moody. I felt he was looking out for me more. He was fussing around me down there now and we were beginning to argue. One night I asked him what we could do about Mr Jones. He sat in his chair by the fire and puffed his pipe, gazing into the fire.

'Nothing, *bach*. How do you comfort a man when he cannot forgive himself, even if it was a terrible accident?' There was pain in his voice. 'If that were you I could not live with it. You make sure you're safe down there. Listen to me and don't do anything foolish boy. You're our future and you'll be safe if I have anything to do about it.' He spat at the fire and it hissed back. 'This mine is hell and I wish it was that you were not there,' he sighed. 'If the farm had survived, we'd have been alright, but there we are.'

'Why did you come to Frongoch?' I asked.

'Money,' he snapped 'It all started as a way of earning outside of harvest, work in the winter and then come back and farm when it was needed. Then we lost a few crops and it became all the time to keep us out the poor house.'

'Must have been a busy time down the farm?' I said and he chuckled, as did Mam from her sewing.

'Oh yes,' he said 'There was always something needed doing, tend the flock, grow the crops, repairs. Dad even brewed his own beer from wheat to earn extra. Nice drop too. The pigs got the waste.'

'Aye, drunk as Lords they were,' said Mam. 'Your Nain and I came back from market the one time to find the old sow staggering in the road.

Nain muttered then if that's the state of the pig, I dread to think what the men are like.'

We all laughed then stopped to listen, as Myfanwy moved in her sleep in the roof above our bedroom. She hadn't woken, so we carried on. Dad struck a flame and relit his pipe.

'My poor Dad,' he muttered. 'The farm failed as the mine on the hill above poisoned the land. Not there when he built it, but soon killed us off. He blamed himself for that and for losing his Bessie to that Spanish sod all those years back.'

Mam clucked at that, but Dad continued. 'Even if that Spaniard is my true father, he took Mam and never came back to check on her. Never forgave him for that.'

'Nain did though,' I said softly.

'What you know of it?' Mam asked.

82

'I remember them talking, they thought I was asleep - but I heard everything.'

'You wait for me, for I could not go to Heaven without you. That's what Nain said'

'I will be there, Bess,' Taid replied. *'With apples for us to eat and a rug for us to sit on the grass and we will watch the clouds drift by together.'*

Dad was silent for a time after. Mam sighed and looked to the fire, her eyes filled with tears.

'Taid died and Nain was true to her word.' Mam whispered. 'She wasted away after him and became very withdrawn. She died in her sleep, but with such a look of pleasure and a lovely smile, knowing as she did the apples that were picked for her ahead.'

'Why did you come here?' I asked again. 'You could have worked at the mine above the farm.'

'Because the agent there was a scoundrel,' Dad replied. 'He wouldn't pay his men for weeks and then when he did, he'd pay them in goods from his shop. Cheese, barley and beer only and at high prices. If they wanted anything else, they had to sell the stuff back to him at a lower price. May he rot in hell.'

'Language!' Mam whispered.

'I would walk miles and work for John Taylor as he's an honest man. Pays his men in coin and on time and he doesn't fleece us at the shop. No man's ever been turned out of his house for debt neither.' Dad puffed on his pipe for a while.

'He's a good Cornish boy and a gentleman and the men would follow him to hell and back. You stay in this mine and the old man will see you right, but I hope you don't.'

'Why, Dad?'

He leaned forward 'Mining doesn't give us long on this earth,' he said pointing his pipe to make the point. 'If it's wet and the water turns to acid, it will rot your boots, your clothes and your lungs. You get what the doctor calls consumption. If it's too dry, you get the cough, like a ball on your chest. Lots of boys drink for that...'

'That's what they say anyhow,' said Mam. 'You see Pont Rhyd-y-Groes at throwing out time after *Sadwrn sistans* and everyone's staggering around looking for a fight and saying the good Lord's name in vain. Women and men mind you.

Then they are up on the Sunday, all holy of holies and praising God to the heavens. That's their entertainment. Pah! Look what it done to Gomer Hughes and his boys.'

'It's another Hughes he would look at,' said Dad all innocent, and I ground my teeth in embarrassment.

'Aye, that's as well. Good girl is Ceridwen Hughes, but you be careful and look out for her snakes of brothers and all.'

'She's not my sweetheart,' I said defensively. 'I'm not interested in women.'

The silence was only for my parents to gather themselves and not laugh in my face at my words.

'Yes, well there we are then,' said Dad sounding choked.

'Why you so against the mine then?' I said.

'I'm not, Owain,' replied Dad. 'I'm not. Look son, I want to see you grow up and marry. I want your son bouncing on my knee. There's times the mine scares me though and you'll forgive me when I seem to be treating you like a child, when you are most of a man. I want you alive, I want you out of there and away from this life. We can talk of this again, it's late now. Just get out before the dust gets you, that's all.

Richard may have died, but he got a quick death, not a slow one coughing his lungs up with dust like the rest of us.'

The room was silent then, except the ticking of the clock on the dresser, time marching on and so much for us to do and say.

Dad sighed. 'It's late now and it's time for sleep. We got a busy day tomorrow and I'll not have you asleep and falling off the ladders. Your Mam would give me hell.'

I bade them good night and began to move to my bed. The added roof space had allowed us to fashion two there, where Myfanwy now muttered away to herself in her dreams. I was glad she had not been listening. The subject was not a happy one and she was still a child.

'What about the New World then?' I said as I stood up.

'Well now that's a thing. There is the New World at that. America or Australia,' said Mam.

'They do say that the conditions are better there. The men are paid a good honest wage and there is no dust, but I think that's just tales.'

'Then there's Patagonia. The Welsh community at Trelew always wants people although you'd have to learn a trade. I could always teach you roofing, mind you. Yes, there's a thing, we'll talk about that some other time.'

I went to my room, turning briefly to see Mam and Dad in a full embrace. Dad's head was on Mam's shoulder and from the way he was standing it looked as if he was crying. Richard's death had scared him and for the first time I saw my Dad for who he was. A strong man, but desperate to keep his family provided for and terrified that he would end up like his father.

Chapter Six

An Accident

I got used to the many dangers working underground. Some were simple, like falling off ladders or flooding, but hang-fire was by far the most frightening.

After you primed your blast holes, the last thing to do was to lay a fuse from the dynamite. It was long so's you had time to reach the safe hole where your boys were crouched waiting. From there you could watch as the flame moved along the fuse, spitting its way on to its doom. I was always one for hiding way before then.

Sometimes the powder did not blow. It might be a slow burner and sit there for a while longer than you expected before it went. It might be damp, that was a real danger. It would dry out all primed and ready to go off. In the jumble of rock after a blast, it was difficult to see where the charge had been. It would lie there, then a miner comes along to a pile of rocks with shovel and pick to clear them. A small spark and that was that.

You never knew if it would happen, like a silent snake waiting in the rocks for you. It was always a thought in the back of your mind when you started a new *bargen* on a patch that had been worked before.

There was always the question, 'What if there's still powder in the rocks?' The light was bad for us down there, the candles faintly flickering in the bad air, so you kept your eye out as best you could for signs. What else could you do?

'Just get on with it,' Mam told me. 'Or quit and walk out your house and into the workhouse in poverty. It's a hard life and no mistake, but it's what we're put on God's earth for.'

Later that year, in November, William Jenkins was caught by hang-fire. He died the following day. They had even got him up the shaft and the doctor had taken him to his home in the carriage, but he'd still not lasted. Again, it was 117 level.

'Poor man,' said David, as we waited our turn down the ladders in the cold and wet soon after the death.

'A bit *twp*, if you ask me,' said Dad. They had primed three charges and only one went off. He went back after twenty minutes to look, while the other boys stayed put like they should.'

'Everyone knows you do wait a full day before you go back,' muttered Ben. 'It do let any slow fuse blow and the dust settle. He was just too keen for his *bargen.*'

'No bloody use if you're not around to share it,' David said with a grim smile.

His father grunted in agreement, but this had a strange effect on Dad. His face grew red with anger; as if someone had let off his fuse and them days it had stopped being a slow burner and all.

'I tell you this now,' he spat out. 'I'll not strike no more *bargen* on 117. That's two deaths in one year, cursed it is. Another thing, we'll not go in so far from now on.

Not losing two hours work a day for fear of choking through bad air. Not losing a man's work because he has to fan the time candle just to keep it going. Waste of a man that is.' His mouth tightened then. 'Plenty of pickings elsewhere, don't need no nonsense.'

Ben came up and clapped him on the shoulder. 'Fine, we do do as you say Gareth,' he said softly.

Dad sighed. 'Alright old man, you always been the calm one. Angry I am at the waste of life, that's all. Quick off the mark these days I know, boys. Just that every time one of us miners is killed, it reminds me that life is such a precious thing and how we waste it so damned cheaply underground. We'll take care of ourselves from now on.'

He was not the only one, all the pare leaders had tightened up since the last accident. Many had been ready to ignore the rules for the extra cash, but at least for now everyone worked as they should.

Death was never far away from us. We died early, worn out and coughing with the dust or consumption. Many babies were lost to working families before they could walk, for that was the time when they were most at danger.

Deaths at the mine were rare though and 1876 was a bad run for us. All we could do was hope the next year would be better.

I had not seen Ceri for a while. The revival folk had moved indoors down in Pont Rhyd-y-Groes over winter and it was difficult to lose ourselves unnoticed from the crowd.

I knew that word would get back to Gomer if I went and it would be bad for Ceri, so I stayed away.

Never got word to her, so God knows what she thought. Didn't want to tell Myfanwy, I knew she'd be off clecking and the whole valley would be knowing soon enough. I was still wary of this Tom Griffiths and remembered Sion Parry's words.

I thought he'd changed, Parry. Well for a moment. One time I was at the ore chute and he had pushed the tram up for loading. He looked around in the gloom, then whispered urgently.

'Hey, *Tomos Shaneg bach*, you want a sweet?'

He held out his hand and dropped a small sticky sweet in my hand. I got a call soon after, so slipped it in my pocket for later. In truth, I forgot about the whole damn thing until after the climb back up that day. David found me at the top looking at it in my hand.

'Why you holding a sheep turd?' he asked all curious.

'Present from Sion Parry,' I said, flicking it away.

David shook his head and smiled. 'He's really got it in for you, hasn't he? Don't worry, you're a stronger boy than him and you know how to look after yourself.'

My days were busier now, there was the small holding to work and the house to repair. Dad had a mind to fill the walls of the house with more clom to stop the draught and make it warmer. We were working out the right mix of mud, stone, straw and cattle blood for it to set like stone and fill the gaps.

The spring arrived and we were looking forward to warm sunny days and a good harvest. Funny, though, that the mine would ever wish the opposite.

Hot summers meant the water ran out at the pools. Without water, we could not pump the mine or mill the ore.

The lower workings would flood, as we waited for the pools to fill again before the pumps could clear it all. Then we could start working proper again. We needed the water to raise the water from the mine. God has a sense of humour sometimes.

The mine used the time for maintenance, even making Llyn Frongoch bigger later on, when they took the trammers out of the mine to help then because there was less work below. When there was no work at Frongoch, there was plenty to do at home.

We all had crops to save and animals to keep alive, so we farmed and searched high and low for what water we could get to keep us. Cabbages and potatoes, beans and peas, leeks and so on all need God's gift of water to grow. Mind you, with no money coming in, they were difficult times. Many would go into debt at the shop. Old man Taylor never put a man out for that when others would, for that he was a saint.

It was not until May 1877 that I saw Ceri again. That month our pare were working at a higher level, so we were close to first out at the end of the shift. As we came out one day, we heard a fuss by the mill.

Fearing for Mam and Myfanwy, I started to walk over and when I heard a scream, I was running for the crowd. The scream sounded again. It just carried on like there was nothing left.

I got through the crowd and found Ceri. Her fists were bunched, eyes wild and tears streaming down her face as she wailed and wailed like there was no stopping her. People just stood and watched, not knowing what to do, until Mam stepped forward and slapped her about the cheek.

Ceri's head whipped to one side and her eyes opened in surprise. She stopped screaming though and just stood there sobbing. Mam spied me and pushed Ceri, so she damn near fell in my arms.

'There's been an accident here Owain. We're alright, but the girl's a bit shaken. Take her home *bach*, so she can rest. It's been a big shock for her.'

Ceri stumbled past me while Mam was lost in the crowd before I could ask what was going on. I caught up with Ceri and took her hand, gently guiding her down past the reservoir and on to New Row. As we reached the road, I felt free of crowds and stopped. Ceri had followed me as if blind, holding my hand as if I was her last hope. She was still sobbing quietly, lips trembling. Slowly she looked up and as her dull eyes met mine, I saw the pain. I reached for her and took her into my arms, so she was in my shoulder and crying like a new-born. Her whole body shook, and I just held her and tried to stroke her hair. It was matted and grey with dust.

She smelt of dried sweat, but I could only think of her warmth and a desire swept over me to make it right for her.

We stood there a while before Ceri broke away and raised a tiny smile, though the pain still showed.

She took my arm and we walked back to the village. She didn't speak and I didn't think it right to ask what was wrong. I could not find the words anyway, so we walked in silence through a world of running streams, rustling trees and birdsong.

We reached the village and made our way towards the group of small cottages where the Hughes family lived.

As we neared them, I saw Gomer Hughes come out towards us. It was early and he was still sober. I could see his face turning red and his brows darken as he recognised me.

'What's this?' he growled.

'There's been an accident at the mill.' I said evenly, 'I was told to take Ceri home, as she's got fright.'

'Aye and docked wages for leaving early, I'll bargain,' was his acid reply.

I shrugged. 'Work's done for the day anyhow.'

Gomer looked at me with for a while; our eyes locked for a moment before he jerked his thumb behind him. 'Ceridwen. In the house, now. There's food to make.'

Ceri stumbled past him in a daze, pausing behind him to look back at me. Her eyes looked at me, telling me a message I could not understand then she left.

Gomer stood in front of me, thumbs in his belt, and glared at me.

'So, Gareth Thomas's boy's come to save us once more,' he mocked, then cursed and spat, his manner changing as he brought his loathing of me under control.

'Look boy,' he said, trying to sound reasonable. 'You're decent enough. I know you're trying to help and all, but I don't want you round here, understand?

I nodded.

'You seem alright, but your Dad got me fired at Frongoch and I'll not have my Ceridwen mixing with your family, alright?'

'I heard tell he offered you a place in his pare, but you threw it back at him.' I said cold as a tomb, stung by the insult.

'To my face, perhaps. But he wouldn't have been such a noble man when I wasn't there,' sneered Gomer. 'Just stay away boy!' He walked past me towards the village to lose his soul once more in a jug of ale.

When I got home, I found out what had happened. One of the mill boys had been crushed between the cogs of a waterwheel. I wanted so much then to find Ceri and talk to her, to see what I could do to help, but I did not see her for ages.

It was as if she had disappeared. I was on the verge of even going down to the house and facing Gomer again, but it was Myfanwy that stopped me.

We were in the garden working together, when she said without warning,   'She's still upset you know?'

'Who?'

'Your girl of course. She saw the boy fall in. Real fright she got.' She gave me a look. 'You two been courting then?'

'Don't be dull, girl. She's walking out with another. What made you say that?'

'Only that she asked me to give you a message. David's hat, she said. Is that the revival meeting on the Banc again?'

'Yes, we're really close to God, so be off with you before I get him to send you a plague of boils,' I said with irritation.

She skipped away, singing, 'Ceridwen Hughes,' as she went.

On the Sunday, I made for the Banc and saw Ceri waiting by the road. When I got there, she wouldn't look at me, her eyes red as if she'd been weeping. She tried to smile, but the side of her mouth trembled. I just reached out to hug her again. She sobbed and clung to me like a child.

She broke away after a while and sniffed, 'I'm sorry Owain,' she said in a small voice. 'I just feel so bad and I don't know who to talk to.'

That made me feel all brotherly, so I gave her a warm smile and a squeeze on her arm. 'That's alright, Ceri *bach*,' I tried to sound bright. 'You know you can talk to me anytime. Worried for you, I was. Been looking for you.'

She smiled her weak smile again, 'I'm sorry. I been hiding, just doing the work and running home.' She bit her lip.

'I been away also,' I replied. 'Stopped going to them meetings for fear of loose talk about us. You know what folks are like.'

She nodded sadly but didn't reply.

In a softer voice, I asked her. 'It's the boy, isn't it? You knew him?'

She swallowed and nodded, 'I saw him,' she said softly, 'when he...'

She bit her lip as it trembled. 'David Richards it was and yes, I knew him. Didn't see him fall, but I heard the cry and I turned and… and… he… his head was stuck and it just…'

She started to sob again, so I held her close, whispering gently. '*Hisht* now girl, it's all gone now. He's off to a better place. *Hisht.*'

I knew the tale; he had fallen into the cogs of a waterwheel and his head had been crushed. Ceri seemed to be reliving it again and again and I felt helpless to stop it as she cried in my arms.

'Come on; you,' I said as I gently broke the embrace. 'Let's go walk and talk. You take my arm and we'll be off. Cwm Newydion and then back down New Row, right? The weather is good and we can watch out for birds or we'll race clouds. You choose one, I'll choose one and we'll see which one is first to Graig Goch. What do you think?'

She smiled, wiping her tears nodding and we set off. I talked about anything and everything. Ceri just listened, clung to my arm and smiled as I tried to make light of the world. We reached a point where the road passed a patch of grass on a rise. Ceri went to sit by there and I joined her. The sun shone and she shook her head as if to warm the curls of her hair. She closed her eyes and raised her head to the sun's warmth as a flower would, smiling with it.

'You are good to me, Owain. I have been so bad since the accident. I been losing sleep, scared of the nightmares I am. I hear the screams echo in my mind and…' Her face clouded with the memory.

'Now then, don't get all worked up again. We'll just sit here and talk, alright? Grass is dry and the sun is warm.'

She had taken out a handkerchief, it looked scrubbed clean. Carefully, she opened it to reveal some food.

'Bread and jam?' she said shyly, 'I brought it special.'

I took some and we ate in silence. A gentle warm breeze added relief from the warm sun. We finished the food and Ceri yawned and stretched.

'Oh Owain, I could just sleep here now.'

'Why not? There's no harm and I'm here to chase away the spirits, so you'll have no nightmares. You rest your head a while and I'll watch over you.'

She snuggled up close and was asleep in seconds, as if she had not slept for a week. I let her lie there, even though my arm tingled with the pressure of her body on it.

She slept an hour at least and I sat there with her and let my mind drift. I looked at the beauty of the land and was sad that I never saw it most days. In that at least, I had envy for the farmer.

At least he could greet every dawn and watch every sunset. He could feel the wind on his face and breathe the air pure and clear of dust.

I looked at Ceri and smiled, I had the urge to stroke her hair, but feared that it would wake her. I looked at her small nose, slightly upturned, her faint freckles and her lovely dark eyebrows. The way her mouth now curved into a relaxed smile. Even then, I knew she was beautiful and I enjoyed looking at her face and watching her move. I thought how lucky I was to have such a pretty girl as a friend. I felt sorry that she had such a man as Gomer as her father. I wished that it could be different but
had no idea how to make it so.

As if to stop my worrying, Ceri began to stir, then woke up stretching away the stiffness of her limbs. Her eyes were slow to open and she rubbed them, yawning, and then stretched once more. She looked around and then smiled at me.

'That was the best sleep I had in ages, thank you.'

'That's alright Ceri, you needed it,' I looked at the sun. 'It's late afternoon, we best start back, for your Dad will wonder where you are.'

She shook her head. 'Not today. They gone up in the hills to a cock fight in a farm somewhere, away from prying eyes. They all gone except me and they'll drink there, so won't be back until late.'

'Well even so, I'll not have people talking.'

She giggled, 'There's a gentleman you are now.'

We got up and started off back down the valley, walking slower now, as we enjoyed each other's company.

By the time we reached New Row, the sun was touching the valley sides and as we passed the chapel, we saw people moving to the evening service.

'Let's go in,' said Ceri all of a sudden.

'But that's Capel Saeson,' I stammered, 'they do it all in English there.'

'Yes, but I want to hear it, it would be nice. It's a musical language.'

'Not the way them boys say it,' I muttered. Then I gave a deep sigh. 'Alright Ceri, let's go in. I'm sure the Cornish boys won't throw us out.'

'Capel Saeson is such a name, *the English chapel*,' she said in a poor impression of gentry. 'What's it really called?'

'Ty'n-y-Groes I think.'

'That's much nicer. Come on then, boy, let's go sneak round the back.'

It was a tiny place, some steep steps up from the road and a little porch leading to the chapel inside. The pulpit seemed squashed between the deacon's pews to the side and the family pews in front.

We tried to sit at the back, by the door for a quick escape. It was nonsense, but I sat there feeling like I would be shouted at for not speaking English, and bundled out. Nobody showed any bad feeling though, it was just my silly thoughts. As we sat there, I felt a tap on my shoulder.

'Welcome to God's house, my boy.' It was Ben.

'Hope they don't mind,' I said nodding at the deacons.

'Never you mind them,' he said. 'I'll nudge you when you do stand and sit and you mime your words like most of them do.' He chuckled and someone gave him a dirty look, which only made him chuckle some more.

We sat and watched the service.

'I always thought that it would all be different somehow,' I whispered. 'But it feels the same as Trisant.'

Ceri gave me a look and I made a face. 'Well it's not as if I go round checking each other's chapels for how they do things, is it? People stay with what they grow up with mostly. Mind you, there were some who would change their chapel to that of the mine captain to try for a better pitch and *bargen*.'

Ceri flushed and someone cleared his throat. A warning for me to be quiet.

I knew Ceri had wanted more time away from her house and so I was happy to give her that. Besides, I liked being with her. I had some English even then, through the Cornish boys at the mine, so I followed the service a bit and guessed the rest.

The minister was a powerful man with big sideburns, making up for his lack of hair on top. His voice carried like a spell and they all hung on his every word. I didn't know if Ceri understood but she watched every movement in awe.

101

The service ended and we all made to leave. The minister came to the door to wish everyone God speed. As we passed, he greeted us and shook my hand.

'You are new here,' he said in English.

'Yes,' I answered, 'from Trisant.'

'Well Wesley's roots lie deep up there also,' he said in Welsh with a smile. 'Visiting then, is it?'

'Yes sir.'

'Well, you are welcome here. Remember that, My name is Rowlands.'

'I am Owain Thomas and Ceri is…'

'Your friend, yes,' He smiled a fatherly smile. 'Well perhaps we'll see you again some time.'

We wished him good-night and reached the bottom of the stairs, where the Treveglos family waited.

'It's a thought I do have that I should escort young Miss Hughes back home,' said Ben. 'Can't be too careful and I'll not be having people talking.'

I nodded thanks, at least I would not be facing Gomer again.

Ceri's eyes brimmed with warmth. 'Thank you Owain. You have been more help than you know,' she smiled and before I could think stepped up and kissed me on the cheek. Then she was off down the road with Ben.

I found David and we walked back to New Row together.

'So, you courting now?' he asked.

'No, just friends like. She's been really bad after that accident.'

'And a kiss and a cuddle makes it better,' he said with a grin.

'*Cer o'r ffordd!*' I growled and he ducked at my playful swipe. 'She's walking with Tom Griffiths she says and I'll respect that.'

David looked at me like I was telling him the moon was cheese.

'What about Gwenllian Lewis then?' I teased. 'Talk is you've lost your soul to her.'

'It's true my friend,' David said with a sigh and I knew he was not joking any more. 'She's the world to me and no mistake. I just... I don't know. I want to ask her dad for us to marry, but I don't know how he will react or even how she will.'

'Why don't you ask her?'

'What if she says no?'

'What if she says yes? Come on you big brave Cornish boy, you're going to have to someday. If you think you're ready, then do it.'

David smiled, all shy of a sudden. 'But I'm only seventeen.'

'Aye and you earn a tidy wage in the mine, boy, considering all other working folk around us. If she didn't want you around, you'd be back down the hill throwing mud at the Logaulas boys by now. With the children.'

David tried a playful slap which I batted away and we both laughed.

'Follow your heart David, it'll tell you what's right.'

We had reached the steps to the houses and he stood at the bottom and then grinned at me. 'I will Owain boy, I will. But you do the same yourself.'

'I will when the time comes, Davy boy.'

'Alright my friend, but it may arrive sooner than you think.'

'Don't be dull Davy, it's not there with me. I'm too young and she's too young and all. Definite! Besides, she's forever talking of this Tom Griffiths and how he brings her daisies and the like. Then there's others like Sion Parry warning me off. What's this Tom like anyhow?'

'Lump of a boy, slow and clumsy. Leastways that what sister Mary have said.'

David smiled, but then he went all serious. 'Look, I'm not teasing you too much, I just have a feeling. I never seen anyone look at me like she looks at you. Now's time to start thinking about the future my friend. Don't lose your way because you can't see what's in front of your nose.'

Chapter Seven

Emigration

There was a dark atmosphere after those three deaths. The funerals were well; it was times like this when the community came together in grief and folk did what they could to help. A *cymorth* was made to collect what coin people could spare for the families, but that never brings back the dead, does it? The sadness was left hanging in the air for ages after. There had been many accidents before this, for mining is a dangerous business. Deaths were not common though and losing three, especially the young ones, caused much heartache. I pray that they all rest in peace, freed as they are from this terrible toil.

Ceri had recovered slowly from the shock and I had managed to start to meet her once more. Her blasphemous family were now off to the gambling dens in the hills. Gwil went with them, more for appearances Ceri said. There was not much love around within that family, with a father who wished he were dead.

Sion Parry still had it in for me, forever throwing me a dirty look when he saw me. He wouldn't come close when others were around, but he caught hold of me when we were out of earshot one break and grabbed my throat.

'I thought I told you to stay away,'
'From who?' I said as best I could.

105

'You know damn well who,' he said. 'I told you enough times she's walking out with another. I had enough of you, you come in here, take the miner's job from those who deserve and all because of your father.' His sneer got louder. 'I'm going to sort you out good and proper you Spanish bastard.'

I had enough of him now and it was time to end it. I pushed him back tripping him as I went. He lost balance which meant I had him up against the other wall in no time.

'Two things I'll say,' I spat. 'One you're not working in my place as you're not good enough. Two, I'll talk to who the bloody hell I like.'

'Time to go,' David's voice echoed as he reached us. 'You've been found out here Sioni *bach*, take your bullying somewhere else.'

Sion wrenched free and stumbled away, casting a sour look at me. It didn't make him work any better, but it had sorted my little problem with him at work at least. He never spoke another word to me.

My Dad and Ben always seemed to be talking over the news. The two of them would each buy a newspaper every week and take the whole seven days to read it.

Dad read *Y Cymro* and encouraged me also, then halfway through the week, he would swap for Ben's English newspaper. Dad struggled with the words, not being English speaking by nature, but it never stopped him.

They would read every line and enjoy discussing the reports with each other over breaks. By the next Friday, it was time to start again and use the old paper for firelighters. The fuel for discussion then became the fuel for the fire.

The local newspapers of the time were weekly and contained all the important news from outside as well as inside the area. There was also the tittle-tattle, to keep folk clecking for days. Dad and Ben weren't the only ones to do this.

The tunnels echoed with political debate at times. Very aware of the world were the boys of Frongoch and willing to debate all day if allowed to. The local politicians would even go so far as to come to Trisant of an election for our votes – and look out anyone who thought they could win us with fancy words and cheap promises. Most went for the *Y Cymro* or *Yr Amserau,* but Ben was champion of the *Aberystwyth Observer.*

'The editor be a bit of a firebrand with his thoughts and I like a man who's not afraid to speak his mind.' Ben would say.

'So, you are not one for the *Cambrian News* then?' I asked.

'No problems with that one. Only we were sent the Bala edition in the past on occasion. Some news for here I grant you, but I'm not so worried about what happens in Dolgellau.'

'Do they not print one for round here?' I asked in surprise.

'Course they do, Owain.' Dad said. 'It's alright, but I'm taken with the *Observer* now.'

Dad had cooled down as time moved on from those dreadful accidents. The worry was always there in his eyes though and he would never be one to take risks. Times had changed now, and other worries were growing, for we were seeing a drop in the *bargen*.

The yield of ore was still high from the mine, but there was a worry that it was starting to level off and we would have to shift out more waste rock to get at the ore.

Some large finds in the New World had flooded the markets with cheaper lead and the prices were still falling. This meant our *bargen* rates were lower, so we was getting less for what we got out anyway.

There was me; always one for an opinion. Forever speaking out about anything I thought was bad to anyone with half an ear to listen. I didn't know the first thing about managing mind you, but it didn't stop me talking about it.

David let me say my piece, the good humour he was blessed with rose above all the bad that I showed. Dad put up with my talk but was quick to put me in my place when I started to talk with others.

He made sure I knew one evening, as we sat with Mam taking our brief quiet time by the fire before bed.

'What's the matter with you Owain?' Mam began. 'You've become quite a miserable wretch these days. What's going on, now?'

'You know what's wrong,' I replied. 'We still produce the same, but now we get less. The *bargen's* shrinking, while the Taylor's grow fat on the profit.'

'Well, we got serious competition these days, son,' Dad said puffing on his pipe. 'There's large ore bodies found in Australia at Broken Hill. It even made the newspaper. The lead's cheap now because it's easy to buy. Lots of it for sale.'

'You know Dad, there's talk of them even wanting to sell up or try and close us down. It is known that the Taylor's need to redo the lease with Lord Lisburne and there's talk that they may leave out Frongoch. How do you think that sits with people? There's hundreds of us families that survive on the mine to earn a crust.'

'Now look son, Old man Taylor took up the mine in 1842 and since then him and his boys have run the place tidy. They've not cheated us before, so why should they start now? They're good Cornish stock and mining is in their blood.

From Gwennap they are, like Nankivell and he'll have nothing said against them.'

'Why not?' I said moodily. 'What's stopping them from taking their share and going back to Cornwall? Don't need no owners or gentry anyway, could run it ourselves, I reckon.'

There was a silence for a while after that outburst. Dad looked at me calmly, as he puffed away at his pipe, he tapped the old baccy out on the fire and started filling it again.

'Who's been filling your head with nonsense boy?' he said quietly. He always called me boy when he was angry with me and at that age it made my blood boil, as I sat and fumed in silence.

'You don't know nothing here,' he continued, waving his pipe to make the point. 'Prices are falling. That means we have to sell for less or not sell at all. That means the mine makes less money. That makes the profit less for Taylor's and the *bargen* is set less for us. You do talk nonsense sometimes!'

'We should not work for less, we cannot afford it. I say we should demand what is our rightful share and strike if they do not pay it.'

Dad puffed away for a while, while I smoked in anger.

'Look son, the old man's done us right up to now and no mistake. Always been fair them Taylors. I've talked to some who work in other mines and they are fleeced.

They get cheated by the truck shop. They get thrown out of their houses for debt or even for saying things, like you have said just now.'

'Fair do's to the Taylors, they been looking after us for years. Remember '74? The yield was low and the pools dried up in the summer, so they couldn't use the machines? They made sure we didn't starve. Now they've got problems and not of their making.

So, we've got to knuckle down and help out as best we can. When the prices go back up, we'll get our rewards. You'll see.'

'So, you wouldn't strike then. You would go against your fellow workers if it came to a fight?'

'Not now. Not for this. I would strike if I felt the cause was just, but now? It would be foolish. Someone's been talking nonsense to you boy. You strike now, what happens? We starve. You want that? If you won, what would happen? In six months time, the mine would go out of business and we starve just as much. You want that? Better you think out the full story before you do anything drastic. We need cool heads for now, while the storms rage around us.'

'So, you would walk through a strike then? You would betray your friends and let the managers win' Dad sighed and shook his head.

'There'd be no winners here boy and you're a fool to think otherwise. Yes, when I decide to work, I'll work and to hell with anyone who stands in my way'

'And I'll break the heads of any who touches my Gareth,' muttered Mam from her knitting.

'And I will,' squeaked little Myfanwy from the roof where she was supposed to be asleep. That took the heat out of the argument. Dad started coughing, he was sounding bad these days. Worse at morning as the muck that formed in his sleep all came out in one huge gob. It was the miner's curse, a sign that the sun was setting for you when that happened.

'Myfanwy, sleep girl. There's a lamb,' said Mam gently from her chair. A rustle of bedclothes answered this, as Myfanwy turned over. We waited a while to listen and make sure she was away before we carried on.

I looked at the old boy and felt respect for him. The mine would do for him in the end, but he would defend it to the death. It would do for me and all in the end, I knew.

'They would have to walk through me to get to you also Dad,' I said gently. 'It is sorry I am. I just fear for the future and what little we have going to the bailiff and us in the workhouse.'

Dad puffed away on his pipe and closed his eyes. The place was silent now, save the ticking of the clock and the crackle of the fire.

'Look Owain, know you this. I know this mine better than most and it will feed and clothe us for years to come. Ben and and Captain Nankivell, agree with me. Lead is dying, but the future is brighter here than anywhere else in Cardiganshire.

Cwmystwyth, Cwmrheidol, Goginan. They got nothing on us.'

He looked over to Mam, who gave him a nod of understanding. 'The Taylors have been careful not to work out the black in the lode and you mark my words. The world is changing, zinc have got a future and it's going to be our salvation. So less talk about rebellion boy. You work for the Taylors and they'll see you right. You cross them mind and you'll be out on your ear.'

112

He paused for a while, looking in the fire. 'But I'd still wish you would go from this life.' He added softly.

'Gareth,' Mam chided him gently. 'Not now, it's late.'

'No, there's much said now but still much to say and it's as well it is done now. You see me, Owain?' He held open his arms to show his chest. 'I'm done for. The dust have got inside me and the years are catching up with me. When I was young, I could run like the wind. Now, I'm out of breath just walking home.

As time goes on, I'll be worse. My breath will shorten. My coughing will bring up more than muck. One day, I'll not have the energy to get up from bed and that'll be it.'

'Dad,' I whispered, tears reaching my eyes. 'What you saying?'

'Oh, it won't happen tomorrow. Maybe that's my point. It'll take years and years and that is the torture of it.'

Mam coughed then also. 'Don't expect your woman to be any better if she works in the mill,' she said quietly. 'We got enough dust flowing in there for us to get the cough also. Even if it's less than a miner's lot, we can get it just as bad.'

'What can I do?' I was getting quite upset by now.

'Leave,' Dad replied. 'Emigrate, move to America or Australia. Go to Patagonia perhaps. Start a new trade and a new life.'

'But you...'

'We'll be fine,' said Mam. 'You're the future, not us. Over there you are freer than you ever will be here.'

'But what trade?'

'Well, that's up to you now,' said Dad. 'Maybe a thatcher, you learned very quickly the skills on this roof and could get someone to hire you as an apprentice until you were ready.'

'So far to go…'

'Well, that's where it all is. Patagonia was in my mind before now. Good Welsh god-fearing community out there. They've had their problems, mind you. Harvest failed last year and even the government here was telling people not to go last Summer. There's other places with small Welsh communities in other lands also, mind. Pennsylvania for one.'

'But the travel…'

Dad chuckled away. 'Now don't tell me the spirit of your grandfather is not in you. We all should long for the sea, the salt is in our blood.'

'I always fancied the roaming spirit was in you Thomas men,' teased Mam.

I wanted to leave the subject now, as I felt uneasy. I was also curious about the famous Spanish sailor.

'What was he?' I asked. 'Only you never talk about him at all. What I never understand how Nain came to meet a Spaniard and how they made a child.'

'Well, you know that much by now, don't you?' scoffed Dad, making me red.

'Course I do, I meant how did it all happen?'

'What you want me to be storyteller now?' Dad said with a smile. 'Well, let me see, where do I start?' he poked the fire a bit to get it going some, then sat back.

'Your Nain was a good woman, but she was lonely. Your Taid was away from the farm a lot looking out for his sheep on the hills above Barmouth. Grazing was away a bit from the farm and he needed sometimes to go out and look out for vermin; foxes…and bad folk that would steal a sheep without a by-your-leave. They could not afford a shepherd most times, so he was forever out and leaving Nain at home to run the farmhouse.'

'Poor thing,' muttered Mam. 'Lonely she was and scared on her own most nights. She told me one time, it was worse than a prison.'

'Nain would go to market with the wool they had made and one day she bumped into this Spanish sailor.

Foreign boats were not common in them days, what with Napoleon wars and all that. Even by 1816, visits were few.

Anyway, this Spanish boat had pulled in for repairs after a great storm. The Captain he was, who bumped into Nain and she looked at his coal-black eyes of his and went all a do-da. Forgot her vows and fell head over heels with this bastard.'

115

'It was a fate worse than death!' said Mam. 'The shame! A woman's weakness is a man's opportunity. That's what his kind think, may he rot in hell.'

Dad hid a smile over this righteous outburst.

'Well, I don't even know what he was like. Mam never talked on it and I never met him. He could have fallen in love there and then. I know he asked her to come with him back to Spain no less.'

'He spent his time while the ship was repaired chasing my Mam around. They would meet for walks by the harbour and at long last, her loneliness and his charm had the better of her.'

'She forgot her marriage vows and he had his wicked way with her,' snapped Mam. 'The shame of it, the pirate!'

Dad looked at her a little angry now, 'Aye, the shame, but she was lonely and sad. My Dad was never there for her and he was not a tender man. Had a brutal upbringing and could never show his feelings.

She was alone and for that moment, she let herself down and God punished her with a baby. Me.' He looked directly at Mam and she blushed.

'I mean no offence, Gareth, for I loved her well as you know. That this man should do such a thing and just leave and never return. It's a sin.'

'Aye and yet you never know if he survived his voyage. There's many a sailor's wife who walks the harbour paths looking out to sea with children in tow, wondering if their man will return.'

116

'How do you know it was his?' I asked, desperate to keep the story going.

Dad grunted. 'Well, it's not respectful to talk on it. Let's just say Nain and Taid tried and it never happened. The Lord did not see fit to bless them with a child.'

'But it might have…'

'Look at me Owain,' Dad leant forward. 'Dark face, brown eyes. My dad was of fair face and eyes of blue as was his family. It was not his.'

'So what happened?'

'Dad saw the baby was not his. He started asking questions in the town and found out about Nain's meetings with the Spanish Captain. In the end he asked her outright and she admitted it.'

'And he kept her,' said Mam. 'A lesser man would have turned her out on the street for her wickedness, but he kept her and took the baby in his name, to avoid the scandal.'

'Many a man has nursed another man's child on his knee,' said Dad and caught the glare that Mam threw him.

'In this case, he knew of it at least. He was a good man and he felt the guilt for leaving her for so long. They sold up and moved to the Rheidol valley to start afresh. It saved them as a couple but killed Dad in the end.' He sighed, 'the bastard work kills us all in the end.'

'Gareth,' muttered Mam. 'Language now.'

Dad sighed. 'Alright Rhian girl, Owain's grown past that now. He hears worse things underground.'

'I never repeat them,' I replied quick as you like and Mam's eyes narrowed.

'It's a heavy heart I do have for my Mam and Dad. They loved each other so much, but fate was not with them.'

'Your Dad?'

'Not the Spaniard, my real Dad brought me up and raised me as a son. The other was never seen again.'

'Do you hate him?'

Dad chuckled. 'Nothing to hate there. I never knew him and I don't know what happened. He was never part of my life.'

'You're a gentle fellow at heart, Gareth Thomas - why I married you.' Mam whispered.

That brought the room to silence and I swear that Dad blushed, then he cleared his throat. 'Anyway, that's the story of my Mam and Dad. I reckon that old Spanish blood have given us a different feeling for things mind. There's many that have roots here from way back, hundreds of years. They'd never move, unless forced.

There's others who come here for work and will not leave for the fear of what the future will bring. Me? I would leave tomorrow, if I was young and healthy like you, boy.'

'Why didn't you go Dad?'

'For raising you children and keeping my Dad safe,' he replied sharply. 'Don't leave it too late like me, go before your roots get put down.'

'What do you mean the call of the sea?'

'One day you should go to Aberystwyth, Owain. Stand at Rofawr, breathe the air and watch the waves. Then you'll know.'

I was really confused by all this. Did they really expect me to just walk away alone? My feelings were strong for my family and even Trisant.

Even so, in the back of my mind, a little thought was saying 'why not?' and spinning me dreams of adventures on the seas. I watched the birds as I walked to the mine and the feeling was in me, as I saw them glide over the hills and cry their freedom with joy.

I asked David what he thought and he frowned for once.

'It's crossed my mind, Owain, it has. There's Cornish gone all over the world, even South Africa and Australia. We make the British Empire work! The *bargen*'s not so good and I don't know how long it will be before I should worry about it, but… I'll not go without Gwen. She's part of me now.'

'You really big with it these days, aren't you?' I teased and he smiled shyly.

'Yes and she feels the same.' His smile broke like a rising sun. 'Now all I need to do is talk to her father, before he finds out for himself.'

'What you fretting on? Caleb Lewis is alright. He's a tributer, just like you and me.'

'Aye, well. I'm never sure how you Welsh boys feel about mixed marriages. Me being foreign and all.'

David spoke Welsh like a man born in our land did. He was really one of us, but deep down inside, Kernow's fire reigned in his heart and always would.

'Don't be dull, Cornish boy, you're as Cardi as them hills. Don't let words put you off now.'

'I suppose so,' he grinned again. 'What say we emigrate together? Me and Gwen and you and Ceri?' he waited for my outburst and roared with laughter

'*Wyt ti weld bat?*' he mocked

'No, I'm seeing better than a bat,' I snapped. 'We're just pals, alright?'

He held up his hands in mock surrender. 'As you say, but maybe we should. Treveglos and Thomas has a ring to it.'

'Yes, sounds like a roving band of undertakers.'

'Well, it's a job boy. No, Mine Captains we'd be. With a name like mine, we could go anywhere.'

'Fancy yourself in a white coat, do you?'

'Fancy myself away from this work at least.'

'Aye, but could you leave here?'

David smiled his smile. 'No boy, I don't think I could ever leave here. They'll have to carry me out in a box. The work is hell, but the land is heaven and I could not swap these here green hills for the bustle of town and the crowds in them.'

'You never see it, David. You spend most of your life underground.'

'Grant you that, Owain, but that makes the air fresher and the breeze keener when I do get out. Even in the rain, the land here is a thing to cherish. If I was a rich man, I would travel Wales like George Borrow did, but I doubt if I'd find me a home. Remember his book? It was read to us in school.'

'Not in Trisant, it was not religious.'

'Well *duw duw*, and him the son of a preacher at that.'

'Not for me to argue, mind.'

'Owain, would you leave? Serious now.'

I sighed 'I can't see if there is a future here anymore, but something in my heart tells me to go and find better.' I smiled, 'we'll see, Davy boy, we'll see how it goes. Maybe I'll get time to learn the skills of a thatcher for when the *bargen* runs low and you and Gwen need a roof in your *ty un nos*.'

'Not so poor, Owain. I'm going to build a mansion out of waste. With thick walls, so when I'm too old and past it, I can lie in bed with my pick and carve a stope out of the side of the house for Frongoch to dress.'

'Maybe you should just set up home on 78 level then. It's not too wet and you never have any roof problems then.'

'I just might do that, Owain, but do you think my Gwen would take it.'

'No. maybe we should all catch the boat to the New World then and be done with it.'

Chapter Eight

A Cross-eyed Man

There were times that made me glad to be alive. When I came out of Frongoch in late summer to the cool evening air and the reddish light of the setting sun casting shadows all round. The heat still coming off the ground after a day's baking sun, on the back of a gentle breeze. Once or twice I even walked down to Wemyss mine to see the sun set over the valley.

Winter days were not so magical to me. True, the land looked beautiful with its white coat and a strange silence would fill the air as if the world was in awe of the snow. What with the birds having left for the season and wild animals sleeping over the winter, even the farm animals seemed to hold a revered silence for the cold.

What I didn't enjoy were the heavy drifts that I struggled to get through. Some days, the lakes and pools were just a solid block of ice, so you had no water to run the wheels and machinery. You could go down and work on your stope, stack the trucks with ore, but there was no way to lift the kibbles and the ore stayed below waiting for the weather to warm.

That was the time to hammer in new stulls and pack waste rock under them for support. Perhaps shoring up the workings to make it safer. There was always something to do down below.

On cold winter days, your fingers were like ice. At really bad times, you felt that your hands stuck to iron. No gloves, so you wrapped rags around your hands. Make do, always make do.

There were many days like these and many a miner went around with a bad gash on the hand, as he had not felt the pain of injury. We were always told to keep an eye out for that, lest a man bleed to death or lose a limb from infection.

I remember one cold morning like this. It was a day when a superstition came to the fore. It showed me how fragile the trust was with things we could see. It was a tough winter and snow lay on the ground. The ice had seized the machinery. I had left early to give them a hand, as the ice needed chipping off the wheel itself also to get the thing moving. Besides, the pennies came handy, a bit of extra cash for the rebel.

The walk to work was a nightmare. Even though I went as fast as I could in the dark to get to Frongoch, the snow was thick. Before long my socks were sopping wet. My lamp was on a low wick, for the moon was bright as to light up the land in its silver glow away from the hollows and shadows.

I carried on down the road, loathing every step but rushing to get to work quick in the hope that I could thaw out with the boiler men at the Cornish engine before I had to start work.

I became aware of a shape on the road ahead. It was a man shuffling towards me, along the path with a strange walk, not quite a limp, not quite a stoop. Not much noise either, not any come to think of it.

Strange, I thought, that such would be walking to Trisant so early. The closer I got, the stranger he looked. He was shabbily dressed in rags and a badly stitched cloak. He was using his staff for support and his back was bent forward as he moved along.

On his back was a sack, from which I could hear the clink of iron. Pots no doubt, I thought. His hair was a tangle of matted filth that hung down like rags. He smelt like a dung heap, worse than a man ever should.

As we passed, our eyes met. Cautiously I nodded and bade him 'Sh' Maè'. His eyes were black and glistened in the lamplight. One eye stared back at me, the other seemed to look inward towards the first. More like they seemed to stare at each other.

The cross-eyed man crowed back. 'And a good day to you kind sir.' He tugged his forelock in a mock salute and then cackled, showing off blackened gums with remnants of teeth within. His breath washed over me like the smell of a dead animal and I gagged without thinking.

I carried on walking quickly past and looked back, only to find he had disappeared from view round a bend in the road. It gave me a great feeling of wrong.

What were tramps doing around this time of the morning? Most would be dossing in a barn somewhere, trying to keep warm or sleeping off the contents of a gin bottle.

Perhaps he was up to no good? A worry gripped me that he was off in the direction of Trisant and what mischief he might undertake there.

Then I relaxed a bit, thinking that Dad was still to leave and would have that one for breakfast before he managed to put a foot wrong in our village. I reached the mine and made straight for the Cornish engine to melt the blocks of ice that were my feet. The glow of the fire came from the door and I opened it to be hit by a warm blast of air.

In I went, quick as you like, to see Jones the boiler. He was a man who always appeared to be covered in soot, save white streaks on his brow, where he had spent a lifetime frowning. He picked up yet another load of coal with his shovel and put it in the boiler. Sweat gleamed off his back, covered only by a vest, as he stood up from his work at the icy breath of air from my entrance. On seeing me, he grinned and shouted.

'Tomos *Sbaneg bach. Sh' Mae* boy, there's a brew on the stove. Pour us both one!'

The engine was off-limits for most, but Jones was good to me. I'd helped him repair his roof a few months back before the bad winter had set in and he'd not forgotten. Always had a pot on the brew did that one, only way to keep going he said.

I found two tin mugs - almost clean, sluiced them with some water then poured two cups of tea. He stopped his work and took one gratefully, sipping it whilst the flames of the fire danced in a pattern of shadows next too him giving his face an orange glow.

'God's got a sense of humour,' I said nodding to the door and outside.

'Well, we need the water Owain, the pools are low after all that dry weather summer last.'

'Yes, but does it have to water on me Jones boy. Anyway, it's alright for you snug here in the warm.'

Jones chuckled. 'You come here in August, when the sun beats down and I get a fair roasting. You'll never be here for a tea then, *bychan*.'

'Yes, yes. Don't be my mother now. It's the folk in the mill I pity, they work there in all weather. No heat or protection from the cold. It's bad for them.'

'True, true. But then old Ben was telling me about some of the mines at his home. Over by St. Just, the mill is on the cliff above the sea. The bal-maidens work there in all weather for their pay.

Nasty when the storm comes off the sea and tries to blow you off the cliff it is. There's always someone worse off then you boy.'

He started shovelling the coal again.

'Funny you should say that,' I shouted over the noise of the boiler, 'I passed one just now. Filthy tramp he was, all rags. Cross-eyed too, probably had problems working out which path to take, him seeing double and all.'

126

Jones stopped and a funny look came over his face. 'Cross-eyed you say? You see anyone else on your way?'

'No, too early for that.'

Jones voice got more urgent. 'You sure boy? You see no one else but this man at all today? You sure now?'

'Well yes…' I started, 'no light in the house for fear of waking the family, so he's the first I saw before here.' A chill ran down my spine as Ceri's words came back and haunted me,

Look out for the cross-eyed man.'

Surely this wasn't happening?

'Iesu Grist!' said Jones crossing himself. '*Tylwyth Teg!*' He threw the shovel down and went to the boiler and pulled a cord. A hooter deafened us above as the steam escaped through it.

'Wait!' I shouted over the din. 'It was just a man, it's only stories about bad luck and that. I don't want to cause no trouble now.'

'No bugger will go down the shaft now Owain,' shouted Jones back. '*Tylwyth Teg.* Bad Omen, seen it before myself. There's enough problems without the knockers on your back.'

The door burst open and Evans Vaughan shaft's head looked in. Must have run all the way from the shaft, the way he was panting. 'What's up Jones?' he shouted.

'Tomos *Shaneg Bach* saw a cross-eyed man on his way in. First man he saw.'

'*Diwedd y byd!* That's me. I'm going nowhere near that bloody shaft today.' The head was gone in an instant and I could hear him shouting away outside.

I was in a cold sweat now and started asking myself what it was had happened. Surely I'd seen someone before him? Was he really cross-eyed? I was in even more of a lather when I went out and saw the commotion.

People were arriving and the word had sent a panic everywhere. I could hear the buzz of voices and the words 'cross-eyed' and 'Tomos *Shaneg bach*' all around.

In my panic. I could see me being in the *Aberystwyth Observer*, with the editor raging out about ne'er-do-wells like me bringing such a great mine to a standstill.

'I saw him too,' said a voice from the crowd. 'Evil bugger he was. Bad Omen!'

People were milling over to the office area and I could see Captain Nankivell. He strode out and looked around the growing mass until he spied me. Calling my name, he marched out wading through the crowd towards me.

The whole scene would look comical to a townie. A burly man in a white jacket pushing through a forest of men wearing grey clothes and felt hats with a candle stuck on the brim and spares tied to their jackets. With them were the women holding their cobbing hammers, like small picks. The Captain pushed his way through until he got to me

'What did you see Owain?' I told him my tale and he sighed. 'Why did you have to say that? You know we be a superstitious lot Owain. Now I do have a mine that do not work through fear and Mr Taylor do want the head of you for what you have told. Pray God that it be true, young Owain.'

'It was just a word, I thought nothing of it. Then everyone just went mad.'

'Aye and now you do know. Let's hope it can be stopped before it do get out of hand.'

My worry continued as a mix of questions went through my mind again. Was this real? Would they dismiss me? I had never believed in superstitions before, but what if they were right?

Captain Nankivell turned to the crowd and roared 'Silence!' One man against three hundred voices you would have thought would not be heard, but you did not know the Captain and his sermons! The noise died as everyone turned to watch him as he leapt onto the stairs of the office.

The respect for the man was so great that everyone wanted to hear what he had to say. Everyone hoped that he had the power within him to banish the evil spirit that I had the bad luck to see.

'Ye do hear tales of bad omens and you be scared,' he began. There were murmurs of agreement. One man even shouted, 'I saw him too!'

That had others muttering the same, which made me feel a lot better, that I can tell you. For a short while at least, then I happened to glance at the upstairs windows of the office.

John Taylor, owner of the mine, looked straight back at me. His face was a mixture of emotions. Fear of the panic that was bringing the mine to a stop. Anger at the reason for this panic and the anger was felt by me through his gaze, like a hot August sun. It sent a shiver of shock through me. Wretched and helpless to do anything about it, I could only stand and watch the scene play itself out now.

'Yes, you be scared,' continued the Captain. That I do understand. My answer to this do lie in my faith. For it is faith that do keep me strong and I do say to you all now, through God we can banish this ill wind and bless the mine through prayer. If you do only...'

His words tailed off as a large cracking sound was heard at the Vaughan's shaft. The sound of splitting timber below, followed by a huge crash came from the right of the great wheel, where a small dust cloud had thrown up in the air.

The place was silent for moments, as everyone was in shock, but you could see it in their faces. Folk were on the verge of panic and it was Captain Nankivell who saved the day. He pointed to Banc Llety Synod and shouted;

'Everyone to the Banc, now! Steady, no rush, just follow my lead.'

The whole crowd moved as one. There were some screams and some jostling as people tried to get out quickly. The fence was trampled in people's haste. I hung back and tried to help any who had fallen or been injured and ended up with a frightened old woman on my arm.

130

Though judging by the way she held it, it was more that she was taking me up the hill and I was the one slowing her down.

Wiser heads were among the crowd though, shouting for calm, picking up those who had fallen in the rush, lest they be trampled. The mass of people moved uphill, with me at the back still in shock from how the world had gone mad. The old woman was dragging me up the hill now, screaming:

'Quick boy, away! There's no telling what them *tylwyth teg* shall do next!'

Captain Nankivell reached the top and waded straight through everyone to stand on the summit, they all made room for him so he could stand at the top, a white beacon in the mass of grey.

He raised his arms for quiet and once again the noise died down, save panting of breath and some whimpering from the faint hearted. Everyone looked up to him, waiting for his next words. It was the biggest meeting of his life and the Captain was not going to miss the opportunity.

'Stay calm my friends, for calm be what we need now. Yes, we do find the mine cursed this day and it be a sad thing.' There were more murmurs and wails at this and the Captain held up his hands for calm again. 'Yes and it be thanks to Owain Thomas, who did give us warning of these omens, thus saving us from the *tylwyth teg*. But what can we do now? We must fight to lift the curse and make our mine good and safe once again.'

He pointed down to the mine and everyone turned to look. The buildings stood empty and forlorn, like a ghost village. A breeze caught at some of the top of some tailings at the mill and a small powder of dust rose out of the building and Nankivell pointed at it.

'I do see him there. That be Satan's work and it is for us to chase him out from this place and banish him from our lives. We have but the one weapon.'

He lifted his fist up then. 'But it be mighty and it do protect us from all evil. Any mischief the knockers may bring. It is the power of the Cross, Our Lord and his Son Jesus Christ.'

He took out two twigs and swiftly bound them with twine to make a cross. Then he held it high, holding the knot and me praying like mad that he did not let go and the twigs fall apart. The omen would be enough to cause a riot.

'A prayer shall be our armour,' he continued. 'Then we shall go back. I will ask the tributers to leave an extra bit of food for the knockers this day. Keep the good spirits happy, but not too much of a gift, boys, for I do not wish them to be greedy and us suffer this devil once more.'

'Join me now in prayer and come pray with me on Sunday at this place. Then we do go back to Frongoch, heads high in pride, following the cross and singing with joy to our Lord God. Now all join hands and bow your heads in prayer.'

A shuffle of movement followed, as everyone reached to their neighbours and held hands. Had he wanted, Nankivell could have had them all baptised, christened and made priests that day, so fierce was the way folk clung to each other and the belief that Jesus would save them.

'Almighty father, deliver us from the evil that we do see this day. Protect your servants with your love and let us work without fear. In the name of Jesus Christ our Lord. Amen.'

All mumbled Amen and the Captain moved downhill through them holding his cross high in front of him. He began to sing the lovely hymn, *Calon Lan* and everyone joined in. The mood began to relax and some began to smile again as the beauty of the music touched their hearts and cast away the shadows in their souls.

The Captain passed close by me and whispered for my ear alone:

'A good day's work for God, but you do be damned lucky boy. Remember that and be careful what you do say from now on.'

A few of the folk had stood back, to wait for the crowd to lessen, so they could reach their work with ease. Two such were Ceri and David, who stood waiting for me at the mine gates.

'So, it's you to thank for the evil spirits, is it?' Said David, 'I always saw you as a magnet for them.'

'Told you to avoid cross-eyed men,' giggled Ceri. 'Why you never listen?'

I sighed 'Aw, come on you, fair play. All I said was I saw this tramp and the world went bonkers!'

They laughed and David clapped my shoulder. 'That it was. Still you were lucky that fall happened when it did. Old man Taylor was ready to boot you out. I heard him raging about that fool who would be out the gate on his ear before the morning was out. At least you'll be safe in the job now. How can he sack the hero of the mine?'

'I don't want reminding. Still, you've got to respect the Captain. He was sharp to use it for a quick sermon.'

Ceri looked back at the hill. 'He's not dull, that one, but he saved the day also. Them folk were ready to run to Devil's Bridge and people could have been hurt.'

We began to walk back to work and Ceri nestled in closer to me, more than normal. For once, my body felt warm and I liked the feeling. 'So, you going to take me to the wedding then?' She said sweetly

'What wedding?'

David laughed. 'Mine actually. Gwenllian and I have been walking out these past months and now finally, I have asked her Dad for her hand. He said yes!'

'Old man Lewis must have been pissed. There's a miracle and no mistake. You being a foreigner and all that. No wonder you been hiding all these weeks. How the hell have you managed that and me not knowing then?

I could have least had a chance to tell him all about you. Would have needed a week for that alone. I don't know if I should, seeing as my friend keeps me in the dark about such frightening news.'

'You better come, Owain, I want you to be *gwahoddwr*. I expect your speech to be in Cornish naturally'

'Fat chance boy,' I said with a smile 'I don't drop my jaw far enough. Welsh you get or nothing.'

'So, you will then?' he beamed.

'There's a boy in the village does that anyhow. Jones the *gwahoddwr*, I think they call him. Funny name that, do you think it means something?'

'They say he's bad in bed and under the Doctor. Besides, I want you, Owain. I need your beautiful voice and your poetic soul.'

'Aye and I'm a lot cheaper.'

'Naturally, and we are Cardi boys after all. But you would do a good job, even if you were second best.'

I stopped teasing him, I was so pleased to be asked. 'How you got round Caleb Lewis then? Thought you'd took fright.'

'Well, Gwen and I have been seeing each other on the sly and I had to make it official, didn't I? So, one day, I decided to ask Old man Lewis' permission to walk out with her. He was with us a few weeks until he could trust me, but then he left us and when I asked the question, I put on my best suit and bowler. He was so taken aback at the gentleman I was, he could hardly say no!'

135

'Trust you? He must have been asleep,' I ducked from a playful slap. 'I must get to him quick and tell him what a son you will be. Old Ben's been giving me the full story, you know?'

'Well, we'd been walking for months now and I decided no time to hang about, so off I went and asked my Dad and then Mr Lewis and then Gwen.' He said that with a straight face, thinking Ceri didn't know too much, but the look she gave him made him flush.

'What if Gwen had said yes and her father no?' Ceri asked.

'Well, I sort of new already bout Gwen now didn't I. Anyway, you may not like it but that's the tradition and if it keeps the old men happy, I've more chance of getting my darling Gwen.'

'Not as if you don't know her already.' I heard Ceri mutter tartly under her breath.

'Well,' said I, 'smitten and no mistake. I hope she knows what she's let herself in for. You just tell her to ask me and I will oblige with the real man, farts and all.'

Ceri looked at me, eyebrows raised 'Yes Ceri,' and I winked. 'Of course I'll take you.'

She beamed and with a quick shout of joy, hugged my arm and kissed my cheek. The feeling I had then was like none before. A sharp shock went through my heart. I had no worries for walking Tom Griffith's girl to the wedding, for that kiss had made me have no fear of anything in the world.

Chapter Nine

Gwahoddwr

David's wedding was one of the more pleasing things at this time. It gave us all the chance to stop thinking of the problems of the day and of worrying about what may lie ahead. 1878 was to be an eventful year and on more than one occasion, I gave serious thought to emigrating, but always there was something to stop me, another excuse to put off what surely must be done.

To make it worse, the metal prices fell and the lead ore in the lode began to lessen, as if in mourning. The lead we dug out was getting less and less and with it our pay. In July of that year, the Taylors finally gave up and sold their lease. The Taylor family were a fine breed of mining men and their leaving made us all worry. If they had cut their losses and left, what chance did we have? Many took this as a sign to get out and leave the area while they still had money to afford to. Empty houses started to become common, stripped of all that could be carried and no-one there to step in and take them over.

Into Frongoch came a new owner, John Kitto. A Cornishman by birth, Kitto had made his name in the lead mines of the Isle of Man before coming to Mid Wales. I had my worries about an outsider coming in, but Dad and Ben seemed happy enough.

'I'm willing to let things lie while I can still see enough lead and black down there,' said Dad the one time. 'Besides, he's got a name for rescuing mines, look at Brynpostig or any of them Llani mines.'

'And he be a Cornish boy,' added Ben. 'From Perranzabuloe, can't go wrong with a Cornishman in charge.'

If you believed Ben, there'd never been a bad one stepped out of Cornwall. It's true, mind that at the time, Cornish captains were well thought of in my part of the world. There's many a Welsh miner that's as not have any bad word said against them, me included.

Although he lived far away in Llanidloes, Mr. Kitto was to visit us regular. The fifteen-mile trip over them mountains must have been rough for the man. He was not a tall man, but broad and slightly overweight, probably from all those dinners he must have gone to when he was Mayor of Llanidloes.

He had a long beard and sideburns as a gentleman did. Always, a gold watch chain crossed his waistcoat. His broad hands were those of a craftsman and those hands crafted our mine to give it a new life, when others had seemed to leave us to the wolves. He put his life and soul into the mine, and I'd like to think that the boys gave back the same.

138

While all around was poor and the smaller mines began to close up for good, Captain Kitto kept us busy, so we made our *bargen* and had food in our bellies.

The lode was getting harder to break. Dad had worked out that for every hundred tons of rock, we were raising sixteen tons of lead and twelve of zinc. In the past the ore was in simple layers, now it was mixed with quartz. This made it harder to break and to mill - less money for all. More problems on top of the falling prices.

Yet it was in these trying times that David decided to marry. Never bothered David, mind you. The world was a joy for my butty, his smile never far away and I knew he would bring Gwen many years of joy with his good humour.

'I would wait, but then perhaps there'd always be a reason not to, then we'd never be wed,' he told me. 'So best we be done now and let tomorrow take care of itself.'

David was to be married in the Cornish Wesleyan chapel of Ty'n y Groes and such was the talk that it felt as if the whole mine would turn out to see him. Tall, thin and too damned handsome was our Davy and we all loved him. He had asked me to be the *gwahoddwr* and I was so happy to accept. It was part of a tradition now sadly lost from our way of life, though at first I was so scared of the idea. Like the boy I was, my first call was to Mam for guidance. I didn't have an idea where to start. I'd heard of them, mind. I just never seen one perform.

'It's a great honour, Owain,' she said. 'Proud, I am.'

'But I don't know what to do!' I blurted out. 'It's only I'm his friend, like.'

'More than that, Owain,' Mam replied. 'He trusts you.'

'I just want to do it right,' I said lamely, and Mam sat me down.

'Well, you're the bidder. You go visit the neighbours and friends of the bride and groom and bid them to attend the wedding and the feast after. Any strangers that may be visiting at the time are welcome also. I know Cardis are famous for not spending money, or more as like not having money to spend, but we still open our doors to friends and strangers alike at times of celebration.'

'What happens then?' I asked and Mam smiled, she was enjoying the telling.

'Those invited come and bring a present. Mostly this is money, a purse for the marriage dowry. All is entered in a book, so that if the guests are married later on, the gift will be returned as a *Pwython*. Don't worry *bach*, it's not as confusing as it sounds. We've been doing it for hundreds of years, so we must have got it right by now.'

Weddings were times of great joy and the *gwahoddwr* was the cream on the pudding, more the reason why I looked forward to it with a great fear, almost as if I was the one to be married that day. I felt the success of the wedding was down to me and I was more scared than I had ever been about it.

140

The bidder had to dress up for this role and his invitation speech was to be dramatic and amusing for all.

Many areas had people who made their living as a *gwahoddwr* and for those with wit and a silvery tongue; it must have been a wonderful way to make a living. We had one, but at this time he really was bad in bed, so David thought of the next best thing – me. It was very flattering and no mistake, but I was fretting for many weeks before the day wondering where to start and what to wear. I felt like I was walking at the edge of a chasm about to be sucked in.

Luck was there for me, as my friends came to the rescue and helped me prepare for the big event. Gwilym and Ceri turned up on our doorstep a few nights before the bidding. Gwil had carved me a willow wand, stripping its bark to leave the smooth creamy wood. A present from Hafod he said, but I knew he'd been up to no good mind, you always knew that old Gwil walked a thin line between what was right and what was not.

I hadn't seen him for months and he had filled out a bit. Too many days gambling and drinking up the mountains, perhaps. Now at least he looked able to stand up and fight back any of his family who would have a go at him.

Ceri produced some ribbons from I know not where and decorated the staff and my hat. They were all working so hard and what was I doing? Sulkily sitting around grumbling about it all and worrying about my lack of a speech for the bidding night.

In the end Mam kicked me out the house while they dressed everything up. I slunk off to Llyn Frongoch and sat on its banks, trying to fill the lake with skimming stones, which I flung across the smooth surface while I thought on what to say.

This went on for too long, until I decided not to move until I had written something and that did the trick. Finally, I had the words in my mind and was ready to leave the banks of the lake and take part in preparing for the day.

On the night of the bidding, I was happy with the words set in my mind like clom. At last I felt ready to take part, I was even beginning to look forward to it. Mam tied a true lover's knot in the lapel of my jacket, then stepped back to look at her son, the great *gwahoddwr*. There then followed that embarrassing thing that women do, fussing about your hair and clothes that have all men wishing they could be out of it. You can't tell your Mam that, can you now? I ducked and whined about it before she gave me a parting kiss on the cheek and I was off down to New Row to begin.

As I approached, I spied a group of people sitting on the roadside just before the terraces. I could see Gwilym and Ceri, also Ben and David with Gwenllian.

A little cheer went up as I approached and some good-natured laughter. Smiles all round as they looked over my costume, the two girls especially fussing around my jacket and hat, making tart remarks, as women are happy to.

'We've come to see you off,' said David. 'Also, to give you courage.'

'Best not have any of the drink now.' I replied like a deacon.

'No, you dull boy, we are here to hold you up when you faint from the fear and to make sure the *tylwyth teg* don't steal you away. If you lose your voice, we will sing the bidding for you in close harmony.'

'Close harmony?' I raised my eyebrows in mock surprise. 'With your singing, Davy boy, it will more sound like cats on heat!'

'They are saying nonsense,' said Gwenllian. 'They are all so desperate to hear your bidding. They want to hide outside each house and listen.'

A small girl she was and very pretty, quiet spoken, but had that strength inside which showed when she gripped your hand in greeting.

'Now then,' rumbled Ben rising from the ground. 'The night do draw to an end before we be started. Off you go now and we'll be with you my boy.'

Ceri gave me a warm smile and squeezed my arm and I was off to a chorus of mocking meows.

Oh well, nothing for it then! Off to the first house on the list. Enoch Morgan, a miner known for his short temper, who had cursed many a man in his time for even the slightest wrong. I couldn't have started with a more difficult one, even as I approached, I could hear raised voices and children crying.

'Enoch's reputation goes before him,' I muttered to a chorus of giggles from the others delighting at my unease. Fear gripped me, as I swallowed and raised my staff, striking the door three times with it. The house suddenly went quiet.

'Who is it?' A gruff male voice shouted from within.

'It is the *gwahoddwr*,' I replied, deep and as loud as I could. Bit surprised too at my baritone. Where that came from, I do not know.

'He's bad in bed,' shrieked a woman's voice from within. 'Some say he's dying.'

'Ummm, well…' I looked around wildly for help from the grinning faces around me. 'I'm sort of an assistant,' I stumbled in reply. Another silence, then the door unlocked and opened, casting a dim light upon me.

'Oh!' said Enoch. 'The **assistant** gwahoddwr, why'n you say 'en? *Dewch i mewn.*'

In I walked and I swear it was to a chorus of sniggers outside. To the centre of the room I went and banged the floor three times with my staff.

'To the House of Morgan, I bring good news! David Treveglos of this parish shall no more bring fear to the maidens of New Row.'

'He likes boys, does he?' Interrupted Morgan.

'No, he has lost his heart…'

'Where'd he lose it then?' said Enoch's wife, in her shrill voice. Enoch sat down; he was clearly enjoying this.

'Not quite where, but to a maiden fair. To the lovely Gwenllian Lewis, a maid of kindness and virtue. Behave!' I pointed at Enoch's nose as he began to make some saucy remark. Enoch grinned back and chuckled in good humour.

Duw, but this was going to be a long night and no mistake!

'Young David, a Cornish boy by race, though we shall not judge him on this peculiarity…'

'Just as well,' muttered Enoch.

'…has discovered this angel fair and betrothed they are with her father's blessing.'

'Was Old man Lewis pissed?' said Enoch. It was hard work, but at least he was but teasing me. I hoped so, mind you, for who was I to judge? Did a *gwahoddwr* always put up with this, I wondered?

'Well, I asked that question myself,' I said slyly, knowing David could hear me and needing a tease myself. 'But I'm not too sure and perhaps he should face the deacons for it.' I struck my staff to the floor again.

'Now! Your presence is requested for the bidding of this lucky couple. At the house of the young lady's father. Whatever donation you may make, shall be gratefully received and repaid in kind, should the occasion rise. Feasting shall take place, so the earlier you come the better.'

'You having any fish?' said Mrs Morgan in her shrill voice.

'The finest trout in all of Christendom will be there for all, should they wish themselves to be caught. Failing that, some lovely mutton.'

'Not much good if you can't get fish,' muttered Morgan. 'Don't know if I'll go, else.'

'Look, if it makes it better, I'll throw the mutton in the Ystwyth for you first and then it will taste of the river.'

A silence came over the two but it soon broke and they started laughing at the nonsense I had said

'Be at peace, Owain. We shall be glad to come.' He got up to show me to the door. 'Good luck with your night Owain. I believe you have the words for it and the wit to make it entertaining. You will make a fine assistant *gwahoddwr*.'

As the door shut behind me, I was hit by laughter on both sides.

'Behold!' Gwilym shouted. 'The assistant *Gwahoddwr*!'

Everyone outside gave me a round of applause and I stood there with a stupid grin on my face, both embarrassed and proud at the same time.

'Aren't you supposed to do it in rhyme?' asked Ceri.

I snorted. 'There's no rules about that. Besides if you want me to think up a rhyme, you had better cancel the wedding for at least twelve months! Who's next now?'

'Lewis Morgan,' said David. 'Let's see how you get on this time. Poor boy's deaf as a post!'

It was a long night yet made so enjoyable by my friends. We made such a noise of revelry on our walk that at one point we were barred entry to a house.

'Evans! Open up!' I tried, after my knocking had been for nothing.

'Go away!' Came the muffled reply. 'Unholy lot that you are, you'll get nothing from me.'

'Evans! It's me, open up boy!'

'No, it's not. It's bloody *Mari Llwyd* and you'll have no food or money off me and if you do any mischief, I'll have the lot of you. I'll break your bloody heads!'

Mari Llwyd, the old tradition of the man dressed as a horse that came around the houses as part of the celebrations for New Year. He would go around the houses and be given money or food for luck.

In some parts, those who didn't give anything often had some trickery done against them by him and his butties and when the drink was involved it could lead to broken windows or the like. Mind, that was a tradition from the valleys of the South, and this was Mid Wales. Also, it wasn't New Year!

'*Mari Llwyd*, what you on about? It's May. You been drinking boy? It's Owain Thomas here, come to do a bidding for David Treveglos. The *gwahoddwr* is bad in bed...'

'... and he's the assistant,' put in Gwilym to much laughter.

There was a silence, then the turning of keys in a lock and Evans appeared.

'Oh Owain,' he said half asleep and a bit the wear for the drink. 'It is you, I'm sorry *bach*, come in, come in. Mair will get us a brew now. Mair? It's *Tomos Sbaneg bach* come to do a bidding. *Gwahoddwr*, he is.'

In I went, to the sound of laughter behind me, with poor Evans all red about the ears with shame. Poor man, he'd had a bad experience all them years back and we'd woken up some bad memories.

We moved on to the village and carried on with the bidding, entering the houses and receiving warm welcomes whenever I arrived. Then as we passed the Miner's tavern, we were met face to face with Gomer Hughes. He'd taken a skin full of drink and was tottering out of the bar, his sons ambling out behind him like a pack of wolves.

He strode up to us and barred the path, hands on hips and a sneer on his face. His breath stank of the ale that he had drunk.

'What we got here then? Who's this little peacock? Thomas is it? Come on then Thomas, do your little dance then,' he clapped his hands in mock rhythm.

'No, it's a bidding I'm here for. *Gwahoddwr* for the night, as you well know.'

'*Gwahoddwr* is it? And there I was thinking you were a *tylwyth teg*, so ridiculous that you are in that dress.' His sons sniggered in the background, as he turned to them for a response. 'And who is the lucky man?'

'I am,' said David stepping forward. 'And I bid you all welcome to attend and help us celebrate our wedding day.'

'Celebrate?' Gomer spat into the ground. 'What, a good Welsh girl polluted by a dirty foreigner? I think not.'

He looked over us, as if trying to find something or someone. I looked around and Gwil and Ceri had gone, more the better for them that they had. Ben slowly took off his jacket and gave it to me.

'Perhaps my son be more forgiving than I,' he rumbled. 'But I still do remember the boys that suffered from you, Gomer. You do get out of the way now or I'll do what I should have done years back.'

Gomer's mouth curled up in a mocking snarl as he mimicked Ben.

'Think you do take me, Ben Treveglos?'

Ben walked up to stand almost toe to toe with him.

'I know I can take you, drunk or sober,' came the slow, solid reply.

Their eyes locked in a stare of great hatred, then Gomer smiled a smirk and stepped back, sweeping a mocking bow at our path.

'Go then, your marriage is cursed anyway.'

'As yours was,' replied Ben, then ducked as Gomer's fist came flying at him. He planted a punch of his own that had the drunkard sliding to the floor.

Gomer lay there with his back to us for a while and then his shoulder's started heaving. I realised he was laughing to himself. He raised himself up to his feet and looked over to Ben.

'Well boy, you got me one there. Out to punish, is it?'

Ben sighed. 'No, old friend. You do punish yourself enough.'

The two stared at each other again, then Gomer looked away sharply. Turning to his sons, he jerked his thumb in the direction of the tavern. His godless sons followed sulkily, looking at us like we were filth to be swept aside. Then they were gone.

Ben was looking at the ground now, a sad look on his face. 'Friends we were once,' he looked at me. 'Your Dad too, Owain. Gomer was a good man; he be now a broken man. I should not have said what I did.'

'It was wise of Gwil and Ceri to leave,' Gwenllian said, breaking the silence that followed. 'Would have been worse with them around.'

'Aye,' sighed Ben, then he gave a half smile. 'Come, this be a time for celebration. I do have the one more visit for you to make, Owain and we do need to go where I know they be this night.'

A bit of a mystery walk then followed, as Ben led us along until we reached our journey end. I tapped on the door with my staff and we were bathed in light as the door opened.

'Can I help you gentlemen?' said Captain Kitto, peering at us from the door.

'A *gwahoddwr*!' came the familiar voice of Captain Nankivell. 'Come in boys, come in.'

I shuffled in and went into my now well practiced routine. This time there were no smart comments to fight off, both men sat by the fire with cups of tea by their side and listened politely to my speech.

Papers were strewn about, which had obviously been their work for the evening. At the finish, Captain Nankivell guffawed with laughter, whilst Captain Kitto, made some polite applause. A wry smile had crossed his face.

'David Treveglos? About time he be caught,' said Nankivell chuckling. 'I'll be glad to come, if only to be sure that the rascal be tied down. The maidens of the parish will sleep the easier for that.'

'And their fathers, I'll be bound,' remarked Captain Kitto. 'I shall sadly be in Llanidloes for both business and family, so it is very unlikely I should attend.' His Cornish accent was till there in spite of the measured tones of an education. 'Be sure though, that I will make my *pwython* either way. What is your name, *gwahoddwr*?'

'Owain Thomas, sir.'

He nodded, '*Tomos Shaneg*'s boy? More of a man now, I'm thinking. Well, thank you for your entertainment. Perhaps I will see you yet in the poet's chair at the *Eisteddfod*? You look after master David. Your pare has a good reputation and I need you boys hale and whole. We all have a lot to do at Frongoch.'

We went back home after that meeting. David took Gwen back and then him and Ben walked with me as far as New Row, leaving me the last few miles to mull over the events of the night. David asked if I could visit some houses on the Trawscoed road and in Trisant the next evening and I felt good about it.

The whole night had been great fun and I was sorry for it to end and so I welcomed the chance to do it again. I smiled as I remembered Enoch and Evans and the others. The meeting with Gomer was almost forgotten.

Most of all, I had a glow of pleasure for my performance. I felt warm, for all the smiles I had brought to the miners in their grey houses and felt tired yet wide awake with the excitement. I spent most of the night telling Mam and Dad the night's events, before I finally went to my bed for pleasant dreams.

The morning after was still warm for me, as I had many more welcome greetings than normal. People smiled at me and there were words of congratulations on my performance. I felt I was floating with pride.

As I neared the shaft and looked down, the scene brought me away from my dreams. The square cladding of wood along the shaft walls, the long ladder reaching down beyond dark shadows, that I could see in the blackness of the deep shaft. The moisture from green moss, growing on the shaft sides dripped slowly with the overflow from previous day's rain.

The drops slowly fell into the dark emptiness as if showing me the place that I should go to.

My night as *gwahoddwr* had been so enjoyable, like a dream even. Now, as I gazed down into the darkness, the change hit me like a pail of ice-cold water.

I silently thanked David for adding some colour to my dreary life and then grasped the ladder and swung onto it, to descend into the depths once more.

Chapter Ten

David's Wedding

The banns were read in chapel. No-one spoke out, if anything it added to the excitement that people had for the day to come. Before we knew it, it was the night before the wedding, where the gifts that weren't money were brought to the Lewis household. Some families had donated furniture, for when David and Gwen could move to their own dwelling. David was hoping that would be soon.

'Though I'm not going to build a *Ty un nos*,' he said. 'We'll have something solid for the children waiting to come in the world.'

They were to live with the Lewis family in Pont Rhyd-y-Groes for the time being at least, that being the less crowded house of the two. The Lewis family even had plans to make the house bigger for them all. Talk of adding a proper second floor and making the house longer by using the space for the lean-to build a new room in the house. They had many years of work ahead of them and I was sure I would be there to help, for I would always remember that day that David helped put our roof straight.

The morning of the wedding was so crisp and cool. A faint mist rose from the land as the sun rose and warmed away the dew. Clouds approached, but there was no hint of rain.

I could swear there was magic in the air, as I looked out of our house across our small village and the rolling hills beyond. I dressed once again as *gwahoddwr* and made my way to the Lewis house, for the morning would see some of the guests return their *pwython*.

The women were having great fun disguising Gwen, dressing her as an old woman in a heavy shawl holding a baby. This being an omen for long life and children. Superstition ruled our lives, although the chapels did their best to stop it mind and I think some even used it to tame their flock.

Flowers were all around the house and there was an air of joy that day from all who were in that little cottage. Gwen sat with Old man Lewis by the fire. I looked at her and never saw someone so at one with herself. She looked up and her face was so peaceful, as she sighed and then smiled at me.

'It is the day I have dreamed of these many months, Owain, since I first set eyes on him. I cannot wait for us to be wed.'

'Hisht woman,' I said. 'For he has to get in first!'

'Aye,' rumbled Old Man Lewis. 'What use is a man if he can't force his way into his bride's house.' He finished with a sharp bark of a laugh. Man mountain he was and all. What man indeed? A true test of devotion, getting around Old Man Lewis.

For that was the custom in them days. As David approached the door with his friends, I slammed it shut and bolted the lock. Footsteps approached and there was a polite knock.

'Go away!' I shouted.

'I have come for my bride,' I heard David shout from outside.

'Then you must look elsewhere,' said I. 'For the women here are too good for the likes of you, they need someone of fine Welsh blood.'

'Fine Welsh blood my arse!' I heard someone muttering. 'He's one to talk of fine Welsh blood, what with his father a Spanish bastard.'

I marked the voice ready for a few choice blows later on, an accurate description for sure, but there is a way of saying things, after all.

'My bride is inside and I shall have her,' said David with laughter in his voice. 'Should you not open the door, I shall stand here and entertain you with a medley of beautiful Cornish songs. One I am thinking of is at least thirty-five verses, which should keep you amused while you find your wits and let me in.'

I opened the door but barred it with my arm. 'Listen you. No singing, for I know you sing like an owl hunting. You are still not welcome; your bride is not here.'

David's good humour sparkled in his eyes as he tried to push me back and out of the way, while his friends stepped up to join in.

Quick as a flash up jumped all the Lewis men and the doorway was full of men tussling with each other on the threshold of the house.

It was good-natured, but us Celts never keep our tempers for ever, so when it began to get rough, I cried 'Enough!' and all stopped.

'You may enter this house, but the person you seek is not here.'

The Lewis men stood back, and everyone started to dust themselves down and straighten their clothing, as if we were naughty schoolboys. In they all came then. David and his friends looked all around the place. Outside and in, up and down, under beds, in cupboards, even the pig pen outside – all to no avail. In the end David sat by the fire and sighed.

'Ah, old woman, do you not know where my bride has gone?'

'No sir,' whispered Gwen, gently rocking the baby. 'She must be away with the *tylwyth teg*.'

'Oh,' sighed David once more, a bit more dramatic than needed. Then he smiled. 'In that case, would you marry me instead?'

'Sir!' said Gwen, hiding a smile. 'How could you be so false, what with me an old lady at that?'

'Well,' said David stretching his legs. 'It would seem my bride is off with the *tylwyth teg* and given the choice between an old lady and the old sow outside, I would prefer to take my chances with you. I'm dressed up to be wed and it would be a shame to cancel.'

This caused great merriment in the cottage and Gwen blushed and looked up to David staring at her in mock surprise. He fell to his knees as if he had met the Virgin Mary and baby Jesus.

'My bride! It is a miracle! God be praised!'
He took her hand and got a slap round the head
for his trouble, which had everyone roaring with
laughter once more.

We were all smiles now, and tea was made
for those who wished, whilst we waited for all
those who would take part in the procession to
chapel. Cups were borrowed from neighbours and
we stood outside as the sun broke through the
clouds and enjoyed the moment sipping our brew.

'Nervous David?' I asked.

He gave a sort of breathless giggle and
nodded. 'But I am that excited also.'

'Best not drink too much tea then,' I said,
wagging my finger at him. 'You don't want to need
to go when you get in chapel. There's no rocks to
hide behind there boy.'

'Yes,' he smirked. 'Not on shift now, so
can't wave it around like you do. The phantom
pisser of 117 is what they call you.'

'Get off with you,' I blushed. 'Look now,
here comes the guests. Let's behave, shall we?'

When all had arrived, we moved on out to
form the wedding procession to the chapel.
Everyone lined up behind the bride and father,
sitting on a cart that was all cleaned for the
occasion until the brasses shone in the sun. We
started at a slow walk, moving along behind the
trap, nodding to the villagers who had turned out
to look. Then the cart started to quicken its pace
and the walking became brisk for us to keep up.

Slightly quicker we went, and the older folk were soon left behind. Almost at the gates to Hafod, the whip cracked, and the horse took off as fast as it could towards Devils Bridge with us all after it.

Another old custom this, known as marriage by capture and poor David and his friends now had to run after the cart and catch it. The driver was local of course, so he knew how to tease the chasing people. A few times he managed to take the cart back the way he had come, whilst avoiding them all.

This fun lasted until the trap was overtaken and caught by a girl who had cut over a field, chancing that she would not ruin her Sunday best. Although the cart made as if to run her down, she stood her ground, so he was forced to pull up short. This was much to everyone's relief and a hoarse cheer went up, as they knew the chase had finished.

Much to my surprise and indeed pleasure, I saw it was Ceri. Always one for looking ahead she was. The trap stopped and the now breathless party applauded her.

'Another wedding in a year's time then, is it?' A voice from the crowd shouted making Ceri blush prettily. Our eyes met, briefly but enough. We knew. Not in words but in our hearts, we knew. For the first time perhaps, I saw it.

We all moved off to the chapel at a slower pace this time, to be welcomed by the minister.

Most ministers at that time had tried to stop the old traditions, linking them with debauchery, ungodliness, and sin. This man was not so blinkered, he could see the joy that people had in playing these games and knew they would come to chapel in good cheer and listen to him.

Indeed, he was quick to point out that such a healthy party could not fail to lift the roof in praising God that day and he was not disappointed.

That said, the marriage took place amid lots of heavy breathing and coughing from those who had taken part in the chase. It was comical to listen, but it did not spoil the service. I sat with Ceri at my side and enjoyed being close. When everyone left the chapel, it was to the most beautiful afternoon sunshine. The sky was golden, touching everyone's hearts. Many people had gathered outside. A man sat at the gate and he struck up a harp and everyone joined in the tune, singing gladly.

As David and Gwen walked out, they were covered with flowers thrown by many of the people and some of the local children surrounded them with chains of leafy tree branches.

'We won't be letting you go until you pay your footing,' shouted the tallest boy.

'Right you are then,' shouted David back. 'But do not expect any silver now, for a Cornishman I may be, but I as brought up as a Cardi.'

This made everyone laugh. David gave a handful of farthings to the boy and he was off with his friends eagerly surrounding him, as they tried to work out how to divide the money.

'It's as well I didn't give them a shilling,' remarked David. 'For they'd still be here next week working out how to share it.'

We all set off for the wedding feast, passing by the children, who had now begun to argue with each other. Reverend Rowlands moved swiftly as one tried to run off with the coins and two others had started fighting. We left to the sound of a sharp voice and lots of screaming children.

'Don't think you were ever any better,' said Ben slyly as we walked. 'I have many a tale to tell, young David.'

At the Lewis house, many tables and chairs had been brought over and given the glorious day, many set up outside to eat and drink. A shelter had been set up for this purpose, as the house was far too small to house us all, but the day was so beautiful that most were outside anyway.

Speeches were given out and received. The speeches were short, for we were no great speakers like the great Wesleyan preachers. It was mostly to thank people for coming and wish them luck, to toast the couple and bless them and so forth. I had a chance to speak and used it to poke fun at my friend. I gave a good account of my butty honest, trustworthy and the only man I had seen clear all the animals of the woods with his singing.

They were good chapel folk. So, no beer or wine was given, but tea was passed around and drank by the lake full. The amount we drank would have filled Frongoch pool twice over that day. There was much merriment for we had no need for alcohol. A few, mind you, did sneak out to one of the village's many taverns for a quick jug of ale.

Good chapel folk these, they knew how to pray forgiveness, having done so on many a Sunday morning with a hangover.

The food was consumed and as evening took hold, the fiddlers arrived. The tables and chairs were returned or cleared away and the music began. People were dancing inside and out of the small house, cheering and whooping with joy. Gwen could be seen moving between people in her lavender skirts. She span around from jig to jig, laughing away. Her smile brought light to even the darkest corner of the crowded room. David seemed to seek out all the young girls around for a quick hug and a kiss, as if tonight was his last night of freedom and he meant to make the most of it.

He grabbed hold of Ceri and she squealed with delight, as he pulled her up from her seat and off they went to the dancing. I stood at the side and marvelled at the grace of her movement, for until then I had never noticed that before.

She was seventeen now. Whilst I had not paid attention to that fact in the last few years of her growing up, now in the heady atmosphere of the wedding night, I watched her go round the dance floor and I began to wake to my true feelings for her and what she really meant to me.

From that time when she tricked me for a kiss, I had shown her tolerance that slowly grew to friendship. I had thought of her no more than a friend, someone to play with outside of work and home, just as David, Gwilym and many others in my life had been.

Then she was more like a sister to me, young of thought as I was then. My own sister was much more distant, being so much younger than me. Ceri was different, but I was sure that she, as I, had thought of ourselves in no other way than just playmates.

Now I watched her. The way she glided in David's arms. The way she tossed back her head in laughter at some jest, most probably saucy knowing David. Her beautiful dark curls falling back on her shoulders as she lifted her head. It struck me then, like a bolt to the heart that this was the woman for me and always had been.

Others had obviously fallen under her spell. I saw Sion Parry catch her and set her off on another dance, she grinned and laughed at him. At the end, he kissed her lips but before he could continue, off she was with another. Parry's triumphant grin went flat, as he saw his prize lost so quickly and with no regret. He returned to a corner, his brows darkened like a storm cloud.

My stomach felt as if it had hit my ankles as I looked at these men. They looked strong, had a great air of confidence and to my young mind, damn good looking to the girls around, who pointed and giggled at the scene.

Ceri looked so at ease in their arms and fear crashed through my brain that she would soon be caught by one of these louts and won over, with me watching on all helpless to stop it.

'That Tom Griffiths thinks he's a man of the dance,' remarked a voice close by and my heart sank.

The dance ended and the man still held her waist, as he bent to kiss her. I felt sick. Blind to my feelings up until now, I had allowed this to happen and my punishment would be to watch the whole tragedy play out in front of me. I would lose my girl before I had even found her.

The pain in my chest grew as Ceri laughed and moved her head. She wagged her finger at Tom, gently mocking him. He carried on holding her and more words were spoken.

'Looks like you need a drink boy,' Gwilym was now at my side. He passed me a jug 'God is not a merciful man if he does not allow us to relax and enjoy some days is it? Besides, this is the Black Lion's best ale yet and a shame to waste on these. Here now, get this down you.'

In my mood, I just looked for a release, although my eyes could not be drawn from the scene that was breaking my heart. In my young and foolish mind, the story I was watching had only one ending, one that would cut me like a knife. My girl was being snapped away by some stranger, while I stood and watched like a fool and drank the ale like it would numb the pain.

'You done well, Owain boy,' said Gwilym. 'Everyone is saying you are the next *gwahoddwr* of the parish and your speech just now was well done also. Very funny, David will be proud of you, Owain *bach*.'

'Well, he's been a good butty to me. What more can you expect?' I muttered half-heartedly.

Ceri had her hands on the Tom's chest and was laughing still. In my mind, they were almost locked in an embrace, it was only a matter of time. A dark cloud settled slowly on me, one of pain and sorrow. Gwilym's next words cut through it like a knife.

'Owain, don't you worry about her now. She's not interested in any other man than you. Never has been.'

That threw me. It was like someone had thrown a bucket of water over my head and I stepped back so I crashed into the wall. 'But... he's going to win her over in the end. I can see it happening, they're in a hug and all...'

Gwilym clapped my shoulder and grinned. 'You don't know nothing boy. He's got no chance. Don't you worry, cos I know. Twins we are, you see and what we don't know about each other, the priest wouldn't know of his bible!'

'Twins! Don't talk daft Gwil. You don't even look the same.'

Gwilym grinned and shook his head. 'Now don't you go dull on me Owain *bach*, you don't have to look the same to be twins. We had a race out of Mam, and I won by about thirty minutes!

That's twins in my book and I tell you Owain, we are linked in a way. I know her and what she wants - and she knows me. Why do you think I've always been to the meetings on the hill? Taking her there, going off when she wanted time with you. You didn't think I just liked walking on my own, did you? All them times in the wind and rain and snow. Thought I'd found Jesus, is it?'

He threw back his head and laughed. 'She only went on about Tom to stop you from running from her. Like a frightened rabbit you were at times, she said.'

It was like the angel Gabriel had swooped down and shouted **'Hallelujah!'** in my face the way I lit up.

'Well, I'd better go and sort out this one before he gets nasty.' I started towards Ceri and the man, but Gwilym held me back with his hand on my shoulder.

'Don't you worry about her. She'll look after herself, you watch. She's had to live with violence long enough to know how to handle herself.'

Tom had her shoulders now and pulled her close to him to kiss her. A sudden movement from Ceri's leg and he went stiff and screwed his eyes shut. She hopped to the side, as he slipped to the floor in a heap, clutching his privates. Gwilym chuckled.

'Told you. Now come on and help me with this ale. Come boy before it gets too warm just sitting here.'

I took a swig of the jug and savoured the alien taste. Never touched the drink before, but it was like wine from heaven after what Gwilym had said and what I had seen.

Ceri came over to us then, all smiles and smoothing her skirts. 'Come on you. Dancing now, is it?' She tugged me into the fray, and we started. I was as clumsy as could be and when I stepped on her foot, she stopped and gave me a look.

'Come on you, stiff as a board you are. What's the matter? You been sharing that jug with Gwil?'

'Well, first off I can't dance. Second, I'm worried you may see me off like the last one.'

She grinned; I swear like a wolf would and punched me playfully on the shoulder. 'Him? He got what was coming. Trying to go where he was not invited! Dancing now then. We'll go slow and you follow me and don't worry. If you kick me, I'll only kick you back. Only fair isn't it?'

Off we went, and she held me like a doll. I was a truly awful dancer, but you would never have known from her smiles and words as we moved around the ground, outside of the house to the tunes of the fiddlers.

The evening carried on to night and still we were all celebrating. I danced until my feet ached, but only with the one girl. Ceri was my world that night and her body so warm to my touch. Her scent was so marvellous. My heart was gone that night to that girl and that was that.

At last, the party began to end. David looked for his bride, so that they could go to the roof for their first night. Where was she? Once again, the wedding party had concealed her

'Aw come on boys,' said a very tired David, still smiling to the last. 'Anyone would think you buggers just don't want me to have her, the way you keep hiding her.'

Off he went to search once again. Helped, or more probably not, by the crowd who went 'Ooh' when he was close and 'Ah' when he was not.

He searched the house through, up into the loft, under the bed and in the animal shed all followed by the crowd with plenty of advice from them as to which parish David should now look in. Finally, he found her sitting up a tree outside, all in lavender with a pale blue shawl to keep her warm.

'Thought you'd be looking forever there,' she said softly to him. 'I even wondered if it was me you were looking for, the number of girls you had to kiss on the way.'

'How was I to know you'd turn into a bird and go sit in a tree when my back was turned,' came the reply. He picked her out of the tree and held her close with kisses three, to great cheers.

They left and the guests slowly made their way home. Some helped to clear, while others slipped away quick, it was ever thus. I made my way off with Ceri and Gwilym and left them at the track to their house.

'Next week then,' said Ceri, turning to me. Her brown eyes were all a sparkle.

168

'What's happening then?' said I, the stupid Spanish boy.

'The *Neithior*,' she said patiently. 'David and Gwen's wedding feast. You're taking me there, aren't you?'

She smiled, touched my shoulder, then kissed my cheek and was gone into the darkness, leaving me standing in the night listening to the drunken singing and people leaving to go back to their homes. I did not care, for I my cheek still tingled with delight from the touch of her lips.

Chapter Eleven

Hafod

The week passed so quick before the *Neithior*, when David and Gwen had their first guests as a married couple. Once again this was a Welsh tradition now sadly departed. All the old ways are now long gone, our younger folk know nothing of the traditions of the past and I feel sad that I have lived to see such change.

Those with the *hwyl* of religion in them saw it as a threat to our path to righteousness. Many seemed to think that salvation lay in constant worship and being miserable. Not all mind you, for many still knew how to celebrate through joy, but others felt threatened by it. Me? I never thought heaven judged you on what chapel you visited or how many times. It's all about what you do down here. How you treat your fellow man. If not, God must be a strange one.

Religion was not all of it, for people change with time and stop doing things like they used to. The outsiders who came in had an effect too I'm sure, with their different ways of doing things. People coming in with their new ideas did not always sit well with local people. Changes happened, slowly at first, then gathering pace.

Mind you, I can't complain about newcomers, me being Gog and all. In them days though going to Ponterwyd only twelve miles away for the yearly horse fair was foreign to us.

Aberystwyth was our big town, a visit there was talked about for months after.

If you'd have picked me up and dropped me on a street in Cardiff back then, I would have been a little lamb lost. London? Well, where was that then? We read of many places in the newspaper, all over the world. All they were to us, mind, were names in the print.

David and Gwen, now there was a couple so well suited. Always happy, they were. Gwen with her quiet confidence and David with his permanent grin.

It had been raining on the Sunday morning and us fair-weathered sinners all went to chapel that day, rather than stand on the hill and get wet. *Duw!* Did the minister give us a fair roasting. He had more than usual that day and tore into them who put free worship before chapel. Not nice neither.

'You go to Llety Synod, thinking it is the meeting place of the religious', he told us. 'Did you not know the name is *Llety Asynod?* Asyn! Asses! It's where the Abbey monks rested their donkeys! There's donkeys you are at that!'

Suitably ashamed, we came out to find the rain had died and the sun was out to greet us. A fresh smell was in the air, as I went down to meet Ceri at the Ystwyth Bridge and we walked up to the Lewis house, to be received by the happy couple.

Many of you know in them days, it was expected for you to ask the father's permission to walk out with a girl. Even then, some fathers came along with you for a while, to make sure you did not get up to any nonsense.

Even to say hello was a crime and worth a beating, but me and old Gomer had a difference of opinion. He had greeted me once before with a knife and I replied with a punch. So, we left him to his jug of ale and got on with our lives.

There were a few at the house by then and tea and Welsh cakes was the order of the day. We were made most welcome and many was the hand offered to me for my day as *gwahoddwr*.

The women clucked over Gwen like hens. Only one topic mind – babies. Gwen's smile was very secret, but maybe we all guessed then. Another early child was due in the parish. Ceri smiled and chatted away with the women. The smile made me feel itchy. Talk about babies does that to many men.

We bade our farewells in mid afternoon and I walked Ceri down the road. She sighed and looked over at me.

'Such a beautiful day, Owain *bach*. Warm too and it looks as if the evening will be fine. Such a shame to go back now, don't you think?'

'Fine by me girl, where shall we go? Down the miner's bridge?'

'No. Let's sneak into Hafod!'

'What you saying girl? They'll beat us if we get caught there!'

'Oh Owain, beautiful they say it is and I always wanted to see.'

'Well, we can't just walk up the road now, can we? Gatekeeper's going to see us, no bother.'

'Let's go up the hill a bit and past then. Towards the church. I never been there neither. Come on boy, it'll be an adventure!'

She was hard to refuse at any time was that one.

'We'll have a look and see then, but no promises, Ceri. I don't want you in any danger and I've no interest in being chased off land.'

She giggled with delight as we made for the Ystwyth Bridge. We turned right and uphill, past the gatehouse that marked the road to the Hafod estate. The small, square house looked empty, although a thin wisp of smoke from the chimney and a full washing line outside seemed to hint otherwise.

The gatekeeper was a regular busybody, who felt it was his duty to stop and question people on their journey as to their business. It's strange how some folk take their work too seriously. For some in service there was a great snobbery towards us mere working folk, although that day we seemed to have missed out on his attention.

The road steadily climbed until we reached a fork. The Devil's Bridge road curved off down and I asked Ceri where next, but I knew damn well her answer.

Off we went up the other road, climbing through the trees that blocked the sunshine. For ages we walked before we saw houses ahead in the distance.

'Estate workers I think,' said I. 'What say we stop now?'

Ceri walked slowly towards the trees. 'So peaceful, Owain,' she murmured and slowly started making her way to a low wall.

'Ceri!' I hissed, 'Come here, you daft girl.'

Ceri had other ideas, 'come on Owain, it's not going to hurt. Just a peek, is it?'

I looked up the road to see if anyone was coming. When I looked back, she had gone *'Iesu Grist!'* I muttered in frustration and was over the wall and after her as she walked downhill, her curls bouncing up and down with each step. She spread her arms wide, like some woodland goddess feeling the air.

Someone once told me they put mantraps in these woods. What was she playing at? I ran after her so hard that when I caught up, I couldn't stop, missed grabbing her and fell forward to roll down the hill and stop against a tree. I came to rest and looked at her coming to me, hand over mouth to stop a giggle, with me at the base of the tree covered in leaves. What a sight I must have been.

'Oh Owain, there's a state you are,' she said, holding her hand out for me. Then I heard a noise, far off at first but sounding like voices.

'Quick! Down!'

I pulled her down and we grabbed each other as she fell with the sudden movement. I spied a couple of figures with stout sticks coming our way. Their voices became louder and I could make out the words. I felt they must see us, but bracken and brambles hid us from their view.

'Keep low and don't make a sound,' I whispered.

I could hear myself breathing and Ceri's short gasps of breath also.

I could feel her heart beating and realised I was holding her perhaps a bit too high for modesty. I did not dare move a muscle and besides, Ceri had her hands on mine stopping me moving them.

Now I could make out the words, as the men walked by. I gasped for air, my stomach tight with fear.

'You sure they came this way?' a nasal voice snarled.

'Yes! Saw them come by the gatehouse now just,' a deep voice rumbled in reply.

They looked about thirty paces away following a path, swinging stout sticks in front as they went.

'Followed em I did,' said deep voice. 'Up the hill and then they disappeared. Must be down here somewhere.'

'Poachers you reckon?' whined the other.

'No. Lovers more as like. Off for a quick bundle. One was a woman.'

'Then we'll give them a bundle to remember,' said the other with a nasty laugh.

The voices faded off and I looked at Ceri 'What we do now then?' I whispered. 'We can't go back up for them seeing us.'

'Best go down then,' said Ceri. 'Then we can find our way out further along.'

We moved through the woods until we had lost sight of the scene of our encounter. Then we started walking the path, for our clothes were getting damp from brushing past plants and trees. We walked down slowly side by side, enjoying the moment. Our hands brushed and without thinking, I clasped her hand.

All we could hear now was the rustle of wind through the leaves and the birds singing above us. There is a moment that comes to us all, one of great joy and calm. This was mine, holding the hand of the one I loved.

As we walked on, we began to see that there were buildings ahead and so carefully we moved back into the woods. We could see some buildings out by a pond in the clearing. Further on there were what looked like some stables and beyond that was the most amazing house I had ever seen.

I could see a strange room of many sides, capped with a roof like a welsh cake dropped on the skillet before flattening. Behind was the main building and its forest of chimneys, leading to a tall square tower. The building seemed to be shaped like an L turned around.

The tower, well I saw a picture like that once in a book at school. It was of a city that had no roads, but canals for streets so everyone travelled by boat. This tower here could have been in that picture, straight, square, very tall with a bell on top amid great arches beneath its peaked roof. As I look back now, I know the city as Venice. Back then I had no idea, and the scene made me stand still, mouth open in wonder.

'*Iesu*,' whispered Ceri squeezing my hand. 'It's beautiful it is. Let's look a bit closer now.'

I followed her and we crept around the side of the house, my mind still spinning at the sight of it all. Behind the house, tall poplar trees fronted the woods and we made our way behind them.

The house looked empty in the warm afternoon sun, water splashing down a drain was the only hint that there might be someone there.

Then we heard music coming from within the house. Very faintly at first it was, like a piano, but thinner and more metal like in sound, the notes drifted gently over the land. With no signs of life there, the music seemed ghostly, like from the *tylwyth teg*.

'Where now?' I whispered. 'I think the road down there leads to the village. We could take that and make a run for it at the gatehouse. What do you think?'

'Yes, but let's stay here a while and listen to the music. Beautiful it is and so warm here. No-one can see us, we could just hide here if we're careful.'

We sat a while and I put my arm around her shoulders. It seemed so natural now to do that. She snuggled up closer and we lay there just listening to the ghostly music. It stopped after a while and we sighed as the spell broke.

I stood up and put out my hands to pull Ceri up. As she rose, I swooped in and pecked her lips, like we been doing it for years. She smiled back, her eyes all a sparkle and squeezed my hand.

As we set off for the road, I was startled by a sudden shout from the house. Looking, I could see a serving woman leaning out of the window and pointing at us.

'Quick!' I shouted, 'we have to make for the road.'

We moved through the woods now without caring whether we were heard. Then I saw another servant, a man with a walking stick, coming down the road towards us, not fifty paces away.

'Where now?' said Ceri.

I looked around and saw a path leading down to the river, trees caused a shade on one side. 'There!' I pointed and we broke out of the trees onto the road and made quickly for the path.

'Oi! Come here you!' shouted the man.

We broke into a run and nearly fell down the grassy bank and its lovely lawn, towards a point where a fancy wooden bridge crossed the river. Over it we went full pelt, our boots thumping a merry dance on the planks, as we made up the other side and back into woodland once more.

Stopping briefly, I noticed we were not being followed and after we had stopped panting like oxen, we moved on, breathless but glad to have escaped.

'Where we going now?' asked Ceri.

'Don't rightly know,' I gasped in reply.' But if we follow the Ystwyth back, maybe we can cross further up and find the Cwmystwyth road.'

Ceri gasped and looked back. I turned in alarm expecting pursuers. What I saw instead was stunning. The mansion house was easily seen from here, nestled in the hollow of a hillside. Surrounded on three sides by woods and in front of it, the grassy bank gently stepped down to the bridge.

The tall tower stood out like a beacon, the strange tower on the other flank. Like two sentries, one tall and thin, the other small and fat, a wonderful sight and no doubt. We stood there, hand in hand and wished ourselves living there.

The path was long and went deep into the trees. We carried on and a nervous feeling had me go up further into the trees. The path was narrow, but it felt safer. All we could hear now was the birds and our own breathing. I looked at Ceri and she gave me a gentle smile in return, before pulling my hand to go further.

We arrived at a point where the path went up a river valley. The stream was below, not too far a drop, but very urgent about its business. We pushed our way forward, as the path rose and fell steeply along the side.

Eventually, we took ourselves up to where the river cut off the path. A waterfall streamed down the side opposite, yet further ahead there was a loud noise of falling water. It seemed to come from a tunnel in the hillside. I was confused, for there was no mine here. Ceri squeezed my hand.

'Come on, miner boy. Time to be brave.'

We scrambled up and picked our way carefully through the pools of water in the tunnel. Pretty soon, the tunnel curved into daylight and we stopped and gazed in wonder.

The river was ahead of us cascading in narrow streams off the edge of a cliff and cascading down to a pool in front of us. It was a sight that stopped us from talking as we watched.

No words, but our bodies were close enough to touch and neither of us would move apart.

It felt hard to leave this, but the spray was making us wet, so we made our way back down the valley again. After a few wrong turns we could see another bridge, but it led directly to a garden.

'How about crossing back here,' said Ceri.

'No, look. The gardeners would see us,' I said pointing at the men working.

'We could pretend we are working here.'

'Ceri! Even our Sunday best would not be good enough to work here. Especially all wet at the bottom as we are.'

She just stood there and laughed silently at me. Beautiful girl, that one, I thought to myself.

'We'll follow the path down the river and see if there's another bridge later on. Ystwyth can't be so busy back there.'

'No,' she said tartly. 'They say it is but a trickle in Cwmystwyth.'

I slapped her rump and she giggled as we carried on around the meadow.

We reached another bridge, this one of stone. Weary of the woods, we decided to take a chance and took a path in the open directly to it, walking arm in arm like gentry and trying not to laugh with it.

The bridge arched over a busy river about twenty feet below. Ceri was right, we would have been back in Cwmystwyth finding a way out. We crossed and looked back to see that the two men with sticks had come into view.

Luck was with us though and they had not seen us, so we quickly moved down another path following the busy river that we had crossed and back in the woodland.

'We must end up by the church, I am thinking,' said I, Owain the great explorer.

Following this path we found more waterfalls and at the end, where the path finally turned away and curved back up a steep bank, lay a powerful fall that seemed to have split the rock in half with its anger.

The rocks around were cool with moisture, but Ceri found a dry patch round a bank and out of view of our path where we could hide and watch the water. We sat down, grateful for the rest.

I had my arm around her waist now and I looked in her eyes as we sat there.

'There's dull you are Ceri Hughes, talking me into this damn fool adventure.'

Her eyes sparkled with humour. 'There's dull you are Owain Thomas for coming with me on this damn fool adventure.'

I stroked her cheek and drew her head slowly to mine. We kissed proper like and she did not draw back. It was like the waterfall had hit me, the shock and all when I came up for air.

'Ceri!' I gasped. 'I love you girl. You are so beautiful.'

'Oh Owain,' she cried. 'I've loved you since the first time I saw you. I never wanted no other.'

We kissed again as the passion rose up and before we knew it we were taking off our clothes, kissing each other all over.

Duw! Twenty years of hearing about God's laws and here I was about to damn myself in the lust of the moment. But did I care? Not then and not now. She was ever my world and all I wanted.

I am not ashamed to say that we had our bundling, there in the depths of the Hafod estate. Hidden from the path, the noise of the water hid the noise of our passion. Trembling at the end, I held her close and she sobbed gently on my shoulder.

We lay there for a while, dozing in the late afternoon, before she shivered and got up to dress. I sat and watched for a while. Then she grabbed my breeches and threw them at me.

'Get yourself decent boy,' she clucked at me. 'You're not so big when you're cold!'

Blushing I was as I put my shirt and breeches on. A little damp they were, what with all the moisture in the air. Ceri straightened her skirts, and then we climbed back up the path. It wound steeply up the hill, but I soon spied the tower of the church and we made for it.

'Inside, is it?' said Ceri. No stopping her today, it would seem.

'What, to pray forgiveness for our wickedness?'

'No, I want to see. Never been in a church before. We'll tell them we're Cwmystwyth folk and on the way home.'

'And they'll believe us,' I scoffed under my breath.

The church was in the lee of the hill and surrounded by its graveyard. There seemed to be lights inside, so in we went then to the sound of the latch echoing around the walls. Nobody was there. Ceri was all wide-eyed in wonder at the white walls and huge windows. I felt at peace and warm there, even though I could see my breath steaming. Then I saw the statue. Pure white it was, of a group of figures and as we went to it, Ceri let go a sob.

A young woman lay on her bed, her head pointed up as if asleep. One hand was clutched by an older woman, who had buried her head in it in grief. The other was on a book that seemed to be falling from the bed onto a musical instrument and palette below. An older man stood looking down at the young girl, one hand cradling her head, the other on the shoulders of the older woman in comfort. It was so sad to see such grief captured in the statue.

'*To the memory of Marianne…*' I read.

'No,' Ceri said sadly. 'It's Mariamne, I know this tale. *To the memory of Mariamne, only child of Thomas and Jane Johnes…* He built Hafod! *Who died in 1811 after a few days illness.*' She looked at me with tears in her eyes and her lips trembled. 'It's so sad, she died so young and their only child at that. They must have been heartbroken.'

'They were,' said a quiet voice behind us that made us jump.

We turned to see a thin young man, dressed in black. A skullcap covered his hair, but for a few white locks. A small, pointed beard decorated his chin.

'They were devastated,' he continued. 'Chantry has captured it well, don't you think?'

We did not reply. At first, we thought he was the vicar, but his manner and dress were too strange even for high church.

'She was beautiful, witty and intelligent by all accounts' said the man in his quiet way.

'Then she was gone and their whole world had fallen apart. Thomas had built this beautiful house and had harnessed the natural beauty of the land. All for his daughter and now she had gone. When she died, her parents left the house and did not return. The house was sold soon after.'

'So, do you like my church, young lady?' He said with a smile, opening his arms.

'It's beautiful,' whispered Ceri eyes downcast.

'And what of my house, was that also to your liking?'

Well, that shut us up!

'Come, come my friends. The gothic tower, the Indian pagoda, the Grecian villa between. Were you not impressed?'

'We are so sorry sir,' whispered Ceri. 'It was just so beautiful. I wanted to see…'

He chuckled, 'I was not worried, even though my staff has been running around like mice trying to catch you. It has been highly amusing to watch and in truth, they need the exercise. I do not really want for much and they get bored so easily.'

He began to walk back to the door. We followed him like sheep. 'I am sorry the place is such a mess. I have let the gardens go a bit and the statues are neglected and decaying. I do not have many guests you see. I am a private man and like my own company.'

We reached the door and he opened it just as our two pursuers were about to come inside, sticks at the ready.

'Just in time gentlemen. My guests are ready to depart. Jenkins, see that they leave safely, and no harm befalls them.' He turned to us once more.

'To you I say goodnight. I think we shall not meet again, unless of course I am invited to the wedding.' He chuckled and walked back in the church.

The thin one shook his head sadly, 'Nothing surprises me with him these days.'

Jenkins grunted, 'Well what's done is done. You two best come with me and I'll see you back to the Ystwyth Bridge.'

We followed him back down the hill into the estate. Jenkins had lit a lamp for the dusk was gathering in. Too stunned by it we were, we could only follow in silence. At the gatehouse Ceri walked on, but Jenkins stopped me.

'You two are lucky buggars. Sir Henry would have had strips torn from your backs, but this one is an odd fellow and no mistake.'

'We meant no harm,' I said. Jenkins snorted.

'I know, you just wanted to see the beautiful Hafod and got driven deeper and deeper in the grounds. Never mind, you were lucky today. Stay lucky boy.'

'Mr Jenkins, I swear to you that I will not trouble you like this again.'

Jenkins chuckled. 'Aye, I know that lad. I see it in your eyes. You are a good boy and look honest enough for me.'

'Owain Thomas' I said offering my hand and to my surprise he took it.

'Idloes Jenkins. I will look out for you young Owain, it is good sometimes to have conversation. Now you look after that pretty thing. She's made for you.'

He was true to his word as I was to mine. I never went back into Hafod and many a time I stopped and talked to the old man as he watched the world go by at his gates.

I took Ceri back and we parted close by the house. Too public for the kiss I was so desperate to put on her lips. A squeeze of the hand was all and she looked at me with eyes full of sadness.

'I know,' I said. 'It will happen love, we will find a way.'

Then she was gone. I made my way back to Trisant a bag of feelings. Joy for the love inside me and yet sadness at knowing where it would all end.

The evening had settled in by the time I got back home. My father was still up waiting for me.

The others were long in bed, it would seem. He was chipping away at some wood with a knife and did not look up as I entered.

'So, no chapel is it?' he said.

'Sorry Dad,' I mumbled. 'I was away at David's *Neithior*.'

'Yes, so were we, with Ben remarking how quickly you disappeared. You and Ceridwen Hughes.'

I could not answer that, the lie died on my lips.

'Off for a bundle then, was it?'

'Yes, no… I mean I didn't plan to, it just happened.' I told him the story, the words spilling out of my mouth. Dad raised his eyebrows but kept on carving as I spoke.

'You better be careful Owain. You shouldn't do that before your ready, until you find the right one. There are enough bastards in this world already.'

I took a deep breath. 'Dad, I think she is the one. I been friends with her forever it seems and now, I just know.'

Dad put down the wood and looked at me, beckoning me to sit. 'Son, how do you know it's her?'

A moment's silence, then I took a deep breath. 'Whenever she talks to me, it's as if the sun shines. Whenever I think of her, it warms my heart. When I close my eyes, she's with me.'

Dad chuckled. 'Owain *bach*, you should have been in the Eisteddfod with that. When I close my eyes indeed! Well, you picked a fine one and no messing. Good girl she is, though her father is another matter. But that is a problem for tomorrow.'

He stood up and stretched. 'Away to bed with you now, we have an early start and a new pitch to begin.' Dad took two steps forward and then stopped to look at me once more.

'Son, I would ask you to consider this. If she is the one, take her away. The mine may not feed us forever, I'm thinking.'

'But you said the black would keep it alive!'

'Yes, so I did. But the price still drops. Cheaper ore coming from the New World all the time. Even the newspaper tells me it. More than I ever thought it would. I wonder if we may be done in here before long. You may find your skills are served better elsewhere.'

'Away from Trisant? I stammered.

'Away from Ceredigion. Set sail from here, like that old Spanish bastard of a father of mine. I stayed here too long and became too attached. Don't make the same mistake.

There's a ship sailing to the Americas regular from Liverpool and talk of another colony boat to Patagonia soon. Take her away while you can boy. Start afresh.'

We stood in silence a while, watching the fire. Then I reached into a box by the dresser. 'One thing Dad. Could you help,' I said shyly. 'See, I've been trying to make this love spoon…'

The smile on my Dad's face was a picture and I swear the old boy had a tear in his eye.

Chapter Twelve

A New Lodger

I remember the talk that was going around at the time was one of worry for the future. One day sticks out from the rest because of the events that followed. We were on our break and sat with another pare wedged up among the rocks where we worked. Not for us the luxury of a *caban*, as the slate boys in the North had. We had to make do where we could.

Some of the boys were talking of the offer of work given to us. To come off the bargen for digging new shafts at tutworking rates. Steady money at least in such times, but it was not greeted well.

'They're forcing us to accept even lower wages,' said one. 'The *bargen's* low, even though we still ship up the same number of trams full of ore. Now they're trying to push us to work on the shaft.'

'You do know that work on the shaft be to allow easier access to men and ore?' Ben rumbled. 'That and they do say we be going down lower, to 154 fathom even.'

'154?' Scoffed another. 'You'll not catch me there, too much climbing up and down. Would spend most of the day on ladders.'

'But that might be where the good ore lies now,' I offered. 'Lode up here is tough, lead, black and quartz all mixed in. Difficult to work now, not like the past.'

190

There were some grunts of agreement. Dad nodded, as he sucked his piece of clay pipe. Never lit underground, did Dad. Not since Gomer Hughes blew up his pare.

'We still get less, yet our tonnage is the same,' snapped the first miner.

'Look boy,' said David gently. 'It's true that we shift the same number of carts. Good for the fat businessman sitting in his English house, not even able to say Frongoch, let alone spell it.'

That produced some laughter, as David continued. 'But it's not all lead these days, less now than ever before. We shift the same amount of rock with half the ore inside these days. It's mostly black that we get paid for now and it's worth less.'

'Aye, but I don't trust that Kitto,' came the reply. 'He's up to no good, I tell you. Who heard of clearing out worked out stopes of their props? Take out all the support that you can without it falling in? It's not done and it's bad luck also. Should leave all where it is, tools and all if the levels closed. He's cutting his losses and he's forcing us down to beggar's wages. All to get his money back and then he'll close us down and run back to Llani leaving us at the poorhouse.'

There were grunts of agreement to this. Dad took the pipe from his mouth and quietly said,

'I don't agree. I notice Captain Kitto have fed pumping rods from the Wemyss wheel back to the Vaughan shaft, all the way across the mine for more power.

He's driving deeper to get to the better ore. That's not a man ready to run now is it? Using the wastewater to pump more out, that's a man who knows what he's doing.'

Dad stood up and stretched, indicating it was time to get started again.

'David's right boys, we produce more black than lead now and they can get less for it. We done good in the 70's, when it was easy pickings, but now we're on hard times.

But I don't see Captain Kitto trying to run, as in my mind he's doing everything he can to keep the cost down, but how can he pay us the bargen we had when the price for ore is half what it were? I don't think he wants us to starve neither, wouldn't get any work out of us else, we'd all be falling off the ladders.'

'Maybe we will be soon,' said the man back. The other miners got up to leave with him and he patted Dad on the shoulder. 'Shame you were never made Captain, Gareth. You understand us at least.' No hard feelings, we knew where we stood.

'What with mines closing all around and the *bargen* low, the boys are scared,' Dad sighed. 'Who can blame them?'

Feelings ran high then, what with Kitto not in long and so much changing around. That day was tragic anyway and we got another reminder of how dangerous a life we had.

We were on level 90 that day and not too far from the shaft, when we heard a fuss far off. Lots of shouting, more than normal. Word came back slowly, it was trouble on 117 again.

They had been using the pipe down there, a big square tube we used to dump the tailings in the old workings. That waste sand from the mill helped support the level, while getting rid of it. The tube would be brought in ready and then the tailings dumped overnight. Too much dust to work in, else.

Only this time, it seems there had been a blockage in it and without warning, it cleared and caught a man under it. David and me went down there to see what we could do to help, but it was no use. We put kerchief's over our mouths, but the dust was too much to get close. It blinded your eyes, got stuck in your throat and snuffed out the candles. We knew he was lost before we started.

At the end of the shift, David came over to me as I sat on the bank by the wheel house, watching the water wheel on it endless journey, shuffling my hat in my hands and coughing up sand.

'John Lewis, it was,' he said quietly. 'Nothing we could do.'

I ran my fingers through my hair. 'I know that, Davy boy, but I can't stop thinking about it. It scares me, being pushed down by the sand until you can't breathe for the dust. I close my eyes and all I can do is imagine me in that. I'll not use that pipe again and 117 too. Bloody cursed that is, Dad was right.'

'They'll do a *cymmorth.*'

'What bloody use is that?' I snapped 'Man's dead. How do you tell his wife?' I sighed. 'Sorry *bach*, I'm jumpy with all this. Aye, we'll have a collection, only thing we can for his family now, but it don't replace the man, does it?'

'True, Owain, but what else is there?' He sat with me and took off his hat. 'What did you make of that talk before?'

'They're all scared for their jobs, that's for sure. There's many a mine gone now and many a miner left for work elsewhere. Do you blame them? To bring in money for the family? Some even swallowed their pride and gone south to coal.'

'Wouldn't catch me working for black diamonds,' said David with a grin.

'Too much pride, Davy boy,' I replied grimly. 'When your stomach cries out for bread, you would go anywhere.'

'We'll see, Owain. Though it's a bad business with John Lewis. Poor bugger, the world is changing with new ways, but it's still the same, us miners pay for their mistakes.'

Yes, I remember 1879 as the year of change. New ways, new departures and in the meantime, I stayed, I had my reasons mind.

In the spring of that year, when the snow melted into the rivers and snowdrops were flowering by the house, we had a visit up in Trisant. We were preparing things for the warmer season. At the time I was up a ladder, trying to fix a leak in the roof.

194

I was getting good at the work and all, should have took it and made a trade out of it. But then, I was just another stubborn miner.

I was threading in the thatch when there came the sound of some bother below. Men were shouting and women crying. I couldn't see what was going on, but the voices were familiar. With a curse I was down the ladder quick, to meet the unwelcome guests.

The Hughes family were paying a visit, all of them. Gomer had Ceri by the wrist. When he saw me, he threw her forward to fall at my feet.

'There's your slut,' he snarled at me.

Ceri had bruising on her face and blood on her lip. She was sobbing as I tried to lift her up.

'And this is for you, you bastard!' Gomer shouted, wading into me. He threw a punch that was badly aimed, missing my head. It caught my shoulder, sending me down. He pushed Ceri out of the way and stepped over her to finish me off.

I saw Gwilym on one side. He wanted to pile in and defend his twin, but his brothers stood around him. When two of them started towards me, Gwilym broke and he was on one straight away, trying to hold him back. The other carried on further, but my Dad was now out of the house and he floored him with a punch to the jaw. Gethin had hold of Gwil and his brother now, pulling them apart 'Stop this. It's between Dad and the boy,' he growled.

Gomer had reached me by then and aimed a kick at my ribs. I nearly got it and all, but I rolled quickly away with my right hand coming up in defence.

Luck was with me, as my arm swept under his leg, causing him to lose balance and fall, giving me time to get back on my feet.

He was up again, running at me snarling like an animal. I ducked under the punch and jabbed at his ribs. He doubled up with a gasp, but his movement made him butt my head. I fell like a sack, head all spinning. We both rose slowly to our feet. He was at me again and threw a right hook. I parried and lashed one back, taking him on the jaw. He shook his head to clear it and charged me, shoulder into my chest. I was back on the floor.

This time I missed his kick. It took me in the ribs. I heard a crack and it hurt like hell. He stepped back for another kick, but I saw it and rolled over, getting up as quick as I could. I was hurting, but could not stop for fear of what he would do to me. I stepped in to miss his next punch and he tried to butt me again. I started to duck, and his nose broke on my forehead, leaving a jagged cut bleeding down my face. Gomer staggered back holding his nose then as my legs buckled. I couldn't keep it up no more.

I was in a daze but could now see my Dad standing over me. He was shouting at Gomer,

'Back off Gomer, you and all your scum or I'll break you all one by one. You had your fun, now you'll tell me what this is all about. Believe me, it better be good, for I'm in no mood for this today.'

I heard other voices now. Neighbours come over to see what the fuss was.

'You need any help Gareth?' Came a voice.

'No,' Dad shouted back. 'Me and these boys are going to have a quiet chat like gentlemen, to see what's what. Thanks all the same, Griff.'

'I'm only in my garden now,' came the reply.

A splash and I was gasping for breath, covered in ice-cold water. Myfanwy had the presence of mind to throw a bucketful over me. The world came into focus and the pains in my head, jaw and ribs told me I was alive.

Gomer stood in front of my Dad, blood streaming from his nose. My mother had her arms around Ceri, cradling her as she sobbed on the ground. Mam's eyes looked dangerous, as if she would kill that day. I certainly never crossed her when she looked like that.

'You better have good reason for this, Gomer Hughes,' she shouted. 'She's but a child, for you to go slapping around.' Gomer lifted his finger and pointed at me.

'That dog of a boy of yours made my Ceridwen a whore. She's with child and him not even asking my permission to speak with her. All skulking in shadows that one.'

197

There were mutters all around, some over-doing the outrage. It seemed the neighbours had not left, some staying in case we had more trouble, others just keen for the gossip.

'Is this true girl?' I heard Mam asking Ceri. She could only nod in reply. Mam hugged her tighter then, whispering soothing words.

'Oh *bach*, poor girl. We'll make it alright. Don't you worry now.'

Ceri still sobbed as if her heart was breaking.

'Well now,' said Dad after a while. 'What's done is done. Strikes me that he have had his beating for it. He'll do the decent thing, Gomer Hughes, no problem in that, is there now Owain?'

'Mr Hughes.' I could hear myself, but distant in the throbbing of my head. Was I slurring? 'I am sorry, we made a mistake... It all got out of hand and ...truth is, I love her and would want her as wife.'

I took a deep breath. 'Never wanted no-one else neither and if she is with child, I will be happy to be named as the father. I know you think I am skulking in shadows, but I could never talk to you. Always we meet on ill terms. Twice we have met and you attacked me. What else could I do? I just wanted her so much.'

I was nearly crying now, but not with pain. 'If you would accept, I would have her as wife and would spend my life trying to make her happy. Please, I am sorry that it come to this and I deserved a beating, but please I ask you for your blessing. She's the only one I want, now and ever.'

198

Gethin it was who broke the silence. 'Seems as if the boy have had his lesson, Dad. Only thing for it now is to have them married and up in chapel. Only way they'll stay in this valley and not be driven out, anyhow. Even then, some will curse them.'

This changed Gomer, his eldest son having spoken up for me seemed to break him. He no longer seemed mad, just sad and helpless.

Gomer looked at me and then down to the ground, his shoulders perhaps had slumped. He wiped the blood from his nose, gingerly on his sleeve.

'You do not need my blessing, boy, I have no daughter.' He turned to his sons. 'Home boys, let's get out of this hole.' He started limping off back to the road but stopped at my Dad and the look Gomer gave was tragic. 'You should have let me die that day, Gareth Thomas. Every time after then has been hell.'

He limped off down the path, his sons following. Gwil had a quick word and a kiss for his twin, before a sharp call from Gethin had him on his way also.

Gethin stopped at our gate and pointed to me. 'Now we're even boy,' he snapped and then they were all gone.

'You will always be welcome...' I wanted to shout, but the words stuck in my throat and Dad stopped me.

'You leave it now. It would not be taken right. Let it go.'

The whirlwind had gone, almost as soon as it had started.

Mam made to get up and gently lift Ceri. 'Come on you. Let's get you inside for a nice cup of tea and see if we can do something on that lip.'

Mam was ever practical. She started taking a trembling Ceri inside. 'We'll set up the bed and you share with Myfanwy, is it?'

Dad had me up by the wrist and I winced.

'Down to the village for the Doctor then. Give it half hour first and they'll be gone. You fight well boy, but you need to be dirtier.'

'What to do now Dad?'

'First get you strapped up and then we make room for our new guest. Make it as proper as we can, though people ...' He looked over at those who had gathered to watch, now slowly leaving. 'They'll talk anyhow, but at least we'll know we are doing the right thing.'

'Then what?'

'Then we sort out you getting married! Now that'll be a wake up for you and no mistake!' he chuckled to himself as he went back to the house.

By the time I was strapped up and back from the Doctor, the women were all asleep. Dad needed to help me up the ladder to my bed. Funny really, it was only when I had to sleep there that I noticed how stuffy the house was.

Typical Cardi miners house was ours, small windows making it dark and cold air coming in through the gaps of the walls, windows and doors! The chimney did not clear all the smoke leaving a thin veil always hanging in the room.

I spent most of that night trying to breathe with my ribs bound up tight. I lay there and thought about Ceri and what I could do to make it right for my son. Funny that I thought of the baby that way. Somehow I just knew or perhaps I just wished it.

It would have looked dull, mind, if he turned out to be a girl. My mind started planning out all the changes that we needed, and I thrilled at the thought of being wed to the girl I loved.

Then I felt a huge pit open up in my stomach. Not for my ribs, though they were sore as hell, just worries about the future.

Where was the money? Could we manage? Should we emigrate and gamble our lives on the chance of a better future? In the end, I got a few hours kip before my Mam roused me for work.

That day, I wasn't far down the ladders before I couldn't do any more. The stretching of my rib cage was too bad. Dad sent me back up top and home I went. The Doctor had told me that nothing had broken, but bad bruising it was. It became too painful and soon I could hardly lift my left arm for pain. Dad had to help me back up the ladder to make sure I got back up top.

When they returned, I was found cleaning the house like my life depended on it. Ideas were tumbling out of how we could get the chimney better, how we could plug the draughts, make the windows bigger. I even had plans to extend the upstairs to cover the whole house, all to be done when I was better. They tried not to laugh but they could not stop themselves. I must have looked like a revivalist with my wild eyes and big plans.

Ceri was with them, very quiet she was. Her eyes looked sad and she wouldn't look at me. She looked as if she had not stopped crying since.

Ceri did not eat much that day and though I longed to talk with her, Mam stopped me.

'Leave her, boy,' she whispered. 'Now is not the time.'

She was right of course. Mam knows best after all. Ceri was too lost within for words then, and there was nowhere private for us in that small house anyhow.

Rain poured outside blown by the icy wind. There was no real place to take her anyway for a quiet chat. I desperately wanted to take her up in my arms and make it right for her, but everything seemed to be in the way.

It was three days before I got back on work and that took an argument. Without me, the team was not producing so much ore, so I got back as quick as I could to make sure we did not lose more money. It was drilling time and the most I could do was hold the drill. My arms ached, but at least I was there, and we got paid.

Don't get me wrong now, us miners got by. No great riches, but not at the poorhouse door neither. As long as we worked, that is. Like good Cardis, we set money aside to try and tide us over the bad times – illness, death and the like. You never knew when you needed to spend.

On the fourth day, I got to talk to Ceri at last. The morning was clear and cool. We hung back a bit behind the others, as we walked to work. The words were difficult at first, but we soon got going.

'Ceri,' I stumbled. 'You all right girl?' Silently I cursed my lack of words. Ceri nodded, but didn't speak. 'But the baby and all. You still…'

'Baby's fine now, good as gold,' she said quietly.

There was a silence and then, I couldn't contain myself 'Ceri. *Cariad*. What can I do to make it good once more?'

She gave a sad smile and looked at me 'Just be there *bach*, just be there and never change.'

'I'll be there girl, always and when we are married, I will build us a house and…'

She stopped me with a finger to the lips, a small sad smile playing on her face. Tears were in her eyes, but I swear they were of happiness now.

'Owain *cariad*, I was so scared you would run from me when I told you, but you're still here if a bit *dwy 'wech am swllt*.'

I started to speak again but she stopped me with a kiss and that did make me all two sixpences for a shilling.

'All in good time, good boy. Your family house is not that busy just now and we can make our own nest in the roof and put up some screen to give Myfanwy her space.' She then sighed and gave me that look, brows all arched. A tease was coming, I knew.

'Don't know why you're talking bout marriage now. You never asked me yet!'

'Ceri…I thought…Oh!' I dropped to my knees, then gasped in pain as I landed on a rock, jarring my ribs. I tried to propose, but it was all lost in laughter.

'God knows I love you boy, even when you're crying on your knees.'

She accepted though and I was up giving her a big hug and kiss. We carried on, arm in arm now.

'Ceri. I'll go down to your father's and talk to him. Make him see sense.'

She shook her head. 'Don't bother, Owain. He's past redemption that one. Him and his nest of vipers. He hates himself so much. Bitter and twisted are they all…though at least Gethin remembered you for your kindness, which was a blessing.'

She looked sad again and sighed 'I do miss Gwil. He's left in that hell. I miss him terrible.' Her lip began to tremble then. 'And Mam. Oh *Iesu*, I do miss her. She was so lovely. Stayed up all night when we were sick, looking after us.

Loved us all and protected us from Dad when he got drunk after the accident. That's why she got so many beatings.'

204

Ceri smiled, tears in her eyes. 'Know what? When she ran off, I hated her. Not for leaving, like the others did, but for not taking me. I think she knew I could look after myself by then and I could up to now. But I do miss her so much.'

I hugged her again. 'Gwil will be fine, don't you worry bout him now. As for your Mam, I'll ask after the gypsies. Idloes may know at the gate.'

She sighed 'Yes, you're right I'm sure. What about us then? The women at the dresser are already clecking away. How we're living in sin. How you took me every night in the *Gwli* at the back of the house in the village.'

'Well, best for them that Mam don't hear it. She'd box their ears for sure. Tongues will wag, Ceri, I have the men down the pit telling me what an old *Wrgi* I am for getting you with child.'

'You an old rutting dog? I never thought of you like that...'

'Stop it you and don't worry neither. Dad will speak to chapel and we'll be married quick as you like. It will all be right, you'll see.'

Then we were parting at the mine gates. Me to dig up rock and her to dress it. The light in my life that she was replaced by the dark world of candlelight below. With her I felt the world was so open and free, but below was narrow and cramped as I worked in the cracks of the earth.

Down below, Ben and David fussed over me and my purple bruising. I could not think of much that day, but a chapel wedding. Now David could be *gwahoddwr*. See how he likes it!

Chapter Thirteen

The Wedding

'You there! Would you give me a hand?'
The voice broke through my daydream and I ignored it. I was up top at the end of a shift and over by the Cornish engine at the time. A few others were around there - and I was always one to ignore those who had no respect as to not address someone by name,

'I say, Thomas, Owain Thomas? Can you help out one moment?'

I looked around to see Captain Kitto on horseback. Both him and the horse were sweating, as if come from a long ride.

'Hold my horse, will you? She's a bit restless. Gone lame over the mountain, I'm thinking.'

I went up to the horse and held her bridle as best I could. Her head tossed up and down as I tried to stroke it. She was clearly in distress, snorting and pulling at my hold on her.

'Poor girl took to limping on the road. Just hold her now.'

As I tried to calm the horse, he stepped in and lifted a front leg, bent up so he could look at the foot. With a grunt, he took out a small knife and prized out a sharp pebble from the hoof.

'Ah, she's thrown a shoe as well. There it is now, easy girl, all gone.'

He stroked her haunch and took the reins. The horse was beginning to quieten now, with the source of her discomfort gone.

'Damn roads are getting worse, I tell you,' said the Captain, as he calmed her. 'If only the railways had been bolder, eh? I'd have been on the train today at Llani and all the way along to Pont Rhyd-y-Groes in comfort. As it is, I have to rely on the old girl here and though she never lets me down, perhaps tonight she needs a rest.'

He patted her and turned to me. 'My thanks to you, Mr. Thomas, not everyone is so ready to assist these days,' he smiled then. 'And how was the wedding?'

I was taken by surprise and managed to mutter something about it going well.

'That's fine; it's good to help one's friends to make it a day to remember. Right, off to the mine smithy I think, see if he has any shoes amongst his drills and picks. Many thanks again.' He began to walk off, then stopped, turned and gave me a curious look. 'Mr. Thomas, how fare the men?'

Though it was not my place, I told him straight enough. 'Worried sir, wondering if the *bargen* will get any lower and how they will make enough money to eat.'

'Yes, I think we all worry for that,' replied the Captain as he stroked his horse's haunch. 'I can't stop the prices falling, but if there's money to be made here, I'll make damn sure my men don't starve for it. Remember that, Mr. Thomas. Good day.'

Then he was gone, with me cap in hand and ready to follow him to the ends of the earth.

We had started making changes at our house. Changes for the new arrival that was due and preparing for the wedding to come. Ceri was beginning to smile her beautiful smile once more.

Mam bustled around and even my little sister Myfanwy was walking around giggling with the excitement of it all. All too soon though my dreams looked as they were in tatters. Dad burst into the house in a rage one night. He'd been up to Trisant chapel and we would not be married there.

'Told me I should be ashamed to allow such a sin to happen in my house, letting the bride live here. That having Ceri here was an insult to God's laws. Where the hell does he expect her to go? What the hell does he know about it? Nothing! Except what's told to him behind hands by them who have nothing better to do and when our back is turned.'

His muffler was bearing the brunt of his anger as he tore it off.

'To hell with them and their damned circuit priest then. Never like folks up there anyhow, damned pack of busybodies. I'll speak to the minister at Ty'n-y-Groes. It's a beautiful place there and the minister has more common sense in his little finger than any of them deacons up here.'

The next night came and my father was again upset. He'd been down the hill to Ty'n-y-Groes. The minister wanted to marry us. The deacons did not. Too much scandal.

'I think that Gomer Hughes have poisoned their mind with lies, bloody Hypocrites! Many of them have little bastards tucked away somewhere and all, I'll wager. Ben is beside himself with anger and shame for this. Right, to hell with chapel. I shall ask Captain Nankivell if he'll marry you on the Banc. He's honest enough to do the right thing, even if it might be a bit cold up there.'

'Dad,' I said. 'If they don't want us, to hell with them. God surely knows us and what we are trying to do, so I can't see him cursing us for it, but it's you I worry for.'

'No son, it's no bother,' Dad looked more angrier than anything. 'But I'll have you two married in God's sight, if we have to go to Aberystwyth to do it.'

'It's just I don't want you having to go cap in hand to these fools for my mistake.'

The room went silent. Dad stopped and looked at me for a while, then asked me plain. 'You want to marry this girl?'

I met his eyes straight. 'With all my heart.'

I heard a faint gasp from Ceri in the corner and Dad nodded back to me, his voice softened. 'Right then son, there's no mistakes now. What's done is done and you are both sensible enough to want to do the decent thing. As for me, don't worry. I'm not crawling to these people and I'm not done yet neither.

Pride have nothing to do with it here, it's what is right that is important. It will happen, even if I have to knock a few heads together first.

So, we'll ask Captain Nankivell for his good offices and go up the mountain and that's an end to it.'

The good Captain came over the following night at our invitation. He rode up through the wind and rain to our little house from Pont Rhyd-y-Groes and swept inside, his cloak sopping wet, to stand by the fire. He looked tired and sad. We bade him sit down and he eased himself wearily into a chair by the fire.

'Dearly would I love to help,' he said after taking some tea to warm himself. 'Nothing would I like more, but a lay preacher is all I be. I do spread God's word, but it be not official in the eyes of the law or the church. If I do wed you two, it would not count.'

'I care not for law or church then,' I snapped. 'I just want to do what's right and proper. If the law will not let me, then marry us anyway. God will know we have tried and your blessing is enough for me.'

Nankivell smiled sadly at my words. 'Grateful I am for your kind words, but as I do say, the world do not smile on my ministrations. T'would be more than a happy day for me to marry you both, but it would count for naught. To those who do wish to make ill or to those in office, you would be no better off than you do be now.'

Ceri started sobbing and I moved to comfort her, biting my tongue at the injustice, my anger would be misplaced with folk around me wishing us nothing but goodwill.

The room was silent as no one could think of what to say. Dad looked old but still determined and was about to speak, when the spell was suddenly broken by a sharp rap on the door.

'Now who the hell can that be at this hour?' Dad muttered, as he crossed the room to the door. A sharp gust of wind and the pouring rain met him as he pulled it open.

To our surprise, Idloes Jenkins, the Hafod gatekeeper, stood on the threshold with a bright lantern in his hand. Judging by how wet he was, he had walked up from his little cottage to us that night. Rain dripped from his broad rimmed hat like small streams and drops even fell from his nose. He was hustled in quickly to our gathering and we all watched as the new arrival gathered himself to speak. He refused the offer of tea, saying that he could not stay long.

'No thank you, your hospitality is too kind,' he began. 'However, my stay must be brief, for I have my duties to take care of and the night is no longer young. Owain *bach*, my master have heard of your plight and he is sad to see how your fellow men treat you in your hour of need.'

He removed his hat and shook the drops off, then removed his gloves, patting them together to shake off the water. 'In view of the refusal of the nonconformist fraternity, he has asked me to remind you that there is still church. He feels that should you approach the Vicar of Hafod, you may well find a favourable answer.'

'What…?' I began, as I was not understanding the hint that was staring me in the face. I stared open mouthed and all *twp*-like at Idloes, before my mind caught up with why everyone had huge grins on their faces.

Solemn looking though the old boy was, he had a twinkle in his eye, as he winked at me. Well now! Married in High Church! *Crachach* we were now!

'Why have the gentleman of Hafod done this?' I asked. 'I don't understand.'

Idloes chuckled back, 'I believe that your little adventure have caused him great amusement,' he replied. 'Your plight then caused him concern. I think that you will find that Hafod church shall more than provide your needs.'

Now then,' Idloes started to move off to the door just as a particularly nasty gust of wind blew the rain against the house. It made him stop and he turned back to look at us with a smile.

'You know, perhaps I will have that cup of tea after all.'

I heard the movement behind me and caught Ceri quickly wiping her eyes before going off to grab the iron kettle. Her smile was one of salvation, she felt finally accepted at last. Had the old gatekeeper asked, she would have cooked him supper and baked for him that day and all, so happy did she look.

We visited the vicar the following evening and he was only too glad to help, but it would have to be a Saturday evensong service.

Not only that, but it would be that Saturday coming, in two days time.

So now began the rush, David was *gwahoddwr* before he knew it. His bidding caused much amusement to many, including for what he called his Spanish dancing. He invited all to the service Saturday evening and a *neithior* the following week, which would have to be our wedding feast.

However, the talk in the chapels had tainted us and even the well-loved David had problems. Many made excuses for absence. Some did not even answer, the tales that had spread was too much for them. Some even would not set foot in an <u>English</u> church. It was to be that our true friends would be found that day.

Our wedding day began with a cold crisp frost which quickly turned into a cool but sunny morning. I had spent the night at the Treveglos house, for decency's sake, and it was with the warmth of the early morning sun on my back and the crisp air, that I turned up to my own house to claim my bride.

David of course barred the door, but he was not to know that I had loosened some thatch at the back before I had left that night, enough to remove and squeeze through. To his surprise, I gave up on the door and sped off round the back, I was through the hole and into the roof before they knew anything about where I was.

I caught Ceri getting ready to disguise herself and we kissed and laughed silently at the fuss below us, as David and Dad tried to find me.

They caught us both trying to sneak out through the roof. Dad would have none of it though, until I had made good the thatch once more and then we began to ready ourselves for the guests to arrive for the procession to church.

The procession from the house was small and the bride had to walk, there being no cart for such a sinful girl as Ceri. This mattered little to her, and she beamed like the sun as each new arrival added themselves to the line.

David led the way, his bowler dressed in spring flowers. Ben Treveglos acted as Ceri's father and escorted her along. The Treveglos family and my family were at the front as we started to move down towards the mine.

We had not gone too far past Frongoch, when we noticed a small group waiting at the Wemyss end. Fearing an attack from the self-righteous, I tensed at the sight, then relaxed as I saw Captain Nankivell at the front. As we approached, he barked a command and the miners in the group made an arch out of hand drills for us to walk through. Dad thanked them for cleaning them first.

'More than was done at my procession,' Jones boiler grumbled. 'Covered we were in rust and muck.'

Other well-known faces were there, Evans Vaughan shaft was one and I saw the red locks of Dai Cochyn's head and a few others.

Those married brought their wives and children. We moved onto New Row and there waiting was Enoch and his wife, cap in hand.

'I know you don't count us as friends,' he said. 'But we would join you if we may. It was not so long back that you brought laughter to this house as *gwahoddwr* and we would like to pay our respects to you on your special day.'

'Come along. You are more than welcome,' I replied, moved by his simple words.

Down the hill from New Row we went to where Ty'n-y-Groes chapel sits above the road, looking out toward the Ystwyth valley, through the mass of greenery and the stream running by in front. It was such a beautiful place and there admiring the view stood the Minister – Samuel Rowlands.

As we passed, he nodded to us and to our surprise joined the procession. I could hear him say to Dad.

'It may be that I cannot bless this union as a minister, but I can certainly honour it as a man.'

We continued down the hill to the Ystwyth Bridge. The houses around there looked deserted, but ahead was the Hafod gate, where Idloes stood waiting for us. With him to take charge of the gate was the thin man who had chased us in our little adventure, he met my gaze with a polite nod.

'We meet under more pleasant circumstances, Mr. Thomas,' he whined. 'My good wishes go to you both.'

As we began to move past him to take the road up the hill, a shadow darted out from the bridge and grabbed Ceri.

Before we knew it, he had her slung over his shoulder and was away up the road, although he struggled to get up any speed with the weight up the steep hill.

'Marriage by capture!' the figure shouted, straining under the weight

It was Gwilym and we all laughed at the sight of Ceri struggling and hitting his back, not knowing whether to laugh or cry at the sight of her beloved brother. He did not get far mind, as the thin man went to stop him. This caused much amusement as being English, he was not aware of our traditions.

'You'll be married now before the year's out,' shouted David, causing the man to blush red and hurry to the gatehouse, with the sound of our laughter in his ears.

Merry was our party now, but a bit breathless as we moved up the hill and across the ridge above the estate to Hafod church. The path seemed to wind on for ever, but finally we crested a rise and there below us was the small graveyard and the little church, its castled tower standing proud with the welcome flickers of candlelight could be seen inside.

More people were waiting for us, some of the mine and the village. The rest had the look of gypsy on them and stood apart. One of the men started a sweet tune on a fiddle as we arrived. Another took up a shoulder harp.

The children there threw flowers over us as we approached the door, at which two figures were waiting. The vicar was known to me by now, but the small lady dressed as gypsy was not, until she looked up and smiled and met my eyes, then I knew at once who it was.

Ceri took one look at the scene and was off to the woman in a flash, hugging her and crying. As the rest of us caught up with her, it became clear.

'Mam, Oh Mam,' Ceri cried with joy. 'I never thought I'd see you no more. Oh Mam...'

The woman held open her arms for Ceri to run to. 'And where do you expect a good Mam to be on your wedding day? We been travelling half the night to get here and all. Now then, let's look at you.' She stood back and held up Ceri's arms to look at her. 'My, what a picture you are there. All in lavender is it?'

'Rhiannon Hughes gave me her wedding dress,' mumbled Ceri shyly, looking over at my Mam. 'Beautiful it is, I'm lucky to have it for sure.'

'And she fits it so well,' said my Mam so kind. 'Makes me wish for time when I was that thin. I never knew someone to suit something so well as Ceri does. Born to wear that dress, I'm thinking. So beautiful she looks and all.'

Ceri's Mam had no words now and could only mouth *Diolch* to us, smiling through trembling lips.

The vicar politely cleared his throat and politely indicated the church. Gwil took his Mam in, all smiles and tears and all the guests filed in behind, before I finally led my lovely bride down the aisle.

I confess now that I did not see much of this walk, for my eyes were full of tears making the church a blur of colour for me, brought to life with its music. Pure joy is how I remember that day. Pure joy, but we did not start so well.

The thing was, the church was English and while everyone started trying to sing as best they could, there were not many there as knew the words in English, let alone read them, so the noise was more of an embarrassed whisper. In the end the vicar stopped the organ in the middle of the first hymn and looked at us all.

'Please, no more. I know that many of you do not read English. That is as maybe, but the hymns you do know. You hold them dear in your hearts. Shall these two be joined in matrimony without the music of the Lord ringing in their ears? Well, if it shall be Welsh, then so be it. Sing your hearts out in your mother language in praise to God and let his word be proclaimed, while you bless this union with your voices.'

Well! There was at first a few mutterings as those that understood explained to the rest, then I never heard such singing. Beautiful harmonies, there were, and a noise that would have lifted the roof of the church and sent it well on its way down Cwmystwyth.

They did not know it in English, but in Welsh they had every hymn to heart and sang with joy. So, it came to pass that we were married in an English language church, to the sounds of our own language.

The service was lovely. It was a surprise for me that them in High Church use the same words and the same hymns, though by the time we got going, I reckon we sang them better than any church folk. As we left, the smiles of those there would have lit up the church alone.

We walked arm in arm to the church door, past the rows of our friends. I was feeling ten feet tall by then and could not stop beaming. We went outside and were met by the musicians outside, who struck up a merry song. The children made bindings and old Davy boy had to lend me pennies to pay them.

'*Duw!*' he teased. 'Coming here with no pennies, now there's a true Cardi boy and no messing.'

As we stood and took the best wishes of all, I saw my Dad about to make a speech.

'Dad?' I caught up with him. 'What are you doing now?'

'I thought it was time to say a few words of thanks, Owain. After all, them folk have walked a fair way to come here today.'

'Yes Dad, but I will do it. It's for me to be the one to say thanks I'm thinking.'

Dad looked at me with the hint of a smile, gazing at me, then his face softened a bit and he grunted. 'Course it is, son. Good boy, you go do it then, worth the more if it came from you.'

I went up and stood high on the bank and asked for quiet if you please.

'My friends!' I shouted. 'I thank you all for coming today and making this day so special. What has happened was not all our doing.'

That met with a bit of laughter there.

'Well, some of it was, I grant you,' more laughter rang out. 'but nothing that we did not wish to make right. We have no wedding feast, as you know. There was not much time to prepare. But...' I said above the mocking groans, 'our *neithior* is next week, we want to invite our true friends and you all are our true friends, so please, I want you all to come. Come and help us to celebrate. Our house is small, but you will find a big welcome.'

There was applause and the leader of the gypsies stood up. A swarthy man, dark curly hair and dark eyes. A real pirate if ever there was. He addressed the crowd in his bass tones. 'For our part, we cannot stay.' I knew he said it for the crowd, and you could almost see an embarrassment mixed with relief as he continued. 'But I do offer the couple a real gypsy blessing and an invite to you. Stay with us this night, we have a caravan prepared for you under the stars at our camp. Your own caravan for the night and the blessing of an old rogue, such as I. what say you?'

Mutters of surprise came about. Ceri looked at me, eyes pleading.

A quick nod from my Dad as he whispered. 'Go on Owain. There's no harm in being polite now, is there?'

That was enough for me.

'That would be welcome. I thank you for your hospitality' I replied with a bow, followed by a cheer from the gypsy folk.

The others nodded politely, but you knew from the look in many eyes it was thought a strange move.

It took us a while to pass out of the church gates, past so many wanting to wish us luck. At the gates, we finally bade our friends good day and took our leave. With Ceri's Mam arm in arm with us both, we set off for the gypsy camp for some warm food and the start of our adventure of a night under the stars.

Chapter Fourteen

The Gypsy Camp

It no longer surprises me how people come to have funny ideas, especially about things they know nothing of. It makes a lack of trust and fear and you could see it in the faces of the local folk as we left. There'd have been worse if Ceri's Mam had not been among the gypsy folk. Many felt sorry for her, for the tale of her life with Gomer was well known in the area. Even then the whispers were that it had been so bad that she was driven to live with gypsies. That bad? For shame!

My father had blessed our visit, but Mam had a look in her eyes that said. 'I will trust you with my son. Betray me and I will see you dead.'

Dad had always been one to tell me to judge people by what they do, not who they are. He looked so at peace with it all. When I looked over and saw how calm Ceri's Mam looked, while my new wife stood there pleading with her eyes. That was trust enough for me, so with that in mind I was happy to take Ceri over to the gypsy camp.

Gwil came along also. After a while, Ceri's Mam went over to walk with him, and they talked all the way for the rest of the journey. Their leader, Brian, was at their side.

He looked like a bear, with his thick shaggy beard and fierce eyes, but soft was his look every time he glanced at the little lady beside him. Down the road toward Devil's Bridge we went to their camp.

It turned out to be a cluster of caravans, gathered in a crude circle around a roaring fire that was already there to greet us. Many people could be seen in the firelight, all busy with some thing or another. Brian led us into the camp, and we sat down in front of the fire.

'Tonight, we can eat and drink and talk and then you lovebirds can sleep,' he said, pointing at a caravan back in the trees.

Water was brewing over the fire in a pot and some tea was made from it and mugs passed around. A bottle of spirit was also passed around after a while and many took it happily, though we politely said no.

Ceri's Mam had disappeared into a caravan and the place was surprisingly quiet given the number of people around. The crackle of logs and the clink of pots and cups rang out louder than the talking. When I said that to Brian, he took a draw on the spirit, wiped his mouth on his sleeve and grinned.

'Well now, all is not as it seems. A lot is said without words and we cannot have too much noise at night. We have to be careful now and watch for those that would do us harm and there are many who would, especially after they are thrown out of the taverns at night.'

'Where are you from?'

He gave out a laugh. 'Hither and yon. Who knows? We travel so far and wide.'

'How do you trade?'

A broad grin met the question. 'Whatever we can and when we can. Be it barter for food,

223

clothing or coin. We can sharpen knives, repair tools, do odd jobs, and buy rags. Whatever we can.' He took a sip of his tea and wiped his mouth. 'Now I would be mentioning, we do not steal wantonly and do not curse the land we walk on. We keep to the right side of the law as best we can, as most do.' He added with a little twinkle in his eyes, 'Ah, now here's Bethan to join us.'

I heard a rustle and looked up. Ceri's Mam had arrived with blankets and we huddled inside them, as the evening was turning to chill. She sat with us and Ceri grabbed her hand muttering, 'My perfect present. Then with a sleepy smile to me. 'That and my husband. I never thought I could be so happy.'

'So, what does the future hold for Owain Thomas?' Brian asked me. 'Now he has found his love and a young one on the way.'

'I thought that's what your people were good at,' cut in Gwilym between mouthfuls of some dried ham. 'Can't you read his hand or something?'

Brian chuckled and shook his head. Then he took another swig and then shouted toward the caravans to an older woman. 'Would you come and help us this moment?'

She shuffled closer, Brian tossed her a coin and nodded at me. 'This is a present from me. Be careful to listen and take heed as you will.'

The woman walked to me and her hands snapped out to grab both of mine, twisting them open.

224

She stared at them for what felt like forever, moving them from time to time in the firelight. We watched her silently, as if she had cast a spell.

'She can't see for the dirt, Owain boy,' Gwilym teased. He took a swig from the bottle of spirit. 'So, what you saying then old girl? A long journey, riches and save the world, is it?'

'He's taking a journey,' the old woman muttered. 'But if it's long, I don't see it. When sadness reigns in this land then perhaps. You may feel lost in the wilderness, but your kin will find you, do not fear. Rich you may be, but if its money, you're more as like to give it away.'

'That's not like Owain,' started Gwilym and I stopped him with a glare.

I looked at the old woman and into a pair of cool blue eyes. It caused a shock at my spine, for I was expecting the darker eyes of the gypsy.

'Be true to your family, your friends and your heart,' she said. 'Do not worry, for you will know what to do when the time comes. Let your children find their way in life, all will be well.'

She stood up and walked stiffly back towards a caravan without another word. The fire crackled, making more noise than us sitting around it, so struck we were by it all.

'…and she makes a living with that?' Gwilym scoffed, but this as more to clear the air, he looked uneasy with it all.

'Aye, because she tells the truth,' said Brian thoughtfully.

He moved the talk on quickly then and we all relaxed. We talked of work, places, religion, politics even. Finally, we started talking about emigration, the thing that everyone had in mind round our way, what with falling prices and closing mines.

'Owain, have you no thought for the New World?' asked Brian. 'Many look to it as the end to their problems.'

'I don't know,' I replied as honest as I could. 'There's baby to take care of first, don't want to do nothing before then. My Dad is forever going on about it also, for he sees no future here.'

'Yes, but how do you feel?'

'Tell you what,' said Gwilym now sleepily. 'The more I look at it, the more my heart says go. I have a mind to emigrate.' He gave a wisp of a smile. 'Even to Aberystwyth itself.'

I talked about the mine and told the tale of my meeting with Captain Kitto. At the end, Brian tapped his teeth in thought.

'Ah, well now. You trust this man?'

'Yes, I think I do.'

'Well now, you at least have the choice. More than I could say for my starving brethren on the Emerald shore not so long back. For them it was go or starve, some did both and still did not survive to the New World. While you have the choice, make sure you do what's best for you and Ceri now, not what others think is best. And that is for free.'

'What about you?' I asked back. 'Would you go?'

'Perhaps in time, but not now. That time has yet to come.'

We talked long into the night before Ceri needed her bed. Bethan took a lantern, and we made our way over to our caravan at the edge of the camp.

Ceri hugged her once more and went inside. Bethan then hugged me and stepped back to look me over holding my hands.

'You'll do, my boy,' she whispered. 'Your children will be strong and healthy at that.'

'Are you staying here long?' I asked.

She shrugged her shoulders. 'It's always best to move on before people start making a fuss. Especially when my husband wants me dead and says it to all who will listen in the *tafarn*.'

'Are you happy now?'

'Oh yes, Owain bach. The life is hard mind, but I am happy being with Brian. He is loving to me and treats me with respect. I had forgotten what that was like.'

'Sorry I am that you are driven to this life.'

She smiled sadly. 'Don't be. Gomer died inside when they pulled him out of the mine. He was a good man once. Now he has to live with what he did every day. It is hard for him and all whose life he touches. That's his burden,' she touched my cheek. 'Not yours. Now go to your wife.'

I stopped and she giggled, '*Dewch ymlaen!* It is your wedding night, what are you waiting for?'

With another giggle, she was off back to the fire to be with her lover and her son.

Ceri was still awake when I went inside. 'Yes, I heard,' she said. 'There's nothing you can do for my father now. You knew that. Now come in love, it's very cosy so I hope you don't move too much in your sleep, as there's no room for elbows.'

I looked in and she had a single arm outstretched to pull me in. The inside smelt homely, of good wood.

'Unfinished business, my love' she whispered. I went in and closed the door.

I woke up in the middle of the night to the sound of raised voices, a shout of warning, followed by the roar of many others.

Ceri was roused also and sat up, 'What's going on?' she whispered urgently.

'I don't know for sure,' I whispered back. Raising myself I crawled to the door and nudged it open. What I saw made me get straight back in and reach for my breeches.

'What is it?' Ceri asked, more urgent now.

'There's some trouble by the fire, I'm going to make sure its alright.' I replied, her brows furrowed and she stiffened as she saw my face in the glow from outside.

'It's him, isn't it?'

I grabbed hold of her and kissed her gently, 'I'll be back soon love, just want to make sure.'

'*Iesu*! He'll kill her.'

228

'Not if I'm around. Don't let anyone in until I come back now.' I slipped out and closed the door softly behind.

On the stair, I looked out at the fight. A group of men had tried to attack the camp, but the scouts had done their work and the gypsy men were waiting for them.

A sudden whoosh nearby though and I saw a caravan take light. Obviously, all was not good. Bathed in the glow of this new fire, a man raised his torch and roared in triumph, until a stick took him in the stomach. In the middle of it all, goading, snarling and cursing, stood a bulk of a man who I could not mistake.

Gomer Hughes, his face contorted by hatred and shouting looked like a demon in the fire of the blazing brand he carried. He stood back away from the fighting, urging on his men. All around him was violence. People were wrestling, punches, kicks and gouging were the order of the day. The world seemed gone mad, with one man trying to break another. A gypsy man lay on the ground, stunned by a blow to the head. A woman shrieked at his side, as she held his head and tried to stop the bleeding. Brian jumped over them and threw himself at the attacker, roaring like a bear. There was a rustle below me and I looked to see Gwilym creeping to the fray, armed with a stick.

As he was about to launch himself, I gave a low whistle and when he saw me, I jumped to him and we crouched in the grass, watching.

'Gwil boy, what are you doing?' I hissed urgently.

229

Gwilym was fit to burst with anger and to cry with frustration. 'I'm going to kill them all, Owain. That bastard family of mine, I hate them.'

I grabbed his shoulder. 'Don't get involved boy. Let the gypsies handle them. They will get it sorted and you got to live with your family after this. You still have to see them every day and work with them after this night. It will be alright. They don't need our help Gwil.'

Gwil shook his head, tears falling down his face. 'Not now, I put up with a lot, but this is the worst. They got it coming to them, then I'm away. Not after this.'

He made to get up and I pushed him down again. 'Alright boy, alright…' I whispered. He tried to knock away my arm and looked angry.

'No it's not alright. I put up with him for too long and now he's going after Mam. I'm not having it. I'm going to break his head, then I'm off down the valley. I been waiting my time to go when I was ready and had a trade, but now I can't wait no longer.'

I still clung to him, though my grip was slipping, as I desperately tried to think of how to stop him facing his family.

'Right Gwil, alright.'

I let him go and we stood, he turned to look at me and relaxed. Quickly, I grabbed the stick from him and pointed it at his face.

'What you doing?' He was almost shouting in frustration.

'Gwil, you're no coward and on any other time, there's none as I would want with me, but you can't win this fight. They'll be on your back forever after.' I wagged the stick as I talked, making the point.

'I'm going instead, I've got nothing to lose, they hate me already, but I need you to watch out for Ceri. In case any of them has ideas of firing another caravan. Come if you must; but try and listen to what I'm saying. Now is not the time, save it for the future and walk away free from them then when you are ready.'

He looked at me in pain, torn between what he must do and what he felt he should do.

'There'll be another time Gwil, wait for it and it'll happen. I'll go look out for your Mam now, you take care of my wife.'

He nodded then and clapped my shoulder muttering. 'Don't hold back.'

I was off then towards the fray, where I could see two men tussling near the fire. A man had floored a gypsy and stood over him, stick raised to crash down. I was there just in time and my up-swinging stick managed to parry the blow. The shock went all the way down my arm, but it was nothing compared to that on the face of the other man.

'Come on boys! Over here now,' I shouted and beckoned with my arm. I heard Gwil a while off shout a reply. I just about parried another blow from the man and swept up my stick to take him in the stomach. The man fled dropping his stick.

This seemed to break them, it was like watching a ripple on a still pond. The man next to him saw the flight and ran also, fearing a retreat and being left behind. Then the next, then the next. Before you knew it, only the Hughes clan stood there, the others having fled.

Gomer still stood directing and I heard him rage. 'Burn them! Burn it all down.' A gypsy ran to him and he felled him with a punch and kicked him in the stomach.

Then his jaw dropped as he saw me. 'What the hell are you doing?' he gasped.

'Hello father,' I replied as acid as I could. 'I'm looking after my mother and my wife.'

That made him growl and he lashed out with his torch at my face, but I ducked just in time. Someone grabbed me from behind in a hug, pinning my arms. Not too well, mind. I butted back and caught his head; his grip loosened.

I turned to be face to face with Gethin, his eyes dead of emotion and blood running from his nose as he launched a punch at me. I ducked and swung one back, much to his surprise. He lost his balance and fell to the floor. He growled and was back up on his feet and his next punch rang in my head like a church bell.

Then I could faintly hear a woman's voice calling, 'Stop it! Now!'

It seemed the world was in her spell, I could only look on as Bethan calmly walked through the fray and towards her husband, a stout club in her hand.

I saw Brian struggling to reach her. He was being held back by another gypsy.

The wood was silent in my mind, as I watched the slow approach. As she reached Gomer, his mouth tuned to a sneer and he spat at her. 'I want you dead, whore!' he raged.

Bethan calmly walked up and handed him the stick. Gomer took it more in surprise than anything. She stood tall and her words rang loud in the air.

'These people have done you no wrong, Gomer. You have no cause against them. It is me that brings you here this night.'

She moved closer to him. 'You want to hurt me, I know you do and God knows you have beaten me enough in your time. Now let's have an end to it.'

She knelt down in front of him and bowed her head. 'Strike me down now and be done with it. Then go your way. Leave these folk in peace, you will have had your revenge. Come on now, you've never been shy of this before. Strike and be gone.'

'Mam?' Gethin called softly, through the spell. He pushed me out of the way and started forward, but Bethan cut him short.

'Keep out of this boy. Your father is here to do what he came to do.'

'Mam?' Gethin was nearly beside himself with fear. 'Dad, no…' he whispered.

Gomer just looked down at his wife, his eyes wide with fear, his hands shaking. Bethan calmly looked back into his eyes.

'You have told me so many times you would kill me, now put an end to it, Gomer Hughes. You are not the man I married.'

A sudden movement by my side and Gethin rushed forward, straight at his father. He caught his father in an embrace and pushed him back.

'This is too much Dad, let's go home and be done with it?' His word came out in a panic and he tried to smile though his fear. Gomer still stared at his wife, he looked in shock now. The stick slipped from his hands.

'Bethan?'

'Come on boys, we're leaving here. Now!' Gethin had pushed his father back and he was slowly walking away with him now. Gomer showed no resistance, but still looked in despair at his wife.

'Bethan?' The words came out like a cry of the damned. Then they were gone in the gloom of the trees. The cry hanging in the air.

Bethan still knelt on the floor, but her shoulders moved as she sobbed silently. Brian now released, moved forward and gently picked her up in his arms. He moved off to their caravan without a word.

People started clearing up, the caravan ablaze was clearly past saving, but some of the men had managed to move it away from the rest of the group.

I found myself standing alone and hurried off back to the caravan where I had left Ceri and Gwilym.

Gwilym's stick lowered when he saw it was me rushing towards them. They both stood at the bottom of the steps.

Gwil had an arm around Ceri and she was sobbing silently. She ran to me and buried her head in my shoulder, her body shook with her sobbing.

Gwilym looked old in the firelight, as he gazed at the blazing caravan. After a while, he turned back to look at me.

'You'd best get some sleep, Owain. What's left of the night. I'll stand guard outside, then no-one will come near you both.'

'Gwil there's no need. They won't be back.'

'No, you're all right there Owain *bach*. Besides, I got a lot of thinking to do.'

I took Ceri inside and we lay down in each other's arms without undressing. So tired we were, that sleep came straight away.

The morning came all too soon. The sound of crockery, low voices a hissing of a kettle. The door opened and Ceri appeared with two mugs of steaming tea.

'Morning, *cariad*. I hope you're not always going to be this lazy - now that we are married.'

I smiled a sleepy smile and gratefully accepted the brew.

'They are breaking camp, Owain. We have to go home after breakfast.'

'Gwilym?'

'He's staying.'

I dressed quickly and was over to the fire then with my mug, yawning and scratching as I went.

Ceri grabbed me at the bottom of the stairs first nearly sending the tea flying. She straightened my hair, and then launched into a long kiss that had me struggling for air. Then we were over to the gypsies.

There were a few murmurs of greeting as we approached the group. Brian came over with a plate of bacon, which he said cost him a hard bargain.

Bethan was stirring a pot over the fire and the smile she gave us was at peace. Gwilym was there too, but his smile was weary.

We ate and the talk was light around the fire. The last night's trouble seemed forgotten. Someone joked that the burnt caravan was due for it anyway. The axle was beginning to crack, and the horse was fed up of dragging it.

Then it was time to leave. The horses were got ready for the caravans and we stood there with Brian, Bethan and Gwilym and watched the scene.

'Are you hurt?' I asked Bethan.

She smiled and shook her head. 'No if anything it is an end to it. I have broken his hold on me. For him, I think the hell continues. I will pray for him.'

'What you going to do, Gwil?' I said to my new brother.

Gwil shrugged his shoulders, 'I'm going back. We had a long chat, Mam and me. She wants someone there to look out for him, steer him to the right path. Or at least try to.'

He sighed then. 'As best I can. But if anything like this ever happens again, I'm going to reckon up with them all and then I'll be gone from here. He don't know I was here. They just think I'm a coward as it is.'

Ceri kissed him bringing a smile to his sad, brooding face.

The gypsies began to break camp. Bethan came to hug Ceri and Gwil and the three stood there together in silence, the little woman with her arms around the necks of her two devoted twins.

Then Bethan was over to me and though red-eyed and with lips trembling, she could still smile as she reached up and pulled me towards her in a hug. Her grip was like iron and I knew then her spirit and remembered Gomer's look as he was dragged away from her, knowing what he had lost.

We said our goodbyes. Ceri looked over and quietly asked Brian if we would see them again, fearful of the answer.

'Well, I hope so,' he chuckled. 'We may be at Ffair Rhos for the fair, but who knows what the wind will bring. We turn up when least expected and half the time don't even know ourselves when.' He gently touched her cheek, as his voice grew softer. 'Yes, we will be back. Besides, we will have a grandchild to visit.'

They left towards Devil's Bridge for the mountain road to the market towns of the East. Gwilym walked with us to the Ystwyth Bridge before he would take his leave and return to the tragedy of his home.

'You know what?' He said with a painful grin, 'I have a mind to take you to Ffair Rhos, Owain. A new baby will bring you enough to do and a man should be allowed to enjoy his life sometimes! Don't worry you'll be back the same day:

Gyrru, gyrru Ffair yn Rhos
Mynd I'r dydd am nol cyn nos'

'Yes Gwil you boys can go off and play, but you bring him back drunk and there will be hell to pay.' said Ceri.

She had an edge to her voice that would split quartz. Already? We'd only been married a day!

Chapter Fifteen

A Cornish Pin

Ceri and I walked back up the hill towards New Row. It was late Sunday morning, and the air was heavy, as if a light rain may fall. Even the birds seemed to sit quietly waiting for the event. At Ty'n y Groes they were all going to chapel. The Reverend Rowlands saw us arrive and came rushing down the steps.

'My little love birds!' he beamed, arms wide open in greeting. Funny words from such a big man. 'How are you today? Did you sleep well? Did you sleep?' He added with a wink. I had to laugh at that. If ever there was a human face to God, it was the Reverend Rowlands.

'Are you in a hurry?' He asked swiftly.

I looked at Ceri and we shook our heads politely. 'Not really…'

'Come in, will you?' he said quickly. 'For I have a good sermon planned here today, that you can be sure.'

There was a note in his voice that made me think and the look he gave me was odd, so I nodded, said it would be a pleasure and in we went.

It was so funny to see the different welcomes we got. The Reverend's happy manner was not matched by all his flock. Some gave nervous smiles or nods. Others had the look of outrage. They could not look down their noses at us anymore, for fear of falling.

This was the welcome I was expecting at Welsh chapel, let alone the English folk, and far from making me humble or even angry, I found it hard not to laugh at them.

Many tried so hard to sit away from us, but the chapel was such a small thing that a few were forced towards us.

'I do have the leprosy, you know…' I whispered to one woman in my best Cornish accent with a wink. Her gasp of outrage just made me chuckle and I got a dig in the ribs from Ceri for my trouble.

'*Hisht!*' She whispered all red-faced.

'Oh, to hell with them if they can't accept us.' I whispered back. I squeezed her hand and she glowed with pleasure.

A cough made me look up to the tall figure of my butty David looking down his nose at me in mock outrage.

'For shame!' He whispered fiercely. Giggling behind him, I saw Gwen as she looked round his side. They sat down and Gwen reached over to touch Ceri's arm, whisper a greeting and a little giggle at some womanly jest. A tap-tapping from the front, meant one of the deacons was fretting at all this good humour in God's house and calling us all to order.

The deacons sat around the pulpit, slightly raised over the throng, so they could look down on the rest. The elders of the community, they were and charged with the moral guidance of it.

They were fine, upstanding men in truth, though I always thought some took it too seriously - and started playing God too much for my liking. Perhaps, I'm still angry at the way we were treated then, but I never looked at them the same after we were married. In any chapel at that.

I leaned over to look down the pew, to see Ben and the rest of the Treveglos family, so we ended up among friends before the service began.

At the sermon, Mr Rowlands stood tall with the deacons at his side, sitting high with importance and scowling at the world.

'I went to a wedding yesterday,' Mr Rowlands began simply enough, though I could see some of the deacons bristling with annoyance. 'Not here mind… It was not allowed. They had committed the sin of fornication and for that they were not made welcome here.'

'Quite right,' came a mutter from one of the deacons.

Mr Rowlands smiled coldly and then he was opened his bible. 'Today I am going to read you a story from the book of Luke. Jesus' parable of the Prodigal Son.

And he said, "There was a man who had two sons…

The tale began and his words flowed over the chapel. Everyone sat in respectful silence and hung on his every word, for you could have closed your eyes and been there such was the power in his voice.

Some mouthed the words silently as he spoke, for many a chapel goer would now the bible back to front and took great pride in showing it.

As the story unfolded, the Reverend Rowlands grew more and more alive with the telling. The youngest son had taken his share of the family money and left home. He lost it all on pleasure and sin. We all knew the story, but as he came to the end, with the prodigal son returned in shame only to have a celebration made for him, I knew the point.

I suddenly realised what the minister was trying to get over to people and a wave of emotion swept over me. Pride, embarrassment, shame all in one go. The Reverend's voice grew firmer, as he related the anger of the eldest son who had stayed loyal. The father's response was plain as the hills.

And he said to him, 'Son, you are always with me, and all that is mine is yours.

It was fitting to celebrate and be glad, for this your brother was dead, and is alive; he was lost, and is found.'

'Lost and is found,' he said gently, looking all around the crowded chapel. 'Lost and is found…'

The Reverend stood still and gazed at us all in silence for a while, everyone watched him, waiting. He grasped the edges of the pulpit and asked gently.

'And for what reason did Jesus tell that story?'

A forest of children's hands were up, for they enjoyed this game at Sunday school.

'Cos they all complained about him going to Matthew the tax,' said one girl, causing a few chuckles.

'Yes, my dear,' he said with a smile. 'That's about right. Now was Jesus ashamed to visit Matthew the tax? Was he too proud to visit the man? Did he welcome him with open arms back into the fold, as the father did to his prodigal son? Hmm? Yes?'

He tensed his hands then and leant forward and said quietly. 'Well I am ashamed. The crash that followed made everyone jump, as the Reverend slammed one hand down on the pulpit rail.

'I AM ASHAMED!' he bellowed. The little chapel seemed to shake with his venom. 'I am ashamed that where we should be welcoming repentant sinners back to the flock, we bar the door. Not as our Lord Jesus did, he was kinder to a leper than we had to those poor souls, whose wedding I was honoured to attend. They had known they had done wrong - but wished to make it right in God's house. Where we slammed the door in their faces.'

He paused then lowered his tone, 'I am ashamed that I am as guilty in that I did not fight our blindness to it all. I feel ashamed that I was not strong enough. To High Church they went, although they are chapel at heart and it was there they were welcomed back into God's family. For that we should have celebrated, as that father did with his prodigal son.'

It was a mixed reaction, even some of the deacons looked embarrassed, but some were angrier at being ticked off.

'My friends are with us today,' he said with a wave of his hand to us, making a few of the folk turn around and stare. I felt embarrassed by the attention.

'To them, I offer my congratulations. I wish them luck. I welcome them to our congregation. I commend you all to do the same.

For when you do, you follow the teachings of our Lord on forgiveness. Any who may think otherwise,' he said with a wagging finger and a hint of menace, 'are welcome to enter a theological discussion with me. I am sure I will be able to show them the light.'

'Aye, with his fists at that,' a man muttered next to me. 'Handy he is too. Congratulations by the way,' he added quickly with a pat on my arm and a wink at Ceri who gave him her most beautiful smile back.

There was not much more to be said then, there was no need, the chapel was like a tomb. At the end of the service, we all filed out of the little place and down the steps to the road with the stream rushing next to it.

Many had the courage to come and wish us well, the Reverend's words releasing them from the fear of the deacon's wrath. Others still glared darkly at us, bless 'em! Word of the gypsy encounter had probably got round, but I didn't care. I would always follow my own path and to hell with those who objected.

Mr Rowlands came rushing up to us beaming. 'Now I can look you two in the eye once more. I hope you can forgive me for my weakness.'

'I'll never forget that sermon, I think.' I mumbled back.

'Don't, for one day you may have to show the same kindness to someone,' he replied.

With a shake of my hand and a kiss of Ceri's cheek, he was off once more to his flock.

And as you see, I never did forget that sermon. It's clear as a bell in my mind even now.

He had risked the wrath of his employers, the sanctimonious deacons, to try and gain us acceptance and for that, me and the family began to visit that little place for our worship. Not that I'm big on religion, as it has allowed some bad people to hide behind it in the past. There is some good there, mind and the stories are nice. We were certainly more accepted by the whole community from then on and tolerated by those with the airs and graces.

We made our way back up to Trisant, at a slow pace, taking in the day. The rain had not come and we wanted to enjoy our first walk as husband and wife.

Enoch was out of the house shouting greetings as we went past New Row and the store. I'd never seen him look so happy that one. We made our way around the Banc and then up to the culvert where Ceri had found David's hat that day, so long back.

Ceri gazed down the valley and sighed. 'There's lovely it is.' She breathed, pointing at the green hills and the trees down the way, where I had taken her to after she saw the boy crushed.

'What? Even the Graig Goch?' I replied tartly, nodding at the little grey mine cut into the hill.

'She turned to me and her eyes sparkled with love. 'Today *cariad*, even the old wheel at Wemyss is beautiful.'

'Well to some it is,' I replied.

'The height of five men standing on one another from the axle and the same below in the trough. They have folk coming out from Aberystwyth itself to watch it in the summer. They hire a brake and come all the way up, just to watch the wheel turn.'

'There's funny folk around, maybe you should stop playing at being a miner and be a guide to them?' Ceri said with a laugh. She looked up the Banc and saw a small group. 'Shall we go up?' she asked.

I shook my head. 'No, girl, let's go home. I want to see Mam and Dad and share our adventures.'

I waved to the crowd and saw the figure of Captain Nankivell, no mistaking him, wave back. It made me smile. I could hear him shouting - but could not make out the words.

We carried on past the mine and on past the lake. Ceri sighed again. 'Funny now, I see it every day, I do washing there, but I see it now with them birds on it and I feel I am at peace.'

'Let's go home *bach*.' I said, squeezing her arm.

'Mam! Dad! They're back!'

No chance of a surprise with Myfanwy keeping guard in the vegetable patch.

We opened the door to find the table was laid and all the plates down from the dresser. The dresser itself looked empty, leaving the big black bible on the sideboard and the little clock ticking away in the centre.

That old clock. it had survived many years on the dresser watching over us. Telling us that things always changed as time moved on.

We were met with cries and shouts of joy. Hugs from Mam and smiles from Dad as he pumped my hand, holding onto a clay pipe with the other.

We sat down to a good hearty bowl of *cawl*, bread and cheese. Meat was on the table also, they had killed the fattened calf for us it would seem. The meal was lively, as we told them what had happened since we left the church.

'It's not just them English deacons that are the problem, the Welsh ones are just as bad, if not worse.' Dad was not too keen on the heads of the community after the way we had been treated.

'Not so much, Gareth now,' Mam clucked. 'They're only doing what they think is right.'

Dad shook his head. 'Now don't you go sticking up for them after the way they behaved to us. We'll be down Capel Saeson from now on with Owain, Ceri and Ben and his family.'

247

'Don't make a big fuss,' muttered Mam. 'No need to make enemies now.'

'No, I'm not going to do that *bach*,' Dad replied. 'I'll give them the time of day, help them out the way I always have, but we'll go and hear God's word from a man who practices what he preaches and that's my final word on it.'

'Eat some more, girl. You're eating for two now.' Mam was ever practical and quick to change the subject when she lost an argument.

Ceri smiled but shook her head. 'No, I'm fine.'

'Oh *cariad*, you still sad about your Mam and Dad now?'

Mam was worried now, but I knew Ceri. In our house, Mam had been the woman in charge for so long that Ceri felt she did not want to say or do anything for fear of causing a fuss. I told her not to fret, but she still felt small.

The way she had been treated by outsiders had been wrong. A few had even spoken to her about her wickedness for living here. Mam got to hear and she was around giving them hell. Ceri had taken it hard though and she went quiet.

'No, I'm alright,' she said softly. 'Dad is who he is and Mam... well, I was sad to see her go again, but now at least I know she is safe and happy.'

Mam just smiled and patted Ceri's arm, she looked on her a bit different now we'd come back from the wedding. There was less of the mothering in her. The meal drew to an end and Mam stood up to sort everything.

248

'Now then Myfanwy, you clear these plates and you and Ceri can go and wash them. I'll get the room cleaned and we'll be readying ourselves for chapel. Miner's day tomorrow and there's clothes to wash, house to sort and bread to bake.'

'Mrs. Thomas, can I make the bread?' Ceri asked softly.

There was a little silence then, as everyone looked at Mam. The family bread had always been made by her, by rights the woman at the head did it. Mam paused, then she gave a smile.

'Of course you can, *bach*. You used a pot-oven before? Simple enough, it is, just put the dough in the pot and hang it on the chain, then use the lever to drop it down over the fire.'

Ceri fairly glowed with pleasure at being allowed to make the family bread. Mam continued.

'Dad you and Owain move the table back now and put the stockings back on the legs.'

'Why did you take them off in the first place?' grumbled Dad.

'Special dinner today, my son brought his wife home to us. You'd be on your best behaviour for that, whereas normal you'd have your hob-nail boots scratching them legs.'

Dad walked off muttering under his breath. That's what he did when he lost an argument.

'Owain, don't think you got out of it lightly, get the lantern ready for tonight. And you need to chop wood tomorrow for the fire and see what you can do with the damp patch in the roof. Now then, I want us all tidy-like ready for chapel, we have a little walk ahead of us.'

The magic of our wedding had gone, and the family got back to normal, but I was so pleased for the way Mam had included Ceri as my wife and not another child.

It seemed that I spent most of the time while waiting for the baby working with wood. Chopping, sawing, fixing wood at that. By the time Ceri was nearly ready, I had the attic split up with two rooms; one for us and one for Myfanwy. Small rooms and not much space to stand in, but we all still had our privacy and Dad was now making noises of how we should make the lean-to a new room for the house, as if he planned for us to have more children.

I had fashioned a small staircase in the corner, down by the fireplace and had made the downstairs into two areas as well. Another wood screen for Mam and Dad and the rest for us to cook, clean, eat and live in.

Ceri stood in our new room when it was done, holding a candle and looked around. In the gloom, I saw her swelling stomach in the shadow and a warm feeling came over me. My family was just beginning.

I went over to her, as she was looking around the new room, nodding to herself. I had no ceiling, but for the inner thatch, making it a tall room. She still looked at it with a smile and nodded to herself.

'Yes, Owain. This'll do.' Then she gave me a peck on the cheek. 'Our own part of the house, now there's swank.'

'Dad says we can move downstairs to their room after baby is born.' I added.

'Well, I don't know about that, kicking them out of their own bed and all. I'll have it up here if I can.' She smiled then. 'Owain *bach*. You don't know what it's like for me to have my own room, when I've my life sharing with sweaty mining brothers.'

'And now you have a sweaty mining husband.'

'Yes well at least I can tell you to wash and you'll go.'

Ceri got bigger and bigger with the baby, but she put up with it all with good cheer and an inner strength. I was not so clever. At the birth, Ceri had a bad time of it and I was beside myself with worry. I couldn't keep still. I could see I was beginning to annoy Dad, by my pacing around and muttering with nervous glances up the stairs, as he tried to sit by the fire and read his half of the *Observer*. Finally, he clapped his hands and stood up.

'Owain, we need wood,' he said stiffly.

'Wood? But Ceri…'

'We need wood for a fire for Ceri. Go and chop some now.'

'But…but…how much?'

'Lots, quickly now.'

I was off with my axe and my mind was just a blur as I went out to gather a lifetime's worth of wood. I collected all the fallen branches, chopped down some of the scrub trees and stacked it high. I looked at it sadly. Surely, we needed more?

I saw our apple tree, the old thing gave us beautiful apples every year, but now I had to sacrifice it. I needed wood! I made towards it and the axe was on its back swing when Dad came racing out of the house.

'Owain! Stop you! Don't touch that tree.'

'We need the wood,' I replied pointing at the huge pile.

'We got plenty now Owain boy, but I'm desperate for a Cornish pin. It's really important now, Ceri is nearly due. Ben has one, go get it now, will you?'

I was off running down the road before he was done. Desperate to get this pin to help the birth, that had taken an age to happen. It had been twelve hours already and no sign, surely that was too long?

I banged my hand on the door of Ben's house at New Row, a bit too loud for polite and for a while I wondered if I'd damaged it. It seemed to take forever, but after a while, the door opened and David stood there in his shirt and breeches, a look of surprise at the wild man stood before him.

'Owain? What's up boy? Ceri…?'

'Yes,' I swallowed hard. 'I need a Cornish pin now. It's really urgent. Dad said that Ben has one.'

David looked surprised. 'What's that? A Cornish pin? Never heard of that myself.' He frowned. 'Are you sure now?'

'Yes,' I was nearly crying with frustration by now.

'How is Ceri,' David asked gently.

'She's close but making a lot of noise and it's been over twelve hours now. Is Ben there?'

David then smiled a broad smile of understanding, 'Oh, right you are then. Dad? Owain's here, the baby's due and Gareth have sent him down here to get a Cornish pin.'

I heard a shuffle of feet and Ben appeared at the door, scratching his chin. 'Well, I don't rightly know,' he said slowly, making me hop from one foot to another in frustration. 'A <u>Cornish</u> pin you say? Well, there's many a Cornish pin. Did he tell you which colour he be after?'

I stopped then with a look of fear. 'No…is there more than one. Look, can I have all of them; I'll bring them straight back after no messing.'

'Well, there's only so many you can take in one go and different colours do do different things. Best you do go back and ask Gareth which colour he do want.'

'But Ceri's been over twelve hours now!' I shouted. 'And she's crying with it.'

'Well, Gwen took the whole twenty-four hours.' David said with a helpful smile.

'Yes, it do show her time hath come. Now, you do run off back and get your Dad to say what colour and I will get it ready for when you do return.'

The door shut on the house, as I sped back up the road like a madman. I ran and ran as best I could, until I was back at the house, puffing and wheezing like the old Cornish engine.

When I got there, I could hear the crying. I ran through the door, shouting 'Dad! Dad! Ben wants to know what colour pin.'

Then it hit me. The crying, it wasn't Ceri at all, it was a baby. I was up the stairs fast then and there was the Doctor on the bed and lying in it was Ceri. She looked terrible, tired with tear-streaked white face, but she gave me a look that had me rooted to my feet and there in her arms lay a tiny baby, peacefully nuzzling to her breast. Her eyes brimmed with tears as she held out her arm to me.

'Owain, come and meet your son Dafydd,' she whispered.

I came and collapsed to the bed, gazing in awe at the miracle in my love's arms. I reached out to touch her and then looked down to run my finger over the sticky baby. Then it all swept over me and I cried like a child.

Behind me, the Doctor was whispering instructions to Mam, but I couldn't hear the words. All my world was the picture of my darling wife and our son.

I came back downstairs after Ceri and Dafydd had fallen asleep. My Dad sat by the fire in his favourite chair, with his back to the stairs. He still read and was puffing gently on his pipe.

'I had best get back to Ben and tell him we'll not be wanting the Cornish pin, then.'

Dad said nothing but leaned forward on his hand and his shoulders started shaking with sobs.

'Dad?' I started to him, to comfort my Dad, as he was overcome with it all. Only as I knelt down by his side, I saw he was not weeping. He was laughing.

Slowly, he got over his fit and forced the words out, as he bit on his knuckles every time a new fit of laughing came on.

'Owain…Owain. There's no such thing as a Cornish pin! But I had to get you out of the house somehow - before you had us all vexed with your fretting.' Then he was off out the house and the laughter rang in the wind.

Chapter Sixteen

Ffair Rhos

David married Gwen in August of 1879, by February of the following year we were married and in May 1880, little Dafydd came to us. He was not a quick arrival, though other women might disagree, but then I always thought the first thing we should have taught him was how to use a clock.

I really loved watching little Dafydd grow. Ceri tried to take him to work for a while. Many women had to in them days, to keep the family in coin. It did not last though, the memory all those years back of the little boy lost in the cogs of the wheel were too much for her and she could not bear to work there and leave her child for any time, for fear he would do the same.

We were not starving, we were all right; but to keep us all right, we all had to work. You always kept money aside in case. In the end, the family had a think and we worked out that if Dad, Mam, Myfanwy and I went to the mine we would have enough to live on and a tiny bit to save. Ceri would stay back with the baby and work our smallholding to save us having to buy food when we could.

She would be woman of the house, making it all tidy like inside! It worked too, never a jealous word with all those women in all them years.

Two months on and I was still in a bother about it all. The baby cried a lot and I never knew if he was in pain or just hungry. Ceri was getting annoyed with my fretting, so she let me and Gwil go off to Ffair Rhos.

The fair was still there in my time, five times a year, but it was a rough affair. They came from all around to trade goods, horses and drink beer, fight and chase the girls or so Gwil said anyhow! The fair at the last weekend in July was the one that most miners were at and that's the one we went to.

Why? Well, miners were paid on the last Saturday of the month and the Monday after that was always Miner's day, a day off work. In July, this meant an extra day to sleep off Ffair Rhos. Never a big drinker, I was a bit worried bout it all, but Gwil laughed it off.

'Come on boy,' he teased. 'We'll make a man of you yet.'

'He's proven that already,' Ceri snapped back. 'I'll keep him as he is, thank you very much.'

'Look, are you sure?' I said to her back, as she thumped her dolly into and around the washing bucket. She was not happy, I could tell.

'Yes!' she shouted above the noise without turning around, 'I can't have you moping around all a bundle of nerves. I am that fed up with it.'

She turned around then, wiped her hands on her pinny and gave me a peck on the cheek. 'Go work out them demons, then come back fresh,' she said gently. Then she pointed at her brother, smirking in the corner.

'You look after him. If you get him in trouble or bring him back drunk, I'll cut them both off and I'm not talking bout ears, neither!'

'You have my word,' said Gwil with a straight face, which made her see red.

'*Ewch!*' She snapped with a flick of her hand and went back to her washing.

'What's about Ffair Rhos, Mam?' I asked her, later. Her being from south of the county and all. 'They do say it's only a few houses at most.'

Mam nodded but smiled fondly as she knitted by the fire. 'Well, it's a funny place. A crossroads between the village, Tregaron, Bont and the old monk's road to Abbey Cwmhir. The monks of Strata Florida used to run the fair in old times, but they're long gone now. Some king had them out, all about money – when was it ever over something else, mind? Typical men and their greed.'

'Monks?' I said. 'You don't see no monks around here.'

She laughed, even though her hands never stopped, the needles clicking in time like the clock.

'No, you don't. long while back, that was. But they left their mark on our land, you can tell with the names. Pont Rhyd-y-Groes; the bridge over the ford of the cross. Ysbyty Ystwyth; the Ystwyth Hospital run by the monks and the Devil's Bridge passed over the Mynach river falls – the Monk's river, isn't it?'.

I imagined a few old monks having a do outside of the Miners, it didn't feel right.

258

'Mind you, quite what was so blessed about the ford and the bridge called Pont Rhyd Fendigaid, I will never know.' Mam went on to herself. 'Probably why we call it Bont anyway, but we are strange with our names sometimes. It's a fine day, Owain. At least it was in my time. Though your married now and proper with it,' Her voice came sharp as she squinted up from her knitting.

'I'm not interested anyhow,' I said in my defence and her face softened a bit.

'Course not. It's not you *cariad*. That Gwilym Hughes, he's alright, but the devil's in him for mischief.'

I met Gwil outside the Miner's Arms in the village and headed up the road toward Ysbyty. Around the corner, the road went past the old turnpike house, which we spat at in memory of the hated system.

The road curved its way around the Counting House, where we got our pay and the *bargens* were set. The great adit; Lefel Fawr, came out in the garden, which had me wondering how anyone there could ever feel away from the mines.

We headed up to Ysbyty school and then into Ysbyty itself, where the small chapel and its graveyard sat below the High church on the hill above. Like the church boys had to make a point they were so much bigger than us chapel folk, I thought. But then was I chapel now or High Church?

Off through Ysbyty and the road twisted and turned up and down to Ffair Rhos. Baking the day was, like being in an oven by then. It could get that hot underground at times as you worked, but the sun was bad on us white-faced miners and we burnt too easy on days like this.

We were not alone on the road, for moving along that road were many folk walking to the fair. A few passed on horse, a carriage even bumped its way past us. There was a hum of excitement, as everyone made for the fair.

Ffair Rhos was not much bigger than Trisant. A *tafarn* at the cross-roads, a church opposite, and some miners' houses, that's about it. Everyone was making for the fields where the fair was. Hundreds there were. The place was a mad house, all horses and people. Nobody had a care for manners, for many were the folk I walked into, trying to keep up with Gwil.

'Thirsty work this,' said Gwil and off he went to the *tafarn*, returning with two flagons of beer. It was cloudy and I'd tasted better, but they must have been selling beer so fast that they didn't have time for it to settle. You drank the muck within it.

'It's not from the *tafarn*, mind,' shouted Gwil above the noise of the folk all around. 'Couldn't get in for folk. Shame on that, best beer hereabouts. We'll come back later. Let's have a look around then.' His flagon was already drained, as he dragged me off into the crowd.

It was madness. People everywhere, talking different languages. Welsh, English, Irish, all gabbing away, many already drunk and some after a fight and it not even being midday!

We looked in at the stalls, the folk shouting out their goods for us to buy. A little boy dashed out of one with a loaf, closely followed by the stallholder, to laughter and jeers from those around. A few people were selling illegal spirit, even though the bailiff's men were around, but pretending not to be. Wise men they were, it would not have taken much to spark off that mob.

Sitting at one tent and drinking beer were a group of loud and shocking women. Shouting at folk they were and offering their company for the price of a drink. Outrageous!

Gwil laughed out and called back. I hunched my shoulders and wanted none of it. I had no desire to be near these folk.

Another drink came, Gwil was really keen about this beer. He got talking to a girl and had her sitting on his knee

'A shilling and I'm yours,' said a dull voice at my side.

I turned and a young girl was there. Tired eyes looked back at me, trying to look pretty, interested and happy. Those tired eyes were haunting mind, like she had given up on life.

'No girl, I'm taken,' I muttered back. Her lips curled into a mocking smile.

'Married is it? We're all <u>married</u> *bach* that's why we do it. Come buy me a drink now, is it?'

'Listen girl,' I suddenly got a bit angry then. 'I'm married right, I don't want no harlot. I got what I need and don't care for your talk.'

'You causing my girl bother?' growled a lump of a man, coming towards me.

'No, but if she's your girl, best tell her to leave me be. I have no interest.' I snapped back.

'Boys is it then?' sneered the man, making my face all flush with anger. I took a step forward, all fists clenched, but Gwil grabbed me in a big hug and pulled me away and into the fair.

'Off we go now,' he shouted then quieter to me. 'You watch who you pick fights with Owain, that bastard was stroking a knife in his back pocket.'

I turned to look back and the man still stood there, a sneer on his face as he pulled his finger across his throat and pointed at me.

I was angry still at the way I'd been treated by him. The beer was in me and I wanted to rush up and punch that smile off his face, but I was no match for a knife. I glowered back and when I couldn't stand no more for Gwil's pulling, I turned and headed off.

'Look Gwil, this was a big mistake. I don't drink much. I don't want no girls. I should go.'

Gwil clapped my arm and stopped. 'Look Owain, I brought you up here to enjoy it, get your mind off things. Just relax and it will all be fine. Ignore them girls or flirt with them, it don't matter.

Don't you worry for him neither, I know his sort. He's happy to cause trouble, but he's here to make money. We'll steer clear of his part of the fair. Don't you worry now; I'll see you're alright'

That's what worried me.

Funny thing is, I did begin to enjoy it all. Leastways, what I remember of the rest of the day. We played at the stalls, then watched the shows and the horse trading. All the while we sipped beer until we were singing in our cups.

I did remember a few more things, mind. I remember being sick and getting thrown out of the tafarn. I remember walking back and falling off the path into a ditch. It was still damp, and I groped around in its slime retching.

When I finally woke, it felt like great hammers were hitting my head and a cold clammy feel was all around me. I wanted a wash but hated the thought, for fear of being sick once more. The land was still warm, but it was now dark. I was wet and cold. I could not sleep for the hammers, even though it was the thing I wanted most to do.

I found I was lying on a smooth slab of stone. Rolling back, I looked up and found myself looking at another one with strange markings. I reached out to touch them and drew my hand back in shock when I realised. They were letters, I was lying on a grave. I got to my knees quickly and retched and groaned,

'I'm sorry,' I croaked. 'My God, what have I done?'

I started singing a hymn, any hymn. Just to show God how sorry I was and a chapel boy at heart. I think it was *Tydi a Roddaist*. It didn't matter, it was terrible. I sang though like I was standing on the crater of hell and had to sing to stop falling in.

'Yes, what have you done indeed?' a voice in the dark replied, which shut me up quick as I thought that Death had come to claim me. 'I'm sure old Ioan Price would have asked the same thing, seeing as you used his grave as a dossing place.'

A light appeared, adding to the pain in my eyes. I was scared first that I had seen a corpse candle and I hoped to God it wasn't mine.

'And what brings you to disturb the peace of the departed?' The voice asked.

I groaned. I had no idea where I was, when it was and who it was I was talking with, though my head had worked out it wasn't Death. My head hurt and I felt so sick.

'I am so sorry, I am,' I groaned. 'Too much beer... Ffair Rhos... I don't drink.'

'Don't drink? Chapel is it?'

'Yes - but married in High Church.'

Is that so? Well there's a thing. I should have a mind to roll you up to High Church, where you can sleep on their graves.' He sighed then, 'but we are all God's children. Come on you, in the house for a gallon of tea and we'll see how you get on. But you be sick, and you'll spend the morning cleaning it all up!'

'Where am I?' I stumbled.

'Is it that bad?' said the voice in surprise 'You're in 'Sbyty. Where you going?'

'Capel Trisant'

'Good chapel there, choir wins many Eisteddfods. Well, now I'm awake you can tell me all about how a chapel boy marries in High Church before I go off to deliver my own sinners from their sins.

There'll be a few with hangovers as bad as yours, I'm certain. Ffair Rhos may have been the old abbey's doing, but the Devil walks tall around it, taking in the honest and the unwary. Now come you, I'm getting tired standing here and dawn will break soon. I need to be ready, for I have to work on Sundays.'

In the warmth of the priest's cottage, I realised how tired I was. He got a fire going quickly and boiled water for tea. I began to tell him my story, who I was, what I did, Ceri and how we met. It all began to spill out, as the brew warmed me. I talked and talked. In my mind tried to forget how bad I felt. I wished I could sleep, but feared to lie down for being ill.

The priest was a good listener and he let me go on. He asked many questions and I mumbled my replies. One hand was propping up my head as I sat. As I talked a memory came back of the fair. All hazy, like a dream though it was. There had been a fight, I knew. Where was Gwil?

'So, you love her then?' asked the man suddenly.

'With all my heart,' I replied sharply and winced at the pain as I raised my head too fast.

'Then why do you go off drinking at Ffair Rhos and leave her at home with the child?'

'She told me to go,' he looked at me and I stopped. 'No, it's not that. She knew I was having a hard time of the baby and let me go to relax. She can handle having a baby much better than I can for sure.'

'She saw you needed to relax and you have repaid her by getting drunk and not coming home. So how do you think she feels now?'

I felt foolish and nearly in tears, why could I not have been strong and just said no? The fight came flooding back then. *We had sneaked back into the inn after I had been sick, lost in the large noisy crowd. Gwil had gone off with a girl and I had run into that man with a knife. Or perhaps it was planned?*

Gwil had got talking to a girl, while I was getting drunk and singing like a fool. Her face cleared in my mind and it was the girl I had turned down at the fair. I was singing away with the rest of them in the tafarn and when I looked back, I saw Gwil leaving the place, his arm around the girl's waist.

A man pushed through the singing crowd towards me, singing and laughing with them all smiles as he got closer. It was the girl's man. His grin turned vicious as he landed a punch that caught me across the face. I touched my nose, while I remembered this and felt the dried blood still there.

The punch made me fall straight back and skidding towards the fire, I know, because I put out my hand to support me and took it away sharp like, when I touched the hot fireplace.

The man drew his knife, his grin was now of a wolf stalking his prey. I got sober quick then and knowing I could not go back any further, I looked for an escape.

Desperate now, I looked around and saw a poker, still half left in the fire, I grabbed it and swung it round to protect myself. He had moved closer and my swing took him in the face. I remembered the point was still red. I don't know if it got his eye, for he crumpled and screamed. I wasn't going to hang around to find out neither.

I ran to the door then, the crowd melting away in front of me. I was out and half-way down the road before I threw away the poker, hearing it hiss as it hit the ditch. I could not remember which road it was. I may have been going away from home, but the fear just drove me to run until I could run no more.

I walked by the faint light of the stars and the moon. When I began to make out the shadows of houses, I nearly wept with relief, for there was still the fear of a chase. The night was warm, and my chest felt heavy with it all.

I saw a field and felt it would be cooler and perhaps I could sleep, as a weariness had swept over me. It did not take long to realise I was in a graveyard. The shadows cast by the headstones had me dreaming of shade and I thought I should rest a moment by one gravestone.

I still felt hot. My head was now drooping, yet I tried to fight sleep, for the world still spun. My head ducked down once more, and I realised it would be cooler again if I put my head to the floor. This time I drifted off into sleep.

I awoke suddenly and the grave was upside down. The whole world was upside down. I screwed my eyes shut and vowed never to open them again. That was when I slept some more and when I woke later, the priest was coming to find me.

I told the tale to him slowly, as I remembered it bit by bit and he chuckled without humour.

'Well now, all good things come to those that wait it seems and that boy had it coming perhaps? Sounds an evil sort to me, one of them gypsy fellows, I'll be bound. It would be too much to persuade you to turn the other cheek in that instant! Your brother in law was not too clever also. I hope he does not live to regret his actions.'

'No.' I replied firmly then, 'Ceri's Mam is a gypsy and…'

Another memory came back. The man who attacked me had friends, as I ran; I remembered being grabbed and held. They were stopped outside the inn by a group of gypsies. I remembered the voices now; I could not forget Brian's.

'Go home, Owain my boy. We'll hold these boys back. Get home to Ceri, where you should be, you…'

I still winced at his final words.

'No.' I repeated, 'they helped me to escape and I know many have honour. Besides, I was always told to judge a person by what they do, not who they are.'

The priest threw his head back and laughed. 'Chastened in my own house, by a man I found asleep in a graveyard.' He stopped and smiled into the fire. 'And yet your words are true - and I stand corrected.'

He had been mashing some leaves and put them in a cup of hot water.

'Now, here is my remedy for you. Never touch drink. Stay with your family and repay their love. Keep away from fairs. Oh! And drink this, it will help.'

I drank it and nearly sicked it back up, it was so bitter.

'And keep in with Mr Rowlands at Ty'n-y-Groes, he'll see you right,' he added with a chuckle. 'While you're at it, perhaps you should go find young Gwil a good chapel girl also, he is in danger of following his father down the road to hell.'

He had disappeared and came back with a black shirt with a white collar fixed to it.

'Now I have been woken by your awful singing, I am off to chapel to sort things out before the morning service. You can stay here a while to sleep some more, then be off with you to your lovely wife and pray she forgives you.'

I didn't mean to stay, but the fire made me sleepy once more and the drink had made me feel better. My head rested on my hand as I sat in the chair.

I slept a while longer, until the sun was gaining height enough to shine through the window and in my face.

With a bitter taste in the mouth and a strange desire for food, I got off home as the day was filling out. I was back just before midday. Ceri came out to meet me. Dafydd was on her arm, all in white and sleepy. Cool eyes were on her, I was waiting for the slap.

'Where you been then?' she said softly.

I tried to tell her about the fair, but she stopped me.

'Gwil's already been here all a fret. He's out looking for you now. He told us what happened, and I've given him merry hell and wished the pox on him and all. He got a bashing round his ears from my hand, stupid brother of mine'

I told her about the fight and Ysbyty and she gasped. Upset and ashamed she was, but still she would not shout.

'Well, that's no more fairs for you good boy. *Twll* of a place that is and sleeping in a graveyard! *Ych-a-fi!* I'm surprised the old boy didn't chase you off for that.'

'I'm so sorry,' I said wringing my hands. 'I feel as *twp* as a sledge.'

She slapped me then, good and hard. 'Yes, you are,' she snapped, then burst into tears.

'Oh Owain, I been so worried. Up all night fretting I was. I knew I shouldn't have let Gwil take you up there. You're too much away from that nonsense,' she sniffed, 'it's why I love you so much.'

I hugged her then for ages. Mam appeared and took Dafydd away, though her eyes told me a tale of a lambasting to come. Ceri and me went away; not down to the mine, but over the hill where Frongoch had other pools for the waterwheels, where the only sound was the lapping of what water was left and the rustle of dry reeds in the wind.

'Promise me you won't do that again,' she said. 'I need you here, not in some graveyard, especially not on some poor soul's last resting place.'

'I promise Ceri love, I hope I never upset you again.'

She chuckled a bit in her tears. 'Don't be dull boy, how you ever going to keep that promise? Do you still feel bad?'

'Yes, my head hurts and my guts rot.'

'Good!' said my loving wife. 'That'll learn you. Now I got plenty of jobs for you for Miner's day. That'll take your mind off things, best get you cleaned up for chapel now and all. Let's hope no-one finds out.'

'Aye, David will split his sides laughing.' I muttered.

'David will be nothing like if word gets around,' Ceri snapped. 'Think of the shame. They'll be saying that you follow my father's path to ruin. That I have cursed you.'

I flushed and looked at my feet, 'I'm so sorry girl. I should never have gone.'

'Well, you've got some time to sort yourself out boy. Better behave now, if you want to avoid your ears being boxed.' Her smile was tight, but I could see she was slowly coming round.

I gave her a squeeze 'Gwil's still looking for me. Shouldn't I go find him first?'

'Leave him. Walk will do him good. Besides, that'll learn him.'

Chapter Seventeen

A Day Trip to Aberystwyth

That August was so hot that the house cooked up like an oven and everyone was forced to sleep downstairs. I even got up to sleep outside one night such was the heat. Strange isn't it? The one time we wanted a draught there was none, as I had spent the winter patching up all the holes in the walls. It certainly made me work quickly to get more air running through the house but still keep it warm at nights. The chimney got sorted out quick that summer.

Long sunny days had dried up the pools so many of the water wheels had to be stopped. In older times many miners went off gathering the harvest anyway, so things were quieter as there was less ore coming out. In our time, this had stopped and we scrambled to get out as much as we could for a decent shilling.

The mine did what it always had done, it stopped pumping out water and only worked the upper levels. The deep tunnels slowly filled up with water until a change of weather could allow us to pump them out again.

The Cornish engine was used a bit more to pump some of the mine, so the precious water was diverted to the mills.

Coal was dear and had to be brought fifty miles up to Trawscoed by train, so we used it as little as we could. All from the valleys of the South, where you tripped over it. Black diamonds they called them, and everything ran on it. Up Frongoch, we had to cut the peat to heat our house for it was cheaper for families that way.

Things had changed, we were now full-time miners of black for the zinc. We still got some silver-lead out, but now it was just a useful extra, where it had once been our lifeblood. The old Taylors hadn't cleared it out before leaving most of the black down there. It meant we could work the old levels above the rising water once again.

The output was up, but I heard the mine still wasn't paying. People began to leave, for the bargen was not as rich as before. Many swallowed their pride and went South to coal. We stayed, tried to sit it out, do our best whilst giving Dafydd time to grow. Many well-known faces to us went and the chapel congregations got smaller, but we stayed. The thought never left me about going away though. I dreamt of Idaho and Pennsylvania, a new beginning for us all. I knew one day it would come to us, just not now.

There was a big surprise for Ceri and me in September. It all started as a normal month after my adventure at Ffair Rhos. Dad had got us a good pitch and the black was all about us.

There was no need to mess about with narrow levels now, we could widen them. Some were now almost as wide as a man is high.

There was twice as much and then some going up top. We were having a good month and were looking forward to our payday.

The pare was working out a winze, clearing out the loose, with me and David up the top sending down toward Dad and Ben below to shovel it in the chute. I looked down and caught Dad smiling fondly at me. Well, let's say I could see his teeth in the gloom of the candlelight.

'Are you hungry or something?' he shouted.

'What do you mean?' I shouted back, stopping and panting with my effort. It was an oven down there and the sweat ran down my back. There was no way I would get cold by standing still that day.

'I can hear you picking away like a woodpecker and we got plenty now. You boys come down here and give us a hand, we'll get Sion to fill the tram and then take our break.'

We finished the loading sharpish and Sion was away with it before we had even started unpacking our food. He'd no bad words for me anymore, in fact I may as well not have been there.

We all had pasties made. It was mostly vegetables from the garden; potato, carrot, beans and so on. We got a bit of mutton now and then.

All was washed down with water from cans filled from the pool on the way down. We even done tea in a pot if we could make a fire. Course we would need good ventilation and no charges around, for sure.

Dad sat me down and as we snuffed our candles to save the wax, he started a strange chat.

'You never had a honeymoon, did you now?'

'No, well we can't afford that luxury, even as a daytrip. I thought of going up to Devil's Bridge with Ceri, but well…baby got in the way. Too late now, innit.'

'True, true. Just thinking, I was. If you went to Trawscoed in the morning for the train. You could get to Aber and be back by evening. You never really got time together, you two. Get to know each other.'

'Aberystwyth? We can't afford that!'

'Well, look now, we're doing alright here. There'll be a bit more for the *bargen* than normal. We're thinking you can have the spare. I think you should go to Aber,' he paused then, 'Idloes the gate will take you to the station.'

'What?' I stood up too fast and hit the top of the tunnel. Lucky I still wore my hat, but I would be needing a new one the way I was going.

'Well,' said David, 'I got talking to him not so long back. Seems his master has a day visitor arriving by train. He could take you up there to catch the morning one and meet this visitor, then pick you up evening when he has brought them back.'

'Won't he get the sack?'

'Well you never know with that place as to who be the puppet and who be the master,' rumbled Ben from the gloom and we all said aye to that.

'Look, we can't take it boys,' I gasped. 'David never had that, it wouldn't be right.'

'My idea Owain,' said David, slapping me on the back. 'You can't use that one now.'

'Dad, we need the money for other things now. Mam and...'

'Look boy, I talked it through with Mam and we both want it. It's something you really should have, get you out in the world and stop you getting so local. We'll be there for Dafydd, never you mind that.'

'Well, I...' I stumbled, but Dad cut me off.

'Right that's sorted then. You're off to Aberystwyth come Miner's day.'

'...and get me one of them oranges now,' sighed Mam. 'Your Nain was given them by her Spaniard and she never would stop telling me how wonderful they were. Bound to have them in a place like Aberystwyth.'

It was the morning of Miner's Day and me and Ceri were rushing about getting ready.

'Leave him girl,' said Dad in a tired voice. 'They're off on their own adventure, not going down the New Row stores. Get ready you two, Idloes will be soon here.'

'Don't know why I have to wear my Sunday best,' I grumbled, my collar pinching into my neck, 'I'll be steaming like the Cornish engine when the sun gets up.'

Dad was sympathetic as usual. 'No son of mine goes to town without looking his best. You'll not let the family down now.'

276

'He's here!' shrieked Myfanwy from outside and we went outside to look.

Ceri stopped on the way to check on Dafydd, but Mam hurried her away.

'Off you go now, baby will be fine don't you worry.'

'*Bore da*,' said Idloes with a grin, 'you ready now?' He opened the door of the trap and put the step down, then he helped Ceri in like the lady I thought she was.

'We'll keep it clean,' I muttered to him and he grinned.

'Right you are then.' A crack of the whip later and we were off.

We got to the station in time to be more than a handful for the ticket office.

'We want to go to Aberystwyth,' I said in a voice more nervous than I'd hoped.

'Single, is it?' asked the man behind the window.

'No, both of us and we're married,' I answered. Why did he want to know that?

The man took off his spectacles and leaned closer to the window, saying slowly. 'You want to go to Aber and come back on the train, do you?' He must have played out this scene before.

'Yes,' I said with relief and the glasses were back on.

'Two returns then, what class?'

'Mrs. Davies at Lisburne Mines School,' I replied straight away. Curious though, why did he want to know that and all?

He sighed and looked down, rubbing his thumb over the M&M Rly badge on his cap sitting on the desk by him. 'You being funny now?'

Idloes thankfully had seen us and rushed in to help and then we were on the platform and waiting for the train.

A whistle in the distance made me look up and I saw the white puffs of smoke from the engine as it raced down towards us. The engine was working hard and it looked as if it would pass straight through.

The brakes were applied, and the train screeched into the station, in a cloud of dirty white steam. It did not seem to stop with all the coaches at the platform, but no one seemed to notice, as if it happened a lot.

We found third class and some seats. The noise and steam of the train was scary for many people at that time, but it was no worse than the mine machinery to us. The doors were slammed shut and the guard blew his whistle. The train wheezed its way out of the station. Off we went, giving each other a childish grin, as we were at last on our adventure to the big town.

The train clanked and puffed its way along to Aberystwyth and we knew as the train reached a rounded hill with a strange pillar on top, that we were nearly there. As it began to move around this hill, I saw the sea for the first time in my life.

My heart leapt at the sight. A blue-grey mass of water stretched as far as the eye could see. Little white lines of waves were all about it.

A long steep pebble beach lay ahead of us and great cliffs rose further down the coast to become ghostly shadows of a headland in the distance. At the end of the beach was a breakwater and people seemed to be sitting on its side fishing.

The feeling I had for the scene was really strange, like I had come home after a long time. For someone who had never seen the sea, it was like a big lake stretching out forever. I knew of it, but I never thought it was that big.

The train moved on, the track seemed to follow a river until we turned again and got sight of many masts of sailing ships. A siding led down to the water, giving us a quick glimpse of some boats in the harbour and a ruined castle beyond. It made me want to explore it. We were then into a cutting and crossing a road past what smelt like a brewery.

Moving slowly now, the buildings quickly passed to a marshy riverside, we went over this other river into a mass of railway yard and sheds, all alive and leaking steam. Another train passed us as we passed the sheds, on its way out. The black engine and green carriages seemed to gleam compared to our rather dirtier red coaches and gallant little engine. Finally, we stopped. The guard shouted out that we were at Aberystwyth station and all change if you please.

Aberystwyth, and a tidy place at that! We got out and looked around. A mixture of fields and buildings were around us. A cattle market was busy on one side, a church being built on the hill of the other.

Behind us the tracks bent around a group of trees, where a castle tower could be seen, which the other train was now up to and quickly shrinking in the distance. A lot to take in, but nothing prepared us for leaving the station.

Outside, a large row of terraces greeted us, they looked as massive as the mine engines and looked to be full of people. We could see people in the window and people outside. Everywhere was people, like being at the counting house on payday.

Nearby, a foundry was hard at work, steam and smoke coming out from the roof. It was so different from the calmer bustle of the people in front of us. It was if everyone in town had decided to pass the station at that moment, some with carts, some travelling on horse and some walking on a real pavement. A good road and a real pavement, now there's posh! It was like Ffair Rhos, but respectable, you could say.

Where to start? We headed going past houses and shops. Not like the store back home trying to cram in as much as they could. These shops had room and they sold only one thing: clothes or shoes, vegetables or tobacco. As we walked, the sea seemed to call to us, the sound of gulls echoing off the side of buildings. Ahead we could see the street ending in clear blue sky and we walked towards it as if drawn by a magnet, guessing that this would be the sea.

The street ended on a promenade and more people were there. Hundreds were walking up and down or sitting on the beach or even paddling at the shallows.

The richer folk seemed to want to walk and keep the sun from them, the women with parasols, while the men wore hats. Strange on such a hot day.

Many boats were tied to it by iron rings, their ropes stretching down the beach.

'Like long washing lines,' said Ceri.

One was taking people on for trips and an orderly queue had formed down a jetty to a narrow plank where people were being helped in.

I could hear a band playing somewhere, donkeys faithfully plodded with their masters taking children for rides, who squealed with delight. The noise of people was incredible for us and we just stood there and watched the world. The promenade was definitely a happy place, judging by the shouts and shrieks of laughter in the air. Ceri just held my hand and gazed out to sea, head on my shoulder.

'Oh Owain,' she sighed. 'I never really seen the sea before. Beautiful it is and so cool. Let's try it.'

'Don't be *twp* girl, we can't swim.'

She giggled. 'You're the one who's *twp* bach. Shoes and socks off and roll your trousers up, like they are doing.' She pointed at a couple paddling at the edge, 'I raise my skirts a bit and we're still decent, don't need any of them funny bathing machines now.' She pointed at a collection of white gypsy caravans, a man emerged from one in a funny costume and headed to the sea, through a jeering crowd of children.

Off we went onto the grey sands and pebbles of the beach. As we neared the sea, it had become gritty grey sand. We took off our shoes and socks and edged towards the gentle push of the waves. Both of us stood not daring to move, until one big wave had an extra push and came in up to our ankles.

Ceri squealed and I cried out in surprise at how cold it was. We ran off laughing at our courage, but soon we edged back once more until our feet grew used to it.

We paddled slowly, arm in arm sloshing through the sea with our bare feet, nodding at those we passed like everyone else did, until we couldn't stop giggling for it. The air was cool and clean, salty and fresh. It was so beautiful.

Arm in arm, we went down the beach. I saw a big crowd outside the bandstand, listening to the music. Many sat on the beach listening for free, so we joined them in the grand tradition of the Cardi.

A row of large terrace houses stretched towards the cliff, ending with a hotel. Ceri wanted a look, so we brushed away the sand and put our shoes back on. Then we were up the promenade. At the end, more people seemed to be enjoying the beach under the dark cliffs.

'Go up then, is it?' said Ceri, but I shook my head.

'No, them rocks don't look safe. If that was Frongoch, I'd be shoring them up with timber. Let's go back.'

'Always the miner,' giggled my wife in a way that made me want to squeeze her waist. 'How about a bath then?' She giggled, pointing at a house sticking out the promenade with the words PUBLIC BATHS in strong letters on the wall.

'Public? I'll keep my baths private, thank you very much,' I grumbled. 'Tin tub out the back, if you please.' I got a laugh and a kiss in reply.

At the other end was the pier and you could see it was a proud thing, but now looked deserted. Jones Engine had told me it had come down in the storm of '66, or a fire or something, but I was too young to remember any talk of that, being seven at the time. I thought I saw bits of metal girder still standing up from the rocks pleading for it to be linked to its grander past.

'Where now?' I asked. 'I'm a bit bad with all this sitting around on the beach. Makes me feel lazy. Let's look round a bit, I'd like to see more of this town.'

Ceri nodded. 'Let's go down the pier and see if we can go around the coast there, then we'll explore. Still need to find oranges as it is. I don't even know what they look like.'

On the way, we caught a Punch & Judy show. Never seen one of them before, so we spent a while there and laughed at it with the crowd. The pier marked the end of the promenade and we looked along the low sea cliff at the beautiful University perched on its edge. Its castled towers seemed to be in keeping with the castle ruins behind.

'Bet they have fun when the storms bring the sea up,' I thought out loud.

We made our way up the street to the Town Clock and took refreshment at its fountain. It was here we found a stall selling fruit and I thought I'd try my luck when the man asked me what I wanted, 'You got any oranges?'

He looked at me all strange like then. 'What do you mean? You're looking straight at them.'

'Am I?' I didn't know many of the things on that stall. They all looked good, mind. 'I never seen one before,' I said picking up a green fruit.

'Not that,' said the man with a gasp. 'The orange ones, stands to reason, dunnit!'

I flushed and looked around wildly and the man's eyes narrowed. 'Someone put you up to this?'

Ceri took over then, she looked about to cry as she looked at the floor. 'Oh no sir, we mean no harm. Only we never seen anything orange neither.'

She bit her lip and flicked her eyes up to meet his before looking to the floor again. It struck me then that she had done that to me many a time. Knowing this, I knew the man had no chance.

He laughed out loud, then held up his hand. 'No, I'm sorry. You're not from round here are you.?'

She flashed a helpful nervous smile, 'no sir, we're from Trisant.'

'Trisant, is it? Well, I have a cousin up by Aberffrwd in the Rheidol. You near there?'

'Near sir, but over the hill to Pont Rhyd y Groes.'

'Well now,' the man had totally fallen under Ceri's spell. He picked up a strange, coloured round fruit with a waxy outside.

'Now this is an orange and you peel it like so.' The inside looked soft and watery. He split it in half and offered a slice to Ceri. 'Go on girl, try it. It's a little nip on the back of the tongue, but it's like nothing on earth.'

Ceri bit and her eyes widened in shock. Her mouth formed a big 'O'!

The man laughed, 'oh indeed!' He offered me a slice and I took it and bit half. The flavour flooded my mouth, an acid taste but refreshing and leaving me a wanting for more.

'The fruit of the Gods,' said the man. 'Now how many do you want, that one will be for free.'

We bought a bag of oranges, as a present for our family to remind us all of our daytrip.

The man told us how to get to the old castle and so we moved off down the street, eating this wonderful fruit. The castle was a sad place, once proud and now a pale shadow of itself, its towers over-run with ivy and the curious prodding it with an eager ignorance.

We found a strange thing called a *camera obscura* and for once decided to take a look, inside we saw the bay and the town through mirrors. The effect was incredible; it was like flying over the beach, like a swallow swooping down to the shore.

I wanted to have a look at the harbour, the smell of salt in the air was too magical for me. Ceri didn't mind, so we followed the road as far as we could, until the masts and spars we had seen from the train came into view.

It was so good to watch others toil with us just able to watch and relax and enjoy each other's company. Fish was being unloaded and other cargo loaded onto ships. Over the harbour, a ship was being repaired and lime was being fired in kilns. The sweet smell of hops was in the air from the brewery over by a grand river bridge. Behind it we could see moving wisps of smoke, telling us that our stay was not forever. The train was waiting for us at the station.

There was a rush of movement around one of the ships. Ropes were being hauled and sails coming out. Men ran around like ants as the front end moved out and then the ship gently moved away from the quay and towards the harbour entrance. I felt a rush of emotion. The way the ship glided over the calm water, the gentle rise and fall of the prow, the way the sails puffed out as the wind caught them. Something pulled inside me and I wished I was on it.

'Looks dangerous,' said Ceri.

'No, it's just beautiful,' I breathed.

She gave me a look. 'Not going to run away to sea now, are you?'

I grinned, then took her in my arms in a hug. 'Love, you are my harbour and I have no need ever to set sail.'

She giggled at that. 'Well at least I'm good for something.' Her eyes showed her true feelings and I melted before them.

It was time to get back to the train. We made our way to the river bridge with the mills beside it, before getting lost a few times in our rush to return to the station. It was a simple day, but so carefree that we could not help but enjoy it and lift our hearts.

We had not let go of each other's hand since the beach. We had explored, talked and laughed together and neither of us wished the day to end. Then there was the sea. How beautiful it was with the afternoon sun shimmering on it. I wished we could stay to see the sun set over it and watch what happened.

'One day,' said Ceri, 'you will take me here and we will walk the promenade together until sunset. There we will sit on the beach until the sun goes down.' She sighed. 'Oh Owain, let's run away and live here forever.'

'And do what?' I asked.

'Oh, just dream it *cariad*, you can fix the roofs and I will run a tea shop.'

'Didn't see much thatch in Aber girl,' said I tartly.

'Just imagine that we could do it.'

'Ceri *bach*,' I squeezed her arm. 'There's nothing more I'd like than that and have you away from that mine. I'd walk you every night to watch the sunset if I could. Let's give Dafydd time to find his feet first, is it?'

'By that time, I may be gone and you old and grey,' she replied sadly.

'We'll always be together here, *bach*.' I said pointing to her heart.

Give Dafydd time. I wish now my Dad had let me learn another trade, but mining paid well then and I was stubborn enough not to see any other way. Besides if I had changed, I would never have met Ceri.

I just remember that day, so peaceful and warm, my loving wife with me and the delight of exploring the town. My face tingled from salt air and the sea breeze in our faces.

Back home, everyone was all smiles. Myfanwy had looked after Dafydd. Dad proclaimed his first word was *Taid*. David and Gwen had been up visiting with their first born. It was almost like they were the better for us going.

We sat around and slowly ate the oranges together all lost in the tangy taste and our own dreams.

Chapter Eighteen

Hang-Fire

October was a grim one, typical Ceredigion. Wet and windy with rain running down your neck. Your socks and boots always damp, in spite of your best efforts to dry them out of an evening. The cold clawing at your fingertips and toes while you sniffled with a nose full of muck from cold and prayed it was not worse.

The mine was fully working now, the rain had filled up the pools and the wheels were now turning happily. The levels had been pumped out and were as dry as they could ever be, that is still damp but with only trickles of water and drops from the walls and roof. We had a pitch on 117, and I remember Dad coming back from that *bargen*. He saw my face drop when he told us and even Ben and David shuffled uneasily.

'What's up boys?' Dad said trying to sound cheerful.

'I thought you said we'd never go there,' I muttered. 'After all them accidents over the years.'

'Well you and David look as though your wives been feeding you too much, so you need a bit more exercise,' Dad replied with a snort. 'Truth is boys, that's all there was that was decent. There's plenty of black down there and a bit of lead too and at least it's not as far down as 154.

'But there's talk of noises and voices.'

'Nonsense boy, you believe everything you hear?' Dad said with a mocking laugh. Then he sighed. 'Come on boys, we'll do it just this once and then be done with 117 for ever.'

There was no problem, but I still had a bad feeling about 117. The memory of those accidents over the years was too great. The last one, where the pipe had dropped tailings on the poor man and buried him alive, I remembered that the worst. That was the last time I had gone down there and it all came back to me when I stepped off the ladder and walked down the tunnel of level 117.

That day had started with my first bit of bad luck. I was in a line of men going down for the shift, candle on our hats, all a flicker with the movement. A man below leaving the ladder, another above me waiting for me to finish, like links of a chain and the ladder all wet with the water working its way down, drop by drop on you. I was working my way down slowly when I stepped on a rotten rung.

As I put my weight on it and I began to lower my other leg down to the next rung, the damn thing broke and the wire supporting it underneath came away with it. Instinct is to throw your weight forward, I dropped down, but my leg went inside and the next rung below got caught under the back of my knee. The other was dangling in mid-air, all useless. Thank God that rung below held, as I grabbed onto the ladder with my hands for dear life.

There were shouts of warning all around me and a rumble on the ladder and a swaying as someone rushed back up. It was Dad. He shielded my body and put up his leg on a lower rung, to allow my flailing leg to use his knee for support. From then I got myself back up and looked over to him.

'Alright now?' he said with a grin, but his eyes showed the fear. 'Well, that's our bad luck for the day.

'Aye,' I gasped. 'Bloody 117 again.'

I could hear many a superstitious miner mutter a prayer on the ladder above. I was trembling like a leaf now, with my hands shaking through hanging there for so long. I managed to get down to the platform at the tunnel entrance and sat there panting and shaking. I looked over at David and he nodded back.

'Don't you dare die on me, Owain *bach*. I'll not hear of it.' I could only smile in reply.

David hauled me to my feet, and we got ready for the days work.

Our tools and a powder keg came down to us in a kibble and then we made off to our stope. Cheerful we all were that day, after the scare. David and I started swapping notes on how to be good fathers to babies and behind us, the two fathers poured scorn on the words of these experts. There was a reason to be happy, for the stope looked a good one. Dad had picked well; we would get more than a few tram loads of ore out of it.

We started on our pitch and things went well. Quite soon we were at the point of finishing the charge holes and ready to load them with dynamite for our first blasting. We set the charges and came back to shelter. Dad lit the charge. I watched the spitting flame shoot down to the charge before I ducked. When the explosions came and we all counted them as they happened.

'We be one missing,' said Ben.

'No, it was a double I heard, replied Dad. 'Give it thirty minutes now, then we'll go back to check and if it all looks good, we'll be in tomorrow to start clearing it.'

We heard an explosion later on, but it was muffled and far away. I was worried, but Dad just kept puffing at his pipe without a care. Thirty minutes on we checked our winze, it all looked well and the dull gleam of black zinc ore on the ground made us pleased with the days work and looking forward to starting on the pile the following day.

Back at the house, Ceri was also in high spirits.

'Fresh apples from the garden,' she cried, handing me one, Dafydd gurgling away in her lap. 'Go on try, they're lovely.'

I took a bite and the flavour made me smile. I looked at my family and how happy they were together and wondered why I ever thought of leaving.

'Reckon we earned that today,' Dad said as he clapped me on the shoulder.

'Aye that we did,' I managed between bites. 'Do you think there's good pickings for us?'

'There is now and many months to come,' Dad replied with a smile. 'Years, even. Lead may have dropped, but zinc is staying level and the office reckon it will rise. As long as we keep filling them trams like we are, we'll be alright.'

'Dad,' I moved over to him so I could have a quiet word, away from Ceri, even though she was busy dancing Dafydd on her lap and not paying attention. Dafydd bounced up and down chuckling away, as babies do.

'If the mine is producing,' I continued. 'I'd soon as not leave here. I see no reason to leave you and Mam here, when all's well.'

Dad said nothing, but picked up Ben's *Observer*. He leafed through the papers and then tapped his finger on a page.

'See this? Comes in the paper most weeks. It advertises sailings from Aberystwyth to Bristol and Liverpool and then on to New York. Thing is, I've heard tell of the boat, it's not so big as what they try and say. Fits into Aber harbour, no problem, but would it ride well on the ocean? I'm told not.'

'Strikes me Owain, that these things aren't always what they look like. Maybe it's best to stay, least you know what's happening here and you can't always see the truth in what is going on outside.'

I nodded, 'Dad, I got plans. To make the house bigger, what with Myfanwy growing and us…'

He nodded with a glint in his eye. 'Yes, and you may yet have more, I know. We'll eat now, then talk later, else your Mam will be giving us her sermon again.'

That night we talked over making another room where the lean-to was. We planned where we could find the stone, where were the best reeds and thought about the wood. There was a chance that they were clearing some trees in Hafod or over Devil's Bridge. We were both excited by the idea and talked well into the night on it.

The first job of the next day was to check over a part of the wall which Dad had thought was loose and could be dug out with a pick. Seemed a shame to wait for blasting but more important, we didn't want it on our heads as we worked.

I was on a platform, not much packing under me, so I had to be careful where I put my feet for fear of falling. Picking off the loose ore to the floor below, I was, to be cleared up by Ben and David. Dad was on another platform, a few feet away.

'You're making a mess of it,' shouted David cheerily.

'Now there's *Tafod Teg* that you are, Welsh boy.' I shouted back. '*Cer a ffordd* or I'll have you carry it all the way up top on your shoulders.'

David chuckled and went off with Ben down the way to fetch the tram up. Dad was feeling the rock with his hand, small drill in the other and hammer in his belt.

'Lot of loose around here, Owain,' he shouted. 'Best clear it now, before we blast.' He started working on a crack with his drill.

The rock had been making noises all day above us, nothing new in that. Grinding, clicking away every so often it was. The old boys always said it was pixies.

'Knockers are busy today,' I shouted.

'Telling us there's good ore to be had.' Dad shouted back. 'We'll make sure they're well fed today, lovely boys they are.' He took the drill in both hands to start to prod the rock loose.

Explosives is a funny thing really. It has a temper like a flighty woman. Most times it does what you want, but if it is the wrong mix or damp, it will have a mind of its own.

Course it's better with dynamite than in the old days, where men had to light big fires to crack the rock open and then work it loose with poles. We was much quicker and got more out faster. But then the old boys never had hang-fire.

After a blast if your charge did not go off, it did not go away. It could sit there smouldering and then go off later. Blasting was done at the end of the day mostly, so by the morning this was all past and the dust settled, allowing you to see the rock pile and breathe clean air. Most would blow, but what of those that did not? Where the fire had not taken or gone out?

The charge just sat there, as if waiting. You had to be careful when you were next down, as it was hard to try and work out where all the charges had been.

The lie of the area had changed with the blast and in the near dark of candlelight, you could not always work out where your charges had been laid.

It meant some that had fizzled out were still left in the rock, unknown to us. Like a snake in the grass, coiled and waiting to strike. A stray spark or sudden pressure would set it off and without warning, then you had it full in the face.

I was watching Dad prod the rock and there was a loud crack. The world slowed down for me, as I saw a short spark reach out to Dad and the rock followed. His head was covered by a cloud of dust. Then the whole wall seemed to shift. I was lifted off the platform and in the air like someone had punched me.

Falling, falling, falling. All a slow and a second before the candles went out, I looked up and saw the roof seemed to be coming down on me. My ears seemed clogged and a dull rush of noise was all around me, even if it sounded far away.

I had no idea where Dad was, but I knew what was happening. Hang-Fire! What terrified me the most, as I fell backwards in the darkness with flailing limbs, was that I couldn't tell if I was in one of my nightmares or not.

It seemed like I fell forever until I hit the ground hard that made a red cloud flash in front of my eyes and my breath whooshed out of me.

The way my left leg landed was bad and the pain shot through me. I tried to protect myself as the rocks fell around and on my body.

The sharp pain as I tried to move shook me up, as the world now sped back up to normal. With no light, I was prey to the falling rock and had nowhere to hide.

In time, the noise stopped. An eerie silence filled the air. I was now stuck in the rubble, not able to move, not able to breathe fully and spitting dust from my mouth, that was dry with fear. The dust was everywhere, choking me. I tried to call out, but it was only a croak that quickly faded. My breathing was shallow, I knew I would die with this load on me if I did not move - but how?

In what seemed to be far off, I could hear David screaming 'Owain! Owain!' Coughing and shouting. Coughing and shouting. I could hear Ben yelling to a trammer to raise the alarm. All seemed so far away, as if in another room. A sudden tiredness swept over me and my body felt warm.

I managed to open one eye and saw white spots in front of me. They faded after a while and I saw a glimmer of light in the dust cloud. I tried to shout, croak, anything. I could only manage a whisper. The light grew, another appeared closer, then another.

David's calling was faint amid the ringing in my ears from the blast. I just lay there and prayed. I prayed to God like I never done before. Let me see Ceri, God, Let me see her on more time. And my boy, I've got to live for my boy...

The lights were getting closer and I knew then that David was lighting his candles and placing them down as a trail as he went along searching for me.

I still could not move, nor speak to let him know where I was. All I could do was lie there and hope he would find me in the dusty gloom.

I started feeling sleepy and my mind began to drift. Then I heard scrambling above me and a shadow loomed over me. A tall dark figure stood there, shaped like a miner with a candle flickering on his hat. The effect of the dust on the candlelight meant the face was hidden in shadow beneath the hat, or perhaps he had no face? This scared the hell out of me, and I was all for thinking it was Death come to claim me. Then the shadow spoke, and I knew with relief it was my butty.

David scrambled over to me and set a candle nearby 'Owain!' he shouted in panic 'Owain!' He slapped away the loose rock from my face as quick as he could, which let my other eye open.

'Can't breathe,' I wheezed.

David picked up the candle and moved it over the scene to take stock of what was there. A large boulder had rolled on my chest and David cursed at it like I'd never heard him before. He jumped up and embraced it with a snarl of anger, his eyes blazing. With a cry of hatred, David rolled it off so fast as if it were paper.

This rock was huge I'm telling you, yet Davy boy had it off like a pebble and with that I'm damned sure he saved my life. My lungs flooded with air but the relief was short lived as my whole body ached with pain and I begun to cough with the dust, which only added to it. My back now felt on fire.

'Don't you worry boy. We'll have you out in no time' David turned to yell 'Quick! Anyone! Man down over here!'

'What's happening?' coughed a reply.

Dai Cochyn, I knew the voice. A few years younger than me, known for his red hair and the hot temper with it. A demon for work, he was; that man could dig. It was all I needed at that moment.

'It's Owain, he's trapped in a fall.' David shouted back. 'Over here boys, we got to get him out quick'

Another scramble on the rock and the face of Dai appeared, sweat and soot hid his freckles and dust tinged his red hair. His face told the tale of how I must have looked.

'*Iesu Grist*! You stay put Owain, we'll have you out in no time, boy.'

Stay put! The *twp* things people say in a panic. Where was I going to go?

'I'll just be off down the tram lines for a few minutes,' I tried to joke.

'He's gone in the mind, we got to get him out quick,' said Dai.

'Only a joke, mind,' I complained, perhaps it was only in my mind, for nobody reacted.

'Stretcher!' I could hear Ben's voice and others were calling as they rushed in to dig.

I was fading, my mind felt as if it was wrapped in linen and I felt further and further removed from it all. The sharp pain was all that kept me there. That and the thought of Ceri. I saw her then as she had been the previous night, giving me an apple, bouncing my son on her knee.

They got me out, though it took a while. David bound some wounds, tearing his shirt into strips. That saved me bleeding to death. David, I thought even then. One day boy, I'll be there for you and all.

'Too right you bloody will, boy,' David snapped back under the strain and I realised I'd spoken out loud.

He looked at me hard and then the fear left his eyes, and his cheeky grin came back. 'You remember that you owe me, butty.'

'Get that bloody wagon here now!' I heard Ben. 'Is the Doctor called?'

On his way, came the reply.

'Not bloody fast enough,' muttered Ben.

I drifted off again but woke as they moved me.

'*Duw*, thought you'd gone then boy,' said Cochyn with a tired grin. Ben's face swam into view, all concern and fear. He shook my shoulder gently.

I looked around and realised for the first time something didn't quite fit. All my friends around and Dad not by me. I remembered him again, laughing and reaching for the chisel with his hammer. Then I pitched back and was falling once more.

'Dad,' I whispered.

'Gareth! Did you see Gareth? Where is your father Owain?'

I struggled to find the words, my lips parted dry as a bone and the lips stuck to my teeth. Someone splashed a bit of water and I licked the moisture gratefully.

'Owain. Do you know where your father is?' Ben shouted again, more urgently. I looked around again, but I fell back quick. All faces around, all known to me, yet one missing.

I managed two words in reply, 'Hang fire.'

Ben's face seemed to age in front of me.

'Dear God, no,' I heard him whisper, then I collapsed.

I woke again in a warm room, the smell of camphor all about, a fire crackling away nearby. It gave me a nice warm feeling around my body, like it was wrapped in blankets.

I felt stiff around my ribs and realised they were bound. I raised my head with a start and tried to rise, but my shoulder was gently pushed down, and a welcome face came into view.

'Steady boy,' said David. 'You're safe now.'

I'd been brought to the office, to be tended. That was strange and I said so, David chuckled.

'Doctor said you needed warmth and there was nowhere else, as the smith had closed. You're alright now, Doctor says you'll live. Just need some time for your leg to heal. You made a right mess of it, you did.'

'David,' I gripped his arm as best I could. 'Where's Dad?'

David looked away for a while and then sighed and turned to me with a sad smile.

'We don't know boy, but we're still looking. My Dad and Dai Cochyn are down there now. He'll be there, we'll find him. Doctor's ready and waiting.'

I was feeling sleepy again, I wanted to ask, but the words were now harder to come.

'How long...' I started but drifted off again.

Later, much later I remember waking. The old clock was staring at me, faithful thing keeping time for us on the dresser. How strange that it should now be in the mine office, I thought, and the dresser too?

The thought was strange, but I felt comforted by seeing those from home. I closed my eyes and voices drifted over me.

'You leave him where he is now,' said an English voice, educated. 'Bathe the wounds regularly and that will help keep away infection. Try and give him air and feed him lots of fresh vegetables if you can. Keep the bed by the fire, so he is kept as warm as you are able. It's time now that's the healer and that will decide his future.' I heard him pack his bag and then close it. 'I'll be back in a few days to see how he gets on'

'Yes sir' Ceri's voice mumbled in reply. 'Thank you, sir.'

'Alright now, I'll bid you good day Mrs Thomas' I felt the blast of air as the door opened. It shut again and Ceri sobbed, I drifted back to sleep and this time I dreamt.

I was in a field on a beautiful summer's day and I was lying in a meadow. Ceri lay over my chest, it made it tight and hard to breathe, but I didn't care. I liked the touch and her scent. The sun shone above her, through her hair, making it shine. I had to keep my eyes half closed to see her in the glare.

She moved up and lay with one elbow on my chest and the other held a buttercup. She was laughing, we both were. She reached up to tickle my nose. She laughed the more, as I moved my head from side to side, helpless to escape.

I closed my eyes. When I opened them again, the meadow and the sun had gone. The old clock was there, marking its time faithfully on the mantelpiece. I opened my eyes wider and looked upon my home.

Ceri saw me wake and ran to me with a cry, she buried her head in my shoulder and sobbed as if she would never stop. 'My darling, my love' she whispered stammering through her tears.

I wept too, 'I love you' was all I could whisper, over and over again as I faintly stroked her hair. The nightmare was finally over, but one thought remained all along. When we had stopped crying, I managed to whisper it.

'Ceri, where's Dad?'

Chapter Nineteen

Gwylnos

They brought him back to us two days later. My body had stiffened by then, so much that I could hardly move, my muscles were red raw and beginning to darken with bruising. All I could do was lie there by the fire in the living room, where they had set up a bed for me. I could only sit back and look across the room. At the far end was a mirror, Mam's treasure. Through it was now my only link with the outside, for though it I could watch the door opening and closing.

I heard a shriek outside and a commotion, lots of voices raised in anger. I could only listen to the noises and wish I was out there to sort it all out. Then, my sister burst into the house. Fifteen now was Myfanwy and blossoming to womanhood. Her face though was streaked with tears as she ran to my bed.

'Owain' she sobbed 'He's...he's...'

I held out my arms and she buried her head in my shoulder weeping. It hurt like hell when she hit, but not half as much as hearing the truth. My fears were real, Dad was gone.

I felt numb, even though I had expected it. When you think of all the rock that fell on me and him further below.

Even then, I had still held a spark of hope in the back of my mind. Maybe he had found shelter under a boulder that had fallen kindly and protected him by making some impossible cave. Now at least we knew, Dad was dead; and no hope would bring him back.

Cochyn cleared the table for Dad's body and covered it with a blanket. From the look on his face, I knew he wanted to say he was sorry. There was nothing he could have said at that moment and poor Cochyn knew it. He smiled grimly and went to help bring the body in.

Dad was in a shroud and I knew the wounds would be too much for viewing. Ceri came in next, looking red-faced and grim. I knew she'd been crying also. She came over to my bed and gently prised Myfanwy away from my battered and bruised body. Slowly, Ceri led her outside, arms around her shoulders. Myfanwy shrieked and sobbed, she could hardly walk with it all, but Ceri slowly led her away.

Finally, Ben walked in holding my Mam. She looked old that day, lost and in shock. Ben had to support her to the big chair at the fireplace, for she would have collapsed without it. There she sat not moving, staring ahead. David appeared with a blanket and put it around Mam's shoulders, but she just stared into the fire as if he wasn't there.

'Doctor reckoned he took the blast full on,' said Cochyn nervously, eager to break the silence. 'He didn't think Gareth knew anything about it. Said it was quick mind.'

The doorway was open now and that old mirror gave me sight of the outside. I could see Ben was now sitting on our wall weeping helplessly. He was iron was old Ben Treveglos, but even iron breaks under pressure and digging out his butty from the rocks was too much to bear.

He just sat on our wall and cried, with David's arm around him, as if he was father and Ben the weeping son. All I could do was watch the scene, helpless to do anything about it.

It was my Ceri who was the strong one for us all. First, she thanked the men, as they stood awkwardly outside and took their leave. Then she sat down with Ben and put her arm around him, then after a few words, she bade David take him home.

Ceri came back in and set Myfanwy on tasks to take her mind off things, I was told to lie back and rest, not that I had much choice then. I was still weak from the fall and had slept most of the time since, as it was. Ceri left Mam by the fire, lost in her grief. As the day carried on she was persuaded to eat some *cawl*. Mam sat in the chair sipping the soup, but her face was still blank and the eyes dull. I tried to speak to her, but she didn't answer. I had lost her at that time.

The local minister from Trisant called in the evening but was given short thrift. Ceri had carried us all through the day, but she was hurting also and in no mood for nonsense.

'May I speak to the woman of the house?' The priest began gently when Ceri opened the door.

'For this moment, that would be myself,' Ceri replied quietly, but I heard a tightness in her voice.

The minister looked hard at her. 'My dear, even in this dark time that is not your role, you should not presume.'

'Well,' said my darling wife, cold as snow. 'My husband lies broken. His sister is beside herself and his mother is lost to us in despair. The only man who acted to me as father lies dead on the table. My *role* as you put it, is not one I wish, but as the only able-bodied person here, it is one I have. There is no choice, I *presume* nothing.'

The minister stood back in shock, then he tried to compose himself. 'You must forgive my choice of words. I suppose that I am at fault, as many are due to the manner in which you became...'

'Became what?' snapped Ceri back. 'Tell me, or am I too *twp* to know? Due to the manner that I became wife? That what I did was wrong and sinful? Aye that it was and yet it was not our intent to go against the teachings of the bible.

We did though and we have worked damned hard to put right that day. We have married to make sure our baby would be born in wedlock, as others have done before but many do not. That, in spite of those who would close their chapel doors to us, as you and your kind did.'

I could see the minister open and close his mouth in surprise, but no words came out and he had no chance anyway. Ceri had had months of being treated bad by them all and now it had just got too much for her.

'I am not ashamed of my son,' she continued, 'for he is the proof of our love for each other. Yes, we have committed the sin of fornication and for that I pray every Sunday in chapel for forgiveness. Whether I am forgiven is God's will on my judgement day, not yours and certainly not those who affect themselves airs and graces like *crachach* and turn their faces from me. They have no right to judge me, as you just did. Good day, sir.'

'Aye to all that,' I croaked as Ceri shut the door on the shocked clergyman. She walked over to me and I could see she was crying.

'Oh, my dear,' I sighed. 'To hell with them if they can't see you for who you are. We got friends and we don't need them.'

'Made me feel like I trapped you, Owain,' she sobbed.

I passed a trembling hand over her eyes, to wipe the tears. 'Well I don't agree and I'm not one to complain.'

There was another knock at the door and Ceri got up to open it, drying her eyes as she went. It was the minister again, but this time he had removed his hat and looked chastened.

'Mrs. Thomas, I owe you an apology. I was too hasty and have listened too much to wagging tongues. I am the one who is supposed to teach people to love their neighbours and yet I have not seen fit to know you first. And now I see I have made you cry. It is bad with me for sure.'

'What changed your mind?' asked Ceri.

'Seeing the door shut in my face,' replied the minister. 'It taught me a lesson and one I aim to pass on to my flock, come Sunday.'

Ceri smiled and rubbed her tears away. 'Would you take tea with us?'

'Ah, I never say no to a tea. Such a heart-warming drink.' The minister replied and they both laughed. The man came in and bowed to Mam and me, while Ceri moved off to make him tea, her smile was one of relief mixed with triumph. I winked back at her.

He was good company and we felt lifted by his talk. He did not preach nor teach us, but we felt stronger for his conversation.

'May I call from time to time?' he asked. 'I am sure Owain may need the company.'

'Thank you, sir, that would be most kind,' replied Ceri simply.

'I also wish to offer you the use of our graveyard, although I more than understand if you wish to take him elsewhere. Please know that Gareth was well-respected here and you have many friends, even if you feel there are none since you were wed.'

This was a good gesture from a good man and the only reason we never took it was we were now with the English Wesleyans. In them days, it was like being a different people in God's kingdom. Some swapped around as to whichever chapel was used by their mine Captain. All to keep in and be nice to the man who might give you the better *bargen*. Our reasons were more honest at least.

A bit later on, Reverend Rowlands called. The minister, whose name was Edwards, was still with us, talking away. He was eager to hear tales of my father, almost as if to bring out the good memories within us to help our grief.

'Stealing my congregation now, is it?' Reverend Rowlands said smiling, shaking his hand.

'Make sure you keep them,' came the reply. 'For they are gold.' The Reverend Edwards then got up to leave.

Reverend Rowlands spent most of his time with Mam. He talked softly to her about Heaven and Earth. How her Gareth was not gone but waiting for her. It was nice, but not what we needed that day and to be honest, friend though he was, I was glad to see him leave so we could grieve in private at last.

Ceri packed the women off to bed then came to me and we slept as best we could. She knew there was nothing to say, but her body so close was the best comfort for me at that time. Even through the pain of my body and the pain of my loss, I shone with pride that day, for the world had begun to see my Ceri's strength.

For three days, Dad lay in the house, as was the custom. Then the funeral eve was upon us and Mam wanted to hold a candle vigil. Myfanwy was packed off to bed, which was not a problem. She was finding it hard to deal with her grief and living with the body there. She had cried a lot and I thought it would do her good for the funeral to be done.

After another long day organising, Ceri followed. At least then one of us had strength for the day after and God knows she was the only one of us who had any strength. I sat there in the bed and shared the vigil with Mam, candles lit around us and the fire low in the grate.

We were silent for a long while, for Mam had not spoken much since they brought Dad home. She sighed a lot but would spend most of the time sitting in her chair, staring at the fire. I started to talk, but once more was met with silence.

She was tough as old boots was my Mam, but even boots cannot take punishment for ever. We were like this for hours, then she sighed.

'For a long time, he wanted you out of that bloody mine,' she said. I jumped at the sound and my Mam swearing at that.

'Yes,' she continued slowly, wearily. 'He knew how foolish it was, dangerous, dirty and cold. He wanted you out before something like this happened.' She bit her lip then to stop sobbing. 'Course, now we're stuck. One less to work and you bad in bed. We'll struggle this winter.'

'I'll work double as soon as I get back in' I started, and her head looked up sharp.

'Don't be a bloody fool boy!' she snapped eyes blazing. 'You go straight back like that and we'll be burying you by next Christmas.' She bit her lip and tears fell. The pain was all there to see. She sighed again and reached out to hold my hand.

'You do what you can *cariad*,' she said softly. 'Damn mine's got us stuck in its web now. Too late for you *cariad*, just look out for yourself down there and promise me you will make Dafydd follow another path when he's old enough.'

'But how…?' I began.

'Just promise me,' she hissed through gritted teeth. 'I need something to live for.'

'I promise Mam,' I whispered.

She sighed and sat on the edge of the bed sobbing silently for a while. I watched her helpless to do anything. My bruises were going to black now and I was stiff as a tree.

My one leg was bound, a clean break but tied with splints, so as to try to mend it straight. To give me a chance to walk in the future, let alone climb. Mam finally wiped her eyes and sniffed.

'Know what Owain? I'm not here to keep the evil spirits away. Superstitious nonsense, all that is.' She looked over at Dad lying in his box on the floor and smiled sadly, 'I just want as much time as I can have with him before he goes under the ground and is just a memory.'

'Come you, 'I said through my own tears. 'Tell me stories about my Dad. I want to hear good things and a wake we can have as we wait for morning.'

She smiled and moved over to me and I held her as best I could as she sobbed once more. I was there for her like she had been there for me as a child.

We spent the rest of the night having our wake for Gareth Thomas, my father and her husband. She told me how they met, courted and married. How they sneaked time together at the back of the churchyard when their parents weren't looking. I asked her of Nain and Taid and the Spaniard.

'Oh, that rogue! He was a visiting sea captain whose ship came in for repair. She was lonely with Taid farming his sheep up in the mountains six days a week. It wasn't right, she knew that, but she was weak. He took advantage of her, but she would never say a bad word against that man and yet she was still devoted to your Taid right to the end.'

Mam began to brighten now, and she smiled fondly. 'Do you know what Nain's last wish was? An orange. Your Dad wanted to show how much he cared, so he talked his way onto the mine carts going to Aberystwyth, just to buy some. Such was his devotion and love. Nain smiled and closed her eyes in bliss as she ate them.'

Her eyes filled with tears again and I reached for her hand, she took it and held it like it was a sovereign.

'He saved the last one for me and when I offered him some, he said it was only for the special women in his life.' Mam sighed and looked at me. 'That's why I asked you for them when you went off to Aber. If I ever have one again now, it will make me feel closer to him.'

I told her then of my time working with Dad and about when he'd saved my hide from Gomer. Then I wept as I said how I'd never had the time to tell him how I felt.

She touched my cheek then, so gentle. 'Owain, you fool. Don't you think he knew? You showed it every day and he returned it. You never needed words. When did you argue? Never much and for how long? Could you not feel how proud he was of you? He loved your Ceri dearly as a daughter and all. Don't you worry now *bach*, he knew.'

'I miss him Mam,' I cried. 'I always felt safe when he was around. He always seemed to know what to do.'

She gave me a sad smile and then a hug 'Owain *bach*, I look into my heart and there's a black hole where half of it has gone with him. I carry a weight of pain on my shoulders and emptiness in my soul. Now *cariad*, you got yourself a fine woman in Ceri. You take care of her and pray you never lose her and feel as I do now.'

But I lost my father too. I felt like I should say. She was right though, I didn't know half of it and selfish that I was, I prayed I never would neither. Strong was our Mam, but part of her died that day.

That was our *gwylnos*, our wake-night. We sat there together the rest of the night and waited for morning. I began to doze for a while and Mam sat at my bed, resting her head on the mattress. We were roused by Ceri and I looked out of the window at the grey dawn and felt the chill air in the house.

As the light grew brighter, six men came in to bear Dad from the house; Ben, David, Dai Cochyn, Captain Nankivell and two other miners; Sion Parry and Matthew Smith, a Staffordshire man. The wind blew level outside and I could feel the thatch lift, the day looked grey. The Reverend Rowlands was with them and Mam gathered herself to let them in, then went off to get ready. Nobody wanted to talk much and there was many a nervous glance about. Parry eventually came over to me, but his look was cool still.

'Friends we're not, Owain Thomas and I know I've been bad with you. I felt you had taken my place and well, jealous I was for your woman and all. I tell you this, I feel bad for you. I wouldn't wish this on any miner. He was a good man.'

He looked away and my sadness was tinged with relief. He had called me miner, after all them years of never admitting it.

'Sorry you can't make it, butty,' said Cochyn, trying to break the silence. 'I'm sure your Dad would understand.'

Another time and I would have laughed at the foolish words, but I knew his heart was in the right place. 'It's alright Dai, thanks.' I whispered.

'You know what I mean, he knew how you felt and all...'

'Yes, don't you worry now, Myfanwy will stay and look after me.'

Ceri appeared again and made sure everyone had tea and cake. In older times, a cup of stronger stuff would have been passed around, but we had moved to the Wesleyans and tea was the order of the day.

A crowd had now gathered outside our house. I could hear the buzz of their talking, but no-one came in out of respect. Mam and Ceri came downstairs, white faces in black mourning. They both kissed me then they were off out, with the men shuffling out after with the coffin on their shoulders.

The crowd went quiet as Reverend Rowlands said a quick prayer, then there was a chorus of Amens, a shuffle of feet as everyone got in line and the first strains of the beautiful hymn *Tydi a roddaist* started up.

The procession would sing all the way to Capel Trisant, only putting down the coffin to pray as they reached each crossroads, as was the tradition.

It would be a long journey, but I knew that the boys would do it without complaint or strain, in memory of my Dad.

Others would share the burden on the way; Evans shaft, Jones furnace. Everyone wanted to do their bit. I knew Dad would be in good hands.

The sound was haunting. I was told a fair few came over from the mine and thereabouts. Some were friends, some would become friends, while some were ghouls who just liked funerals! The music grew fainter as they moved down the road to Frongoch and I was left in the house with Myfanwy. I needed a nurse and they all felt poor Myf would not bear up to the service, so the two of us were left in silence the singing fading in the distance and us crying our eyes out for our father, who we would never see again.

After a while, I felt tired and warm and drifted asleep into a dream. I found myself back in the mine on a platform. The blast came once more and the fall of rock. I felt once more the feeling of being helpless as I fell back and down and the hurt of the falling rock pounding my body.

I was trapped with only my hand sticking out of the rubble, all around was dark and the rock was crushing me. Then I felt a hand grab mine and pull me clear of the rocks.

It was Dad, he was smiling, and his clothes were so clean and white like the mine captain I always felt he should have been. His candle shone over him like a beacon as he looked down at me with a warm smile.

'There's clean you are,' was all I could think of saying. He laughed at that, all smiles. He patted my shoulder, and the scene began to fade. As I faded back to sleep, I heard his voice. 'You'll do my boy, you'll do.'

I woke up as the door slammed. The wind was rustling in the trees and the rain was pouring down. Myfanwy was shaking my shoulder and shaking with fear for the storm.

I held her hand and told her not to fret, as the rain beat down on the window. Very quickly though, the rain stopped, and the sun broke through the clouds. A fresh smell was on the breeze.

Myfanwy still looked frightened, 'Owain…it went so cold and then the rain and wind and…'

'It's alright Myf,' I said gently. 'It was only Dad; he meant no harm. He's gone now and at peace.'

She clasped my hand and sobbed a deep sigh, 'I miss him so much, Owain. I love him and wish he would come back.'

As she cried onto my shoulder, I patted her gently on the back. 'Don't worry Myf, he'll be waiting for us when we're ready. He's just gone on ahead to build a fire in the grate.'

She laughed then, bless her and wiped her eyes. 'As I must.' Then she gave me a quick hug and she was back to normal. 'Now then boy, best get you well. You're the man of the house now. Cup of tea, is it?'

John Kitto himself was there they tell me and Ceri was told they would hold my job. Ben said he would have no-one else mind, for he would be the leader now. The people had been generous in donating money at the grave for Dad's *Cymorth* This was freely given by all as a mark of respect and alms to help us get by.

We would need the money now. It would tide us over winter but what the future brought after that was a worry and no mistake.

Next miner's day held a surprise for us though. The women were all working; cleaning, working the garden or mending clothes, with me the pathetic bundle in the bed. Then there was a knock at the door and Ben and David came in to greet us, caps in hand.

'Welcome you are,' said Ceri, 'come to see our sick boy?'

What, that lazybones?' said David with a cheeky smile. 'Still waiting for him to get out of bed and do a decent day's work for once.'

'All in good time, you rascal.' Ceri giggled back. Ben cleared his throat and stepped forward.

'It's Rhiannon we be here to see.'

Mam came out from her washing and Ben was almost shaking with fear.

'I do want to talk about the pare Rhiannon' he began. 'See, we be a team and more than that. It be like a family, we do look after one another, especially when we're sick and all. That you do know, for when one of us be bad in bed, we do all cover and he do get his share of the *bargen* come payday.' Ben paused and looked down at his feet. 'Owain should still have his share and Gareth... well he should too,' he added quietly.

There was a silence in the room, Ceri and me were in shock, while Mam just sat looking straight at old Ben, as he played with his cap nervously.

'Ben, no,' Mam whispered. 'We don't need no charity. You know how it is. We have to make do. You have your own families to feed and what of the other boys you got in? Or is it just you and David working now?'

'We had a mind to that,' said David a bit quieter and for once not smiling.

'We took on Matt from tramming and Sion is helping out. We said we'd split our wages alone, but they wanted it like this also. They was the boys who helped dig Owain out and get him up top and Gareth too.'

'And as for our family,' said Ben. 'We talked it through. They do want it also.'

'Ben,' said my Mam so gentle. 'You can't do this for Gareth, he's gone.'

Ben looked at the floor and rubbed the back of his head with his hand.

'Rhiannon' he began, his voice hoarse. 'He was my butty, my brother. I do have to do something...' He stopped and sat there; eyes screwed shut shoulders shuddering as he tried to stop the tears.

After weeks of walking around in a daze, Mam came to life. Gently, she reached out for Ben's hand and clasped it. He gripped it like iron and started sobbing, but Mam was in control now and she just stroked his hand.

'Ben *cariad*, I know you miss him. We all do. And I know you cared, but you got to let go of him now. He's gone and we've all got to pick up our lives and carry on. It's what he would want.'

Ben sniffed a bit, wiped his eyes and nodded.

'Now, we'll take a half share for Owain, seeing as he's in your pare and there's the baby and all, but you boys have still got mouths to feed and bills to pay, so thank you for the offer and we'll say no more on it.'

Ben nodded and David smiled once more.

'I came to ask if I may help in any jobs on the house, while the scamp is in his bed.' He winked at me, 'even if I'm half the roofer he is.'

Mam smiled and said that would be very welcome. She looked at Ben and stroked his cheek.

'Ben, Ben' she sighed 'I know you want to help, and you are. You are a generous man, but do not let it ruin you. Please do not worry, we will get past this and come back the stronger for it. Come and visit us still though, you're always welcome here.'

Ben nodded and got up to leave. 'You do look after yourself Owain, when you be ready to come back, we'll be waiting for you.' Then they were away.

Ceri went to console Mam, but she waved her away with a sad smile. 'Poor Ben,' she whispered. 'Poor Ben…'

Chapter Twenty

Gwilym

That was not the last time that folk came to try and help us, but the very last one was not as welcome nor as honest as Ben.

Gomer Hughes. It seemed that he would always be there to cause us misery, him and his loutish sons. Snakes all, save Gwilym, who was made in the same mould as Ceri and suffered for it. Time had changed Gomer and now the drunken brawler of old had found salvation in temperance and the Cross. This only made him ten times worse, for there is nothing as bad as those converted who have discovered God and wish to change everyone to their thinking. Not all are as bad, but some do try to push their zeal on you. In the case of Gomer, it meant he felt he was always right - and you were wrong.

I had begun to walk by then and was taking my first shaky steps, while my legs tried to remember what they used to do. I was lucky I could walk at all and level 117 had given me a parting gift of a limp to remind me of that terrible day with every step I took.

It had been a few months, but slowly my body had begun to heal. My bruises went black, then purple before fading to yellow and red.

My cuts had healed. There was feeling once more in my left hand, where for so long it had been a dull tingle. It was like my body was waking up once more after a bad dream, to find I'd fallen off a cliff.

My legs were not strong with the weeks of just lying in the bed as my left leg mended, the muscles had softened and shrunk. My mind was also slow from not doing much, apart from socks, that is.

Mam had this idea that I should work at socks and stockings, for we needed them, and they could be sold to friends. A few more pennies to help us while we scraped together what money we could. So, there's me, the big miner, sitting in his bed days on end, making socks and wondering if God was not laughing at me or something.

Both Reverends, Edwards and Rowlands, had been to see me regular. Reverend Rowlands had helped my mind by bringing me old copies of the *Cambrian News*. I used it to slowly understand how English was written. It was a language that I used at the mine, for there were a few English and Cornish at Frongoch and you pick up some words as you go, as they did with Welsh. Now I began to use it as a way to keep my mind working. It gave me news from outside of the area, but in the main I found that the people of Aberystwyth always seemed to have something to complain about.

Strange really, I always thought of it as a fine place myself, but the way they wrote it, the folk were ankle deep in filth and choking with smoke and steam!

Reverend Edwards tried to help me learn to walk again. He knew that my legs had to be built up strong once more and so he began to push me to stand, then to take one step, then two. Before I knew it, I was shuffling around the room with a stick, still shaky but at least I was up.

It was about this time that Gomer arrived on a Miner's Day with a cart and his band of poisonous sons. I heard a fuss outside, as I sat in the chair, tired with walking around the room. I could hear Ceri shouting angrily outside and the sound of her voice made me worry, so I limped to the door as quick as I could.

Ceri stood at the gate holding a pitchfork at her father. He was a changed man from that dark night at the gypsy camp, clean-shaven and dressed for Sunday service and sober with it and all. He was trying to look at peace, but with a painted smile that made my back itch.

'Go away,' said Ceri firmly, voice trembling in anger. 'You are not welcome here.'

'Daughter please, let me have my say,' said Gomer, arms open as if begging forgiveness.

'Have your say and then leave,' I said from the door, leaning on the frame for support.

Gomer's eyes flashed angry. For a second, I saw the old drunk there. Then he smiled.

'You really should show more respect for your father, daughter of mine, but I do forgive, for I was bad to you for so many years. I was a sinner and a drunk and the devil had me in his hands. I treated you no better than cattle…'

He then smiled broadly and took off his hat and held his arms high, looking upwards to the clouds. '…then the Lord spoke to me and told me I would perish in hell, should I not change my evil ways. I am saved now and all I can do is sing great *Hallelujahs* and thank Him for every day in this beautiful world.'

He shouted the last of this little speech and turned around as if to an audience around him. There'd been a few religious preachers who legend had it, could convert even the worst sinner. I'd even seen one or two come to Pont Rhyd-y-Groes in my time, but I felt nothing with Gomer. There was still the feel of a man who was trying to look at peace, while his soul howled with pain. In my mind, it had driven him mad. His eyes blazed in religious zeal. Ceri's however just blazed with anger.

'That may be, and I thank God for it, but I think you have not come all the way here to tell us that.' Her tone was cold and icy and the pitchfork in her hand had not moved an inch. She was a long way from trusting a man who had caused her such pain, only to have changed in so quick a time.

327

'Indeed not,' smiled Gomer, looking respectful. 'For I know of the tragedy that has befallen you. Word has reached me of the accident. Gareth dead, the Lord bless him and Owain sick. It may be that Gareth did not walk in the true light.'

His smile was vicious now, like a fox. He saw Ceri's face darken and the godly man returned. 'It may be, even though he was a good man, but now he is at peace and I pray for his salvation.'

I knew there was a trick coming, but before I could say anything he carried on. 'Then there is Dafydd, my only grandson. What life is it for him in paupery, with no men bringing money into the house come payday?'

He held out his hands again and the smile was broad, 'I offer you the chance to come back to the flock, the prodigal daughter and to my house, which we shall make larger for all. Instead of the wilderness, I will bring you to Pont Rhyd-y-Groes. We will all live there and worship together in the new chapel.' He was getting quite excited now and was shouting once more.

'We can all give thanks together and pray forgiveness for our sins, so the Lord will look kindly on us. Now, come! We have a cart for your things and plenty here to help and we can put up the house by sunset.'

Ceri was stunned. 'You would have us leave here and be put where? A *ty un-nos*?'

'For sure,' Gomer replied as meek as you like. 'For when you are reborn in the light, must you not start anew? The greater the trial, the greater your place come judgement day. You were led astray, and I am here to save you all. Owain Thomas, now is the time also for you to put aside the sins of your fathers and step forth in the light.'

I felt my face flush red at that, 'I tell you now drunkard, stop talking ill of my father or I will send you off to see him and he can spit at you as you descend to hell.'

'Owain, your words are sharp with the grief that you hold. Tell me this, has not this been a punishment for Gareth for his sins and the sins of his father before him?'

'The only mistake my father made was to mistake one of another pare's charges that went off that day,' I growled. 'That was what killed him. His other mistake was to dig you out to curse this land as you have.'

Gomer smiled his vicious smile. 'So you agree with me at that. He interfered with God's work. Well that is a start on your long road to redemption, my son.'

Ceri was in a fury now. 'You talk of sin as if others are to blame. I tell you now the best thing you ever did was throw me out of the house and away from your madness.

You talk so cheaply of a good man as if he was a great sinner, when it was he, not you who practiced what you preached. His only sin in my mind was he rescued you from the mine. *Ewch! Cer a ffordd!'* She fair screamed the words in his face. 'Your words are poison. You are not welcome here. Leave us to our own lives and look to your own salvation.'

Gomer's smile was almost demonic. 'Ah, Ceridwen, you are young and foolish. Gareth was a good man, but he dared interfere with God's work and God will punish him. The Lord had decided I was to die, and Gareth went against his wishes. It was a sin that earned this retribution, but I forgive him for that as I am sure the Lord will on his judgement day. Now you must work hard, for now is your chance to redeem his sin. Through such humble beginnings, you will surely gain redemption.'

'Was it not God's will to have you found?' shouted Myfanwy, coming up to Ceri's side, shaking with fear. 'Do you twist everything to your way of thinking?'

Gomer chuckled and shook his head. 'It is not for us to question God's will, for he doth move in mysterious ways.'

'Take one step on our land and you will be moving in mysterious ways,' I shouted from the doorway.

Gomer smiled and opened his hands. 'My children, I was worried that you would resist God's word in such a manner. Should not families be together in their hour of need? Does it not say so in the Bible?'

Not that I remember, I started to say, but he carried on. 'I hoped it would not come to this, but God's will be done. If it means we destroy this den of sin to make you move, then so be it. You shall follow the true path whether you wish it or not. It is right that you come with us, so gather your belongings on this cart, as we mean to fire this place and destroy all that remains.'

The final revenge for Dad's rescue of Gomer and he was so mad now as to want to cause misery as payment and more than likely kill us in the bargain. All that hiding behind God's name, his twisted plans showed at last. He stood with his sons standing around like a pack of wolves waiting for the kill.

Further up the road, I caught sight of Mam returning from a walk with Dafydd on her shoulders. She had not been seen yet, but stood their unsure as to what to do. She was not like the Mam of old, who would have been in there now tanning their hides. I looked away from her and shouted, 'Mam, to Thomas. Go now!' I hoped that she would understand and seek out the Reverend at the chapel. She moved out of my view, but by then a new danger had taken up my thoughts.

Iorri had come into sight from behind the cart with a flaming torch, he had been working on a flint whilst the argument had gone on. He almost licked his lips as he thought of the damage that he could see would take place.

Gomer's sons had been brought up with nothing but contempt for the world and they seemed to live for the conflict and misery that it brought. All save one and I couldn't see him there. Where's Gwil? I thought. I wished I could see him. I was sure he wouldn't let this happen.

Iorri made off over our wall to the side and started walking towards our cottage and the thatched roof. I moved from the door as fast as I could, but it was not as fast as I expected or needed. My limp was slow, and I cursed my aching legs, as I knew I would not reach him in time. Even if I could, I feared I would not have the strength to do anything.

Iorri's smile was evil as he watched me, youngest of the brood he was the hothead of them all and was enjoying the conflict. He slowed to make sure I could reach him and then knocked me aside with a kick and a laugh full of malice and scorn.

I went down like a stone and he made for the house once more. As he reached the back and was about to toss the brand up high, he was hit from behind by a figure so hard that the torch left his hand with the shock and hit the ground.

Gwilym had appeared from nowhere and was now wrestling on the ground with his brother. Blind fury showed on his face, as he hit his brother again and again until the man lay still. I crawled over to the flaming brand and rolled the torch on the ground until it was out. I made to pass it to Gwil and saw that he had pulled a knife. I held the brand instead and got to my feet to face Gomer, his eyes blazing with hatred. I waited for the start of the battle that must surely come now.

'Gwilym,' shouted his father. 'Are you so much a sinner as to stand in the way of God's work?'

'God's work!' spat Gwilym, 'more like Satan's work from what I can see. I have been to enough chapel to know what is God's work. This is not it. You think everything you do is God's work, but you use the Lord's name for your own ends. This time I will not stand idly by and watch you. I should have had you at the gypsy camp and done us all a favour.'

'Come on then, brother dear.' Gethin sneered. 'There's more of us than you. We'll have you over easy.'

'Come and try, fat man.' Gwil snarled in response.

'Boys! Boys!' Gomer shouted, his hands up to try and calm the brothers. His smile looked fixed now, but like a mask of mud, about to crack.

'Gwilym, would you go against your own father? Would you turn your back on your own kind? Would you stop us from God's work?'

'Were I to leave now, I would be turning my back,' Gwil shouted. 'For Ceri is my own kind and the only kin here worth tuppence. I'll not let you harm her, you drunken bastard.'

Gomer turned purple with rage. 'Then you can suffer with them,' he shouted and started forward.

Ceri was pushed aside and Myfanwy slapped down. Two of the brothers had pounced on Gwil and the one on the floor was now back to his senses and easily knocked me down again. I hit out at him with the torch, but he was up and at me quickly.

Then all hell broke loose, as people appeared everywhere. Ben and David. Old Enoch and Cochyn, even our neighbours. They all piled in and Gomer and his vipers were soon beaten off and running back down the mine road. Cochyn led the chase after them, spitting feathers.

A cheer went up at this and everyone started talking at once. I heard Enoch say he would take the cart back to its owner and would anyone wish for a free ride, causing a roar of laughter. A man helped me to my feet and I saw it was a neighbour, but not one who had looked to know us in the past.

'John Evans is my name, and I am ashamed that we have left it so long without helping you or knowing you before.'

'John *bach*,' I said feeling faint now. 'You picked a fine moment to start, but a welcome one at that.'

John laughed at that, but I was lost in a faint, so I did not hear what he said next.

When I woke up, I was back in bed and the house was full of people all in good cheer. Ceri was at my side, quickly to check that I was alright.

'There you are love, now you rest here,' she soothed. 'It was a fine display that you did, but foolish. You'll undo all the good work of these past months, if you're not careful.'

'Where's Gwil?' I croaked.

'He's here,' she said and called him over. He came and stood with his arm round her and Ceri rested her head on his shoulder, 'He's my hero, Owain. He was locked up by Gethin, but still managed to break free and knock up Ben and David. They rounded up the rest from New Row. Mam got to Capel Trisant and the Reverend was there. He spread the word like wildfire, said they all had a chance to redeem themselves for the way they have treated us. Everyone in the village was more than happy to come along.' She looked over at her brother fondly, 'but Gwil is the man. If they'd have got to the roof, we'd have been lost.'

'Well,' said Gwil all shy and looking at his feet. 'I have let it all go on for so long, I had to stop it all. It have cost me everything, but I'll never go back there.'

'What will you do?' I asked.

At that point, someone tapped a glass for silence. It was Reverend Edwards.

'Quiet now, my friends,' he boomed. 'Mrs. Thomas would like to say something.'

He didn't mean Mam, who looked happier but still so small and lost. No, it was my Ceri he meant, and she stood proud and head high. Nervous and frightened as a rabbit, mind.

'I…I have to say a few words,' she started quietly, then she gathered her strength as I looked on with pride. 'I just want to say thank you. We nearly lost it all here today, because of my father. With Owain injured and Gomer…'

Her eyes were damp with tears and she stopped and swallowed. 'I know my family have been trouble for years. I know that I have come here in a manner which is not how you would wish, but the kindness you have shown in saving us is just…' She bit her lip then for a while and just whispered. 'Thank you.'

There was a murmur of agreement and a spatter of clapping in sympathy. Reverend Edwards then called for quiet once more as loud as Reverend Rowlands he was and everyone stopped straight away.

'Brethren all. I see today as a redemption for us, for in truth we have treated this family with a lack of respect that they have not deserved. It sits bad with me that we did not speak and I regret that we judged too quickly. I hope they can now forgive us our pride.' He looked over to us, I think wanting a word to say all was well. I cleared my throat, I had no idea what to say, but in the silence as they waited, the answer came from Mam.

She looked so small sat in her chair, staring at the fire, all the men stood around. She seemed to be lost in a dream, but her words were what was needed. 'I wish Gareth was here to see this, he knew you were all good men at heart.'

There was a lot of talking then and the Reverend called for quiet once more. 'I would also want to talk of one hero among us. The one who overcame fear and doubt and bondage. Who turned his back on the evil ways and broke free to raise the alarm and carry the fight. This may only be tea, but even so please raise your cups and toast the honour of Gwilym Hughes.'

A huge cry of agreement and a thunder of applause followed. Everyone then turned to Gwil, to hear him speak. He looked nervous, eyes looking this way and that, like a trapped animal, then he cleared his throat.

'I'm no hero,' he said, almost crying with the shame. 'I been with them with all their wickedness. I been cockfighting and gambling on the Sabbath. I been drinking and fighting. Sometimes I hated what I done, but I still went along. I never found the strength to stop. Sometimes, I even enjoyed it... but when he tried to hurt Ceri. When he done that, I knew he had to be stopped. I'm no better than them, but I'll not go back to them at home or down Logaulas again, I'm finished there.'

'You're staying with us' said Ceri firmly. 'And don't you talk nonsense, you never been like them. You always been your own master and you know what's right and wrong. Don't you ever say different.'

'You do come to work with us,' called Ben. 'Sion be moving on and I do need a good miner in his place.'

'Gwil hook his head sadly, 'I can't. You can't reward me for what I done. You should be doing me for what I done before.'

'You're staying and that's final brother,' I said as loud as I could, which was a bit of a croak. 'Or do I have to fight you for it?'

That caused a laugh all round, which broke the spell. Everyone watched him as he stood a while, then he smiled weakly, gave a nod and he was swamped by folk wanting to clap his back and shake his hand. After a while, he was free of it all and he worked his way over to my bed.

'So, you're staying then?' I said with a chuckle.

'Leastways till your well Owain,' said Gwil with a sad smile, he looked around the house at the people inside. 'Then I'm off, this land holds nothing for me.'

'We want him for the pare, Owain.' said David coming into view all a grin. 'He's a good strong boy and a brave one at that.'

I managed to grip Gwilym's arm 'Not bad, eh?'

'No, not bad Tomos *Shaneg bach*' said Gwil, the smile not reaching the pain that showed in his eyes. Family ties are strong, and it had been hard for Gwil to do what he had done. In the end he chose the love for his sister over the duty of his cesspit of a family and for that I would always be grateful.

Gwil moved into the house at Trisant and we worried less about money coming in. As for Gomer, he was never to bother us again. Down by Pont Rhyd-y-Groes, the river Ystwyth cuts its way through a deep gorge, with rocks as sharp as knives.

In the Maenarthur woods, is a bridge called the Miner's Bridge. It is mostly used by the boys on their way to work from the village towards Gwaith Goch.

It seemed that Gomer had gone back home and went straight on the bottle. Heavy with guilt for his action or anger at losing the fight, I do not know. Then he had an argument with Gethin. Gomer wanted to come back here, Gethin had had enough and wanted an end to it.

Gethin it seemed had finally had enough. He'd gone along with it all for too long, stepping in when things were too bad.

Thankfully, I had been helped on more than one occasion. Seems old Gethin never really forgot what I done when I carried him up from the Ystwyth gorge. The more I thought of it, how he had acted when Ceri was thrown out and now with the final meeting, he was always the one who stayed the hand. He had done so for Gwil on a few bad times and all, it seemed. Gethin was more of a man than I had given credit for.

Gomer had argued with Gethin that night. Gomer wanted us crushed, but Gethin knew it was going too far. The talk got ugly and it came to blows. In the end, Gomer walked out into the dark and was gone. A day later they found him.

We learned later on that he had been found in the gorge under Miner's Bridge. He had jumped to his death, for there was no signs of struggle. It was a tragic end to one who could never live with his guilt. His last argument was enough and the pain of another one of his brood standing up to him, perhaps the pain of it being his eldest son, was too much to bear. I pray his soul finds peace, even though he had caused us nothing but harm.

He had tortured himself for so long after the accident at the mine and the pain of guilt had made him turn into the animal he had become. In doing so, he had brought misery and pain to all around him time and time again.

Now at least he had an end to it and could stand before God for his final judgement. I hope the good Lord remembered him for what he was before the madness took him and swallowed his soul.

Chapter Twenty-one

Turn of the Wheel

One Saturday afternoon a few weeks on, Gwil and David were doing some repairing to the roof, sorting out some of the damp top thatch and replacing it with new reeds. I was being useful by sitting outside and shouting orders, knitting my socks.

'So, when you coming back then?' David's question never changed. 'Time you tested that leg of yours on the ladders, isn't it Owain? We need you and besides a hosier's life is not for you.'

'Trying to get rid of me already, Dai Pasty?' Gwil's voice rang out from the other side of the roof. 'I only been down Frongoch five minutes and all.'

'Well,' David said with a smirk, 'you don't work half bad for a <u>Logaulas</u> boy, but well me and Owain got a way of working, that's all.'

Gwilym snorted, 'Owain does all the work, that's why. You just keep yourself pretty in case the bal-maidens come calling.'

'Well he's got a long wait then,' I said. 'For when my Ceri tried to go down Vaughan's the one time she left with a boot up her arse. Seriously boys, you don't need me - and my leg is not strong enough at any rate.'

It were a miracle that I could walk at all and Reverend Edwards was to thank for that. It had been more than a few months and I still walked with a limp, but walking I was.

The good Reverend was a regular visitor and he began to take his daily walk with me in tow. The first day we only reached our gate, but slowly we had got further, and the walks had changed from damnation to salvation.

We were also back in Trisant chapel every Sunday, on account of my leg. They made us very welcome too and I'll not forget their kindness, as they made amends for the past. Ceri in particular was spoilt rotten.

'Your legs is doing alright, Owain boy,' replied David. 'What you need is to go up and down this ladder a few times as practice. You'll be back with us in no time.'

'Perhaps later David, but there's no room for me in the pare now, is there?'

'Always room for you, Owain boy, never say that.' David's smile, warm as always, turned into a broad grin as Gwil's voice sounded out again.

'Aye, maybe we'll get four man's worth of work with you in the team, brother.'

Myfanwy appeared at the front door, arms wet to the elbows with washing suds. 'Owain,' she shouted. 'You seen Mam? Only she said she would help me.'

'No,' I shouted back. 'Out with Dafydd more than as like.'

'Dafydd is with Ceri,' I heard her say as she walked back in.

343

By food time, Mam had not come back. We ate and the boys carried on the work with me up and down the ladder fetching them reeds.

My left leg was sore as hell from the work, but at least now it was strong enough to hold my weight. The day moved on towards early evening and with the job done, David was off back to his family.

'Give a hug and kiss to Gwen from me,' I said, and his grin was broad.

'I'll do more than that, Owain boy. Sorry I never got to see your Mam. Say hello from me now.'

'Yes, she's probably off visiting someone like Reverend Edwards and got talking,' I replied, and David was gone with a cheery wave.

'I'm worried now,' said Ceri after the door was closed. 'She's never gone for long and she never said anything. Where do you think she is now?'

Gwil came bustling in the door from sorting out the tools at the back. 'Your Mam?' he grunted. 'Yes, strange that. Look, give it one hour and we'll be out and search. Less if it looks the light is fading faster than we expect.'

It was less than that when a breathless David burst into the doorway wheezing with the effort. 'Owain!' he called, that fell into a cough. 'She's at the mine, on the bank above the Cornish engine. I just walked past, and she acted like I wasn't there.'

Ceri's hands went up to her mouth and she gasped then, '*Duw!*'

'What's the matter girl?' I said a worry starting to nag at me.

'Don't you know what day it is?' She said with an edge to her voice. 'A year ago to the day of the hang-fire, when you and Dad got caught.'

I hurried down to the mine as quick as my leg would let me, though it was hurting me now with cramp. I was worried now that dusk would be gathering soon, for Mam had no lantern. Perhaps I feared for worse. For a while I couldn't see her and then I saw a grey figure sitting up the bank looking down on the Cornish Engine. As I got to her as fast as my legs could take me, I saw her sitting and hugging her knees. That effort nearly did me in and I fell to her side coughing and wheezing.

'Mam,' I panted. 'Where you been? Worried, I was. Thought...'

Mam blinked like she was coming out of a dream. 'What's that *bach*?' she said faintly.

'I thought you might have come here to jump one of them shafts,' I said straight, not even sure if she didn't still mean to.

She sighed and looked down for a while at the engine, the pumping rod stuck out behind it that disappeared down the dark hole of Engine Shaft for hundreds of fathoms.

'Thought about it at that,' Mam said quietly and then she smiled. 'Quickest way to be with him, isn't it? One step, a fall and we'd be together for ever.'

I looked over to her tear-streaked face and she reached out to touch my cheek.

'No *bach*, I'm not going. Hard it is some days though not to wish it. It's a year now and not a day goes past without me thinking of him, what we had and what may have been. I'll live though, I'll do what is expected.'

She hugged me then and cried on my shoulder for a long while. All those months of grief had built up inside and now she let go. Then, finally she sat back and wiped her nose with another sigh.

'Bless you *cariad*, you're just like him you know. He always knew when to be around.'

'Mam,' I stopped then knowing that my mind was set - but fearing her reaction. 'Mam, I'm going back down Frongoch. Not now, but I'm nearly ready and…'

Mam just patted my shoulder with a sad smile. 'You think I don't know that? Just like my Gareth you are, stubborn to the end. But we need to put bread on the table, for Gwil will not be here forever and a hosier you will never make. Thought for a while you could make a go of a thatcher, but there we are.'

She looked back over the grey wasteland below us. 'I'll go back in the mill too, Owain. When the family is ready. Ceri's a good girl, but her heart is at home, not in that damned mill and I think some heads need knocking the way they been working there.' She paused then and looked at me sadly. 'Dust will get us both at the end, you know that?'

I nodded sadly. I couldn't think of what to say.

346

'Why don't you leave Owain? Take Ceri and Dafydd away from this, breathe some fresh air and be free.'

'I'll not leave you here Mam,' I replied quickly and she nodded.

'You know, your father had this idea that his real father, the Spaniard, had given him the roving spirit. The thought of thinking beyond this land.

He had the choice to leave and start afresh, but like you he chose not to. Your Taid was failing and Gareth wouldn't leave the old boy. I'll tell you what I told him. You look down on some here for not being able to think outside the village and the mine, for not wanting to change for the better. When it comes down to it in the end, you're no different than they are. You're just as trapped, remember that Owain and pray your children fare better.'

We sat a while in silence then, both lost in each other's thoughts. 'So, what do you feel about going back?' Mam asked finally.

I thought a while about it. 'Good to be back with my friends. Good to be doing something, but I worry about it. What if I can't do as much as what I did before? I can't work up top and watch my butties coming and going. I fear that it would kill me inside, but most of all I fear the mine itself if I do work. I fear the drop in the shaft, the tunnels collapsing, hang fire. I fear it all, but it won't stop me facing it and it won't stop me going down there, so I can bring the money in and feel like a man once more.'

Mam nodded. 'Fear is a good thing, Owain. Makes you know your limits, keeps you sensible. Just don't let it control you and you'll survive. In the future, you must make sure that Dafydd is kept well away from this work. Get him to work at school and have a future. Don't let him go through the slow death and worry that we have. Maybe the spark of the Spaniard is in him. I pray that this is so.'

I nodded and shivered as the light had dropped and a chill was filling the air. 'Let's go home Mam, mine's not going anywhere and the light is fading.'

She stood up stiffly. 'All right boy, let's go. Ceri will be wondering where we are by now. I said my goodbyes for now and there are things to do. Oh dear, and I said I would help Myfanwy also.'

'Never mind Mam, she's done now. She'll just be happy to have you back.'

Her smile was sad, but she had come back to life, I could see in her eyes.

'Owain *cariad,* life has its ups and downs, but what is bad now, does not mean that there is not good in the future. Life is like a Turn of that Waterwheel by there, remember that.'

It was time to work things out and first I had to speak with Gwilym. That evening after supper as we sat by the fire I asked him.

'I want to go back to Frongoch, Gwil. I want to go back down the levels, but I don't want you gone neither. You're a boy and a half and I want you to stay with us, I still reckon the land will do for you and you don't need to go.'

Gwil just shook his head. 'It won't Owain, grateful though I am to you. I will only stay until you are back to where you were.'

'Just think on it Gwil, there's a home for you here and we can always make it bigger if we need. I could even put a word in on for you on some of the honest girls in the parish.'

Gwil laughed at that. 'All right boy, I'll let you know how it is. Let's see how you get on first.'

Ben was the next one to approach. I was up for walking to New Row after the work on the roof had proven my leg and so went down a few weeks on after chapel. As I reached the door of his neat terrace, I saw a row of tools outside. Most looked broken, the shaft of the pick was split and the metal of the rusting hammer was pock-marked and twisted. I turned it over in my hand and straight away had a mind as to whose it was.

The door opened and Ben blinked out into the daylight, 'Owain! Well you be a welcome surprise.' He saw me look at the tools then and his voice lowered. 'Aye, they're Gareth's. We got back what we could as we dug for him. Did not know what you would be wanting with them. Some of the heads be fine and the chisels do be good also.'

He was looking for some sort of word from me, so I smiled back as best I could. 'I'll use what I can Ben. Shame to waste and then there's less to buy. Perhaps even I'll feel he's with me when I use them.'

Ben nodded and stood back to let me in. 'We do have a brew going, Owain. Come in and warm yourself. Rest your legs, that walk must have hurt.'

I went in to gratefully accept a chair by the fire. I sat there with a steaming cup of tea and a few Welsh cakes. Typical Welsh way of greeting that, cup of tea and a cake. The Treveglos folk had been here long enough to follow the tradition.

Ben leaned back and took out his pipe to light. 'You be decided then, you do want to come back?'

I nodded. 'Ben, I want to come back, but I don't want you to lose none of the boys neither. I don't even know if I should be asking...'

'Aye you should Owain and right glad would we be to have you. The boys be fine workers, but I be reckoning that we will have you back and we do better as a five until you be strong. Then we do see.'

'Ben, are you sure? I mean I don't want to cause a fuss now, but you are paying for me and all and I want to work it back.'

Ben waved his smoking pipe at me. 'Now don't you be worrying about that. I do speak with Captain Nankivell on the morrow and he will be fine.'

'But five in your pare...?'

Ben smiled at me as a father would.

'Owain, you do have to understand now. We do not know how much work you can be doing. We do not know if you can do the work no more.

With five, we do have the time to build you up and find out and if it do not work...well, we are still a pare as four.'

Fair do's, he offered me the chance and I was grateful for it. When I left, I took his hand and looked him in the eye. 'Ben thanks for the chance. I'll not let you down.'

Ben gripped my hand like iron and grinned. 'Owain boy, you be one of us. Me and David have waited for this day for many a month.'

There was one more that I had not talked to about the mine and Reverend Edwards put it plain to me as we walked along the edges of Frongoch pool on a cold Sunday afternoon.

'Owain, how could you not mention this to Ceri? She's the first one you should have spoken with.'

I flushed with shame at his words, 'I've no excuse sir. I'm just not sure how she'll take it. What if she worries? She calls out some nights in her dreams, though she'll never say why. I'm scared I'll upset her.'

The Reverend snorted. 'Well, there's only one way you get to find out and you'll do it right away, my boy. You tell her straight or I'll have the deacons on you come Sunday.' His eyes glinted with humor, but his voice told me not to cross him.

As I walked in that day, Ceri was at the fire stirring a pot full of soup. She looked up and smiled at me. It was red roses in summer, swaying in the breeze. It was the rainbow of sunlight shining through a waterfall.

I thought of the dance at David's wedding and our first time together by the raging Ystwyth and I knew where my strength lay. In a moment, I was there and her in my arms, her warm body pressed close. We kissed and her face lit up like a spring morning.

'You could have let me put the spoon down first,' she said holding up the dripping ladle.

'Shame to waste the moment, is it?' I said back.

'You're looking stronger every day Owain, almost like the man I fell in love with.'

'Almost?' I frowned. 'What does that mean?'

'When you start work again, then you'll feel complete.'

I could only gasp and she slapped me on the rump and went back to stirring. 'Thought I didn't know? Do you think I'm *twp* or something?'

'No *bach*...'

'Were you just going to sneak down there and not tell me?' Her voice had taken a hard edge and I felt I was losing my grip on the matter.

'No! I just...' I swallowed and had to tell her the truth. 'Ceri, I'm scared. I have to go back, but I'm scared to. I'm scared of what you will say - that you will worry. I don't want you living in fear that I won't be back.'

352

'Scare me?' Her eyebrows shot up.

'You still have nightmares Ceri,' I said quietly.

She stopped then and stared at the fire, nodding slowly. 'Of the mill and the poor boy squashed in the wheel.

Yes, I still see him, I thought our eyes met as he went in. I got a shock, like we shared the fear. I'll never get over that, but I know the world is full of sorrow and it's a rare thing to find a job that's not full of worry and danger round here.'

'Oh Ceri, I wish I could take away the pain,' I said. She kissed my cheek.

'I live with my pain Owain, but it's you who has to face your own demons. You have to go back *bach*. It's who you are, it's what we are – mining folk. We've no other way, the world here is the mine and it's all we know.

Perhaps Dafydd shall have a better path and I pray it be so, but we got to make do with what we have. So, you go down Frongoch with David once more and I'll be waiting for you when you come back.'

We hugged then a long while and I was promising I would be safe.

'Just you look out for yourself Owain, your Dad got bad luck but it don't mean you have to fall the same way. I pray every night that you won't be brought home as he was. Just do what you can to make sure you are not.'

Miner's Day came all too soon and the day after I was up before dawn like the rest of them.

The house was cold without a fire and my breath was steaming. Not many words were said, it was almost a holy silence, but more due to us all being bad with mornings. Ceri whispered to Dafydd as she dressed him, Mam was at the fireplace with the kindling to make a fire for the tea and gruel.

We sat at the table in silence, all in our thoughts. I was worrying if I could get down those ladders in the mine, hoping the *bargen* would be on a high level and wishing Dad was there to see me right. Mam's voice broke through my fretting.

'O Lord, keep us safe this day and bless us in our work. We give thanks to you for bringing Owain back to us. Lord keep him safe as he starts work once more. Amen.'

We ate in silence, but I was beginning to feel fear. Fear of the dark, the drop, the tunnels collapsing.

Most of all I feared letting everyone down. I looked over to Mam to see her watching me like a hawk.

'How do you feel, Owain?'

'Scared Mam,' I replied quiet as a mouse, making Ceri reach out and grip my arm.

'What you going to do?' Mam asked, eyes watching my every move.

'Oh, I'm going down there.' I said, the stronger for Ceri's touch. 'Got to, an I?'

Mam nodded. 'Good boy,' she muttered.

As we all got ready, Gwil opened the front door and moonlight flooded in, lighting up the little clock on the dresser, as it gently ticked away to itself.

Ceri was at the doorway, waiting for me. 'Ready?' she asked.

'Ready,' I replied. She kissed my cheek and I stepped out into the dark to join Mam, Gwil and Myfanwy, who were already starting up the road the swinging light of their lantern in the gloom. The stars were bright, millions still up there, but not the same to me no more without Dad around to name them for me.

We set off for the mine, past branches of small trees that knotted and curved their way at the sides of the path, like white ghostly demons. The train of other lights was ahead of us, but there were no calls of 'Tomos y *Shaneg*' now and I felt empty for it. Mam talked away to Myfanwy about things that needed doing at the mill, Gwil and I walked in silence. After a while he punched my arm and grinned.

'Always wanted to work with you brother,' he grinned, his face looking child-like in the light. I smiled back but could not speak for the demons of doubt that were with me. We all parted at the mine and went our ways to ready ourselves for the day's work.

I went up to stores for the kit I needed to start off once more. A bundle of candles, a tull and some tools that I could not repair from those recovered from the accident.

I looked around the mine and the people rushing around readying for their work in the growing light of morning. Wisps of smoke came from the chimneys, water rushed from the wheels, a faint yellow warm glow coming from the blacksmith. I felt at home and yet a stranger, lost in this crowd, walking around looking for a friendly face, until at last I found my *pare*; Matt, Gwil and David, gabbing away as they waited for Ben to come back with our *bargen*.

'David Treveglos,' I said in a deep voice. 'You wanna fight boy?'

David threw back his head and roared with laughter. 'No, let's be friends instead.'

He came up and lifted me in a huge bear hug. 'Good to see you back, Owain. We're just waiting for Dad to give us news now. I think he'll do a shallow pitch, to break you in.'

At that moment Ben came over, but his face was grim. 'It be 117 boys,' he said straight out. 'There be good pickings for us and I do have extra food for the knockers. Five of us should make easy work of it. What do you say?'

No-one said anything, they all looked over at me. David was shaking his head and was about to speak, but I broke in.

'Fine by me, Ben. If I can't do it now, I'll never do it. Besides, Gwil can carry me home, can't you Gwil *bach*?'

We walked on to the shaft and my mind went through it all. Ben was testing me for sure and it was up to me to prove his trust and make my family proud of what I done.

356

Then it was time to line up and grip the ladder to lower myself rung by rung into the darkness. The first rung felt cold as ice and I could see my hands tremble as I held it and swung myself onto the ladder.

I stood there and sighed to calm myself, before lowering my leg for the first step. My leg felt as if it was dragging down forever and I had to hold down the feeling of panic, then my toe finally found the rung and I moved down.

'Taking the rungs two at a time won't get you down any faster,' said someone above and there was a murmur of laughter.

I made my way down slower than before, my eyes firmly fixed on the wood cladding the shaft. I noted every patch of damp, every piece of moss and every part where the bedrock stuck out. I reached the first platform and stood there shaking. The dark seemed to close in on me and my chest felt tight, as I looked around me and up at the grey light of the morning that was the shaft entrance.

I could see the next ladder leading down through a square hole in the platform. A cool breeze came up from it and made my candle flicker. I could not get my feet to move.

'Are you coming down or what?' A voice rang from below. I was in terror, thinking for sure it was my Dad. Then the ladder started to tremble as someone started climbing it. I could only watch at the ladder moving with each step. I could see the flickering faint light of the candle get brighter.

357

Then the candle itself appeared and the hat. Underneath was David, all a grin.

'Come on Owain *bach*, we haven't got all day. Black won't come out of here on its own now, will it?'

I breathed a sigh of relief and David frowned. 'You alright boy? You're looking a bit pale there.'

I shook my head. 'No, I'm fine now. Just daydreaming, can't do that can I? Let's get on then.'

David grinned and his head disappeared back down. The spell was broken. I moved ready to follow. The climb down seemed to take forever, but I finally got down to find Matt waiting for me.

'Boys told me to wait and bring you along,' he said. He spoke Welsh with a funny accent and his words were not always right, but at least he tried, bless him.

We walked into the level, half crouching at times, until we reached a chamber and I was surprised by the sight of more than a few miners stood ready for me. I could not say how many, at the time it felt like the whole mine was there. Perhaps they were, in spirit.

'Owain, we do want you to say a few words for the memory of your father,' said Ben at the centre of the men. 'It was by here that you did both come to grief.'

I walked up to Ben and took my hat off and there was a rustle as everyone did the same, holding their hats flat as to stop the wax dripping and for keeping the flame safe.

I swallowed as I began. 'Dad, I know you're here and I know you'll look after us. You were all right you know, best Dad you could have I reckon. Be at peace, I'll look after Mam, you keep them knockers in order.'

I put my hat back on and wiped away a tear. A few mutters of 'Amen' came over and then the others made off to their work. I lifted up a large hammer to the side and walked to my pare.

'Right boys, where's the first charge to go then?'

The climb back was hell and it took a while, but the pare was with me and I knew they would always be there. When you're down that mine, you bond like family and you can never break that bond. At the top, Evans shaft grabbed me up and then clapped me on the shoulder.

'You'll do, Tomos *Shaneg*, you'll do.'

Dad gone now and I was the Spaniard. Many nodded and muttered 'Tomos *Shaneg*' in greeting as Gwil and I shuffled off home. Ceri was sitting by the fire waiting and she jumped up to hug me as I walked in.

'Owain,' she smiled and kissed my dirty cheek. 'Straight to the bath for you, tin tub is ready and you're lucky today as I'll help you wash. Won't be doing that in a while, so don't expect it now.'

What you saying?' I asked following her out the back and stripping to get ready. She carried a pan of warm water and put it in the tub.

'Well Owain, now you're back and working, I'll tell you. I think I'm with child once more.' Her smile lit up her face then. 'Seems like you'll be working for more than three now.'

'But how…?'

'Oh *bach*,' she came to hug me again with a mocking smile on her lips. 'If you don't know now then God help us. Ask your Mam.'

I picked her up and she squealed as I took her to the bath. Her thumping me made us both laugh. She only got a bit wet in the end. I settled in the bath then and she poured water over me and started to wash my hair. A wave of warmth washed over me, and I sighed. The warmth of the water, mixed with the love and warmth of family and a new child on the way. A new dawn was beginning and I looked forward to it, as I lay there lazing in the old tin tub.

Chapter Twenty-two

New Beginnings

We had reached 1881 and I was now twenty-one years of age. In my seven years at the mine, I had reached manhood. As my childhood dreams had faded, I had grown in strength. I had gained and I had lost. I had gained a beautiful wife, keeper of my heart, owner of my soul. I had gained a son, who I hoped would grow up strong and whole and prayed that his path would take him away from the life that we lived, a trade that would take him from the clutches of the mine.

I had also gained a cough, a little tickle at the back of the throat for now, a reminder of what was to come. Not like the wheezing thing I have now and the black spit that follows but something that was always there to haunt me. I had lost my father, victim of the perils that the mine held for us. I had lost my guide and now it was all down to me, as head of the family to keep us safe and sound.

I had lost Mam a bit. She was better now, but still distant. A shadow of the strong woman she had been, lost without the man who had been her pillar. I had also lost the father of my love, though this was more of a release for a tormented soul.

In September of that year, David and Gwen christened their son, Nathaniel. We were down at Ty'n-y-Groes to see the little one come into God's house.

Afterwards, I went to David outside, as he leaned on the chapel, beaming at his lovely wife, who stood there gently holding the sleeping babe in her arms.

'Bit of a wailer, that one.' I said tartly and David nodded.

'Right enough, but the Devil's washed from him now, I reckon.'

The sound of children came from the woods beyond the busy stream. Shrieks and shouts and howls of pain.

'Logaulas or the Glogs?' I asked with a smirk and David chuckled.

'Either way, they're on for a beating.'

I shook my head sadly. 'Seems like only yesterday we were down there.'

'Fancy joining in?'

It was my turn to laugh. 'No *bach,* our time has gone. We have to be men now.'

'Too true, we come a long way you and me, Owain.'

'That we have. Why Nathaniel? I had him down for an Owain.'

'Well, I thought that too, but he's not Welsh enough.'

'Yes, he is, Dai Pasty, you just can't see it. I can hear him in the baritones at Trisant already.'

He laughed again and we watched the people outside the chapel, buzzing around Gwen and Ceri like bees. They stood there with their children, proud Mams both.

'You and me, Owain. As long as we're around, nothing will go wrong.'

The words sounded like a prophecy. I looked at David and for once his face was serious, there was a spark in his eyes, and I saw him for the first time as the brother I never had.

'You're right there Davy boy. You and me will sort it out.'

'You two,' said Ceri as she came to us, a dangerous glint in her eye. 'Time to stop skiving and give us a hand. There's people to thank and then back to sort out the tea and food for the guests. Don't think you're getting out of it.'

I'd like to think that David and I would sort it all. Though we were not to know the future or the struggles that we might have, right up to the last dark days of Frongoch itself and beyond. We still felt that we would be there for each other, well that we did. I gazed into Ceri's brown eyes and a wonderful shiver fell down my back.

'Alright girl,' I said gently. 'We weren't hiding, just admiring you both.'

Ceri flushed prettily and punched my shoulder. 'You think that will get you into favour?' she said with eyebrows arched. I kissed her cheek and gave her hands a squeeze.

'Well, I have to start somewhere.'

Ceri gave me a look that said it all and I felt glad to be alive.

A few words on Welsh pronunciation

The Welsh language appears a minefield at first to the uninitiated, but it's a beautiful language and there are some simple rules in pronunciation. The main rule of thumb are all the letters should be pronounced hard. In modern appliance, this does not always happen, but in early 20th century parlance it would. Of these, this is a list of the main ones to consider:

A – is hard like 'apple'

Ch is a guttural word, like the Scottish word 'loch'

Dd -is pronounced like 'the'

E is hard, like 'egg'

F is pronounced hard, like 'Of'

Ff is soft, like 'Off'

I is like 'igloo'

LL is unique to Welsh and so should be approached by placing the tongue behind the front teeth as you exhale. Yes, it does work, so repeat after me… 'Llanelli, Llanelli, Llanelli…'

O is hard, like 'Of' or 'Off'

Rh is like exhaling an R

U is like the I in 'irrigation'

W is a vowel, pronounced like 'oe' in 'does' but with northern English flat vowels

Y is a vowel, pronounced like 'us'

There is no J, K, V, X or Z

Glossary (with English language phonetics where applicable)

Aber – local abbreviation for Aberystwyth.

Aberystwyth – (Abb-er-ust-wiff) The seaside resort in the centre of Cardigan Bay. Also a small commercial port in the 19th Century and the largest town in the area.

Bara brith – A welsh yeast bread, speckled with dried fruit and soaked in tea.

Bach – (pronounced as in JS Bach, the composer) The welsh word for small, used as a friendly address, especially after a person's name.

Bal maiden – Cornish name for the women who worked in the processing of the ore on the surface

Bargen – (bar-genn) A method popular in Welsh metal mining, whereby a team secured a contract for producing ore at a certain price per ton. This was negotiated monthly in the afternoon of payday. Both pay and bargens were set at the Counting House, The local Counting house was at the east end of Pontrhydygroes and the adit 'Lefel fawr' started from its garden, draining four local mines (Glogfawr, Glogfach, Logaulas, Penygist). The garden had a raised patio behind the house, which the managers would stand and declare what bargens were to be had. The pare leaders would gather below and bid.

Bendigedig Ffyddo'r Iesu – A welsh hymn 'let us praise the Lord triumphant'

Bont – Local knickname for Pontrhydfendigaid

Bore Da – (Bor-eh dar) Good morning

Buddle – A narrow cone like structure used for the washing of ore after crushing.

Bychan – (bu-ch-an, using the ch as in loch) welsh word for small, used as a friendly address, especially after a person's name.

Caban – (Kabann) A small underground hut used by the men during their refreshment break. Common in the slate mines of North Wales, but lead miners tended to eat where they were.

Calon Lân – A welsh hymn, translated as 'A pure (lit. clean) heart'

Capel Saeson – English chapel

Cariad – (carry-ad) A fond term of address to one of the opposite sex, meaning darling or sweetheart. 'Cariad ti' means 'love you'.

Cawl – (Cowl) A vegetable soup made of large pieces of root vegetables, occasionally served with a slice of bread and cheese and if you are very lucky, mutton.

Cer a ffordd – Go away

Ceridwen – (Kerrid-wen) The female protagonist and Owain's love, called Ceri (Kerry) for short.

Cochyn – (Coch-in, using ch as in loch) Redhead

Counting House – Cornish term for the building where mine finance was undertaken. Abbreviation of 'Accounting House'. See entry for 'bargen'.

Crachach – (Crach ach – pronounce ch as in loch). Hoi Polloi

Cwm Newydion – (Coom newudion, the 'oo' pronounced like book. A forested and mine area across the gorge from Pontrhydygroes

Cwtch – (cootch, the oo as in 'book') a welsh hug or cuddle, but oh so much more...

Cymorth – (Cummorff) A collection, in this case, to aid the widows and orphans

Dafydd – (Dav-i-the. -Remember to pronounce 'the' not 'fuh'!!!). The welsh version of the name David, Owain's son

Ddrwg gen I – I'm sorry. (literally, it is bad with me)

Devil's Bridge – a small hamlet 12 miles east of Aberystwyth, up the Rheidol valley.

Dewch I mewn – (De-w-ch ee meh-oon, ch as in loch) Come in

Diolch – (Dee-olch, the ch as in 'loch') Thank you

Diwedd y byd – (Dew-evv ur beed) End of the world, an explanation

Drill – A long metal rod, that could be taller than a man. Used to make the hole for the dynamite charge or shot.

Duw (Dew) – God, used as a mild expletive.

Dwy 'wech am swllt –(Dooee wech am soo-llt) Two sixes for a shilling. Away with the fairies. All over the place.

Eisteddfod – A Welsh song and poetry festival or competition, made famous by the National and international Eisteddfods held annually in Wales.

Ewch! – Go! (the ch at the end makes it a command)

Fathom – A measure of depth, equivalent to about 6 feet. The measure is more commonly known in maritime.

FFair Rhos - (Fire Rors) A village near Ysbytty Ystwyth, site of regular fair since the local monks in medieval times

Frongoch – (Vron-gor-ch, as in loch), A large lead mine south west of Devil's Bridge

Gareth – Owain's father

Gethin – (Ge-thin, with a hard 'g') – one of Gomer's sons

Glogfach and Glogfawr – (Glog -farch, with a 'ch' as in loch. Glog – vour) Local lead mines near Pontrhydygroes

Graig Goch – (Gr-aye-g Gorch), with ch as in 'loch') A small mine to the west of Frongoch, further down the valley, that used the water from Frongoch and We myss mills to power its own equipment. Name means 'red rock'

Gomer – (Gom-air) – The antagonist and Owain's drunk miner of a father in law.

Gwahoddwr – (Gwa-hoth-oor) – the bidder. A man appointed to knock on the doors of the village and bid people attend a wedding.

Gwenllian – (Gwen-ll-ian) David's wife

Gwilym - (Gwill-im) – Owain's brother in law, his wife's non-identical twin.

Gwli – (Goo-lee) A narrow passageway between buildings

Gwylnos – (Gooeel-nors) Wake. The night before the burial, normally attended by friends and family, who bring gingerbread to the bereaved

Gyrru, gyrru Ffair yn Rhos, Mynd I'r dydd am nol cyn nos -Driving, driving (to the) Rose Fair. Going (in the) day and back before night

Hafod – (Havod) Local estate, with grounds landscaped by Capability Brown. Today, the mansion is gone, but the woodlands still offer stunning walks.

Hisht – a welsh version of 'shhh'

Hwyl – (Hoo-eel) a stirring feeling of emotional motivation and energy, and yet, so much more…

I bob un sydd ffydlon – (Ee borb een seethe fuvlon) – a welsh hymn 'for everyone who is faithful'. The quote is "To all that are faithful under His banner, Jesus wears a crown in the Kingdom of Heaven."

Idloes – (Idloyss) A man's name

Iesu Grist yn Arglwydd Dduw – (Yessy Greest un are-gloo-eeth view) Jesus Christ and God Almighty

Iolo – (Yollo) A welsh man's name.

Iorri – (Yorry) One of Gomer's sons.

Jigging – A method of ore separation by placing the rock on a vibrating table.

Jones y bont – Given the prevalence of some surnames in Wales, many were given knicknames to distinguish themselves, alluding to their residence, profession or some sort of other feature. Jones y bont, means 'Jones the bridge' and in this case, refers to a character who lived close to a bridge over the river Ystwyth near the village.

Kibble – A large bucket used to lift material from underground up the shaft. In places, the kibble was used to transport men.

Knockers- A Cornish superstition that sprites lived underground and would cause harm if not respected. Any noise from the movement of the rock in situ would be attributed to them.

Leat – A water channel of up to miles in duration, bringing water for use by various machinery and waterwheels.

Lefel Fawr - the main adit for four local mines in Pontrhydygroes. See entry for bargen

Llani – Abbreviated version of Llanidloes

369

Llety Synod – (Ll-ettee Sun-od) or Llety 'Synod, a farmhouse behind Frongoch mine. The name means place of the Asses (Asyn). Has the

Llyn – Welsh word for lake. See notes on welsh pronunciation for the 'll' sound, 'yn' is pronounced 'in' for this example.

Llyn Frongoch – an artificial lake, between Frongoch mine and Trisant to the north, used to supply the mines of the area with water.

Logaulas – (Logeye-las) A local lead mine near Pontrhydygroes

Lord Lisburne – (also Marquess of Londonderry), the land owner whose land most of the mines in the area were leased. Resides in a mansion at Trawscoed.

Mam-gu – (Mam gee, with a hard 'g') South wales word for grandmother.

Mari Llwyd – (Marry Ll-ooeed) A wassailing custom from South East Wales, whereby the long nights were chased away by Mari Llwyd, a man dressed in a white sheet carrying under it a pole on which was mounted a horse's skull, like a hobbyhorse. Mari Llwyd celebrations were known to get rowdy as alcohol was invariably involved.

Mill – The dressing mill was present at larger mines and was where the rock was crushed and the ore separated. Metal ore is heavy, so the purer the end product, the less weight to carry and the higher price got.

Mine Captain – The foreman or superintendent. There could be more than one, depending on how large the mine was. Cornish (and therefore Welsh) metal mines tended to refer to the owners as

Captain also. These men were addressed by the term 'Captain' and then their surname e.g. Captain Nankivell

Miner's Day – The first Monday after payday was traditionally a day off for miners in the region.

Myfanwy – (Muv-an-wee – the 'u' pronounced as in 'uh') Owain's sister.

Neithior – (Neytheyore) – The wedding feast held after the wedding.

New Row – A small line of terraced houses below Frongoch, on the road to Pontrhydygroes. Originally built by John Taylor to house Cornish immigrant miners. Further down the road are the ruins of Capel season, the first English language chapel in Wales, built for the Cornish miners and later used by Italian miners as a catholic church.

Nain – (Nine) North Wales word for grandmother.

Nankivell - A mine captain at Frongoch from Cornwall.

Nant – stream (Nant Cwm Newydion pronounced Nant Coom Newuddion)

Owain – (Owe-ine)The main protagonist for the story, a lead miner at Frongoch

Panad – (Pan-add) A northern welsh slang for a pot of tea. An abbreviation of Panad o de (Pan-add o dare)

Pare – A group on mineworkers who would work as a team for a particular bargen. This would not only be miners, but trammers, carpenters and mill workers.

Penygist – (Pen-ur-gist, with a hard 'g') A local lead mine near Pontrhydygroes

Pont Rhyd-y-Groes or Pontrhydygroes – (Pont-reed-ur-groyss) the central village for the area, south of Devil's Bridge. Nearly a dozen mines surrounded the village, with its stores and taverns.

Pnawn da – (puh-noun dah) Good afternoon (name is a combination of the bridge and ford of the cross)

Pwython – (Pooee thon) The returning of a marriage gift when that person gets married.

Rhian – (Rh-ee-an) short for Rhiannon. Owain's mother

Rofawr – (Ro-vour) An area at Aberystwyth harbour, known for its shipbuilding. Now covered by South Marine Terrace.

Sadwrn Sistans – (Sadoorn Sisstans) The Saturday that was payday for the miners. Normally the last of the month, under John Kitto it became every four weeks.

Sanctaidd – Holy. The title of a well-known Welsh hymn that affords beautiful harmonies in the chorus and amen. The translation of the chorus quoted is:

"Full are the heavens of thy glory,
    Full is the earth, land and sea;
  To be given to thee forever is praise,
    Holy, holy, holy Lord!"

Sbaneg – Spaniard. Tomos y sbaneg, was the name given to Owain's father (Thomas the Spaniard) after his lineage.

Sh'mae – Hello

Shaft- A vertical or diagonal tunnel from the surface to the orebody at a mine

Sosban – (Soss-ban) A saucepan

Tad-cu – (Tad kee) South Wales word for grandfather.

Tafarn – (tav-arn) Welsh word for inn, tavern or pub. The Miners Arms is the only tafarn remaining in Pontrhydygroes.

Tafod teg – fair tongue

Taid – (Tide) North Wales word for grandfather.

Tailings – The waste product after the ore is milled to purity. A fine sand

Trawscoed – (Trouwss- coyd, 'ou' pronounced as in out) A small settlement area and site of the mansion of Lord Lisburne

Treveglos – (Trev-egg-loss) a Cornish surname based on the town Treveglos, meaning Church town. The welsh equivalent is Trefeglwys.

Trisant – (Tree-sant) The small settlement where Owain lives. Just north of Frongoch lake, around a chapel and close to Llantrisant church. Means 'three saints'

Tull – A felt hat used by miners for protection. They would stick a candle on it to provide illumination underground.

Twll – Hole

Twp – (Toop, the oo pronounced as in book) stupid.

Ty un nos – (Tee een norse) One-night house. The tradition was if you could build four walls and a roof overnight on common land and have a fire in the hearth by dawn, you could live in the dwelling. Your land was the distance of an axe throw from each wall. If you stayed in the house for a year and a day, you had the freehold. Not written law and sometimes was quashed by landowners. Plural is Tai un nos (Tie een norse)

Tydi a rhoddaist – Welsh hymn 'O thou that gave'

Tylwyth Teg – Fairy folk

Wemyss – (Wims) The mine adjacent and to the west of Frongoch. Part of the same operation, it became absorbed and in time, was used for the site of a large dressing mill.

Winze – a small shaft connecting two levels

Wrgi – (Oorghee) An old rutting dog.

Wyt ti weld bat? – Do you see like a bat?

Y Cymro – (Uh Cummro) A Welsh language newspaper. ('The Welshman')

Ych a fi! – Yuck!

Yr Amserau – (Ur Amserr-aye) A Welsh language newspaper. ('The Times')

Ysbyty Ystwyth – (Us-butty Us-twiff) A small village east of Pontrhydygroes (Ysbyty meaning hospital or hospice, this was originally a site of healing by the monks of Strata Florida)

Ystafell – (Ust-av-ell, using the welsh 'll' sound) Room or chamber

Ystwyth – (Ust-with) Name of main local river that runs from the Plynlimon Hills to the sea at Aberystwyth.

Author Biography

I grew up in Aberystwyth until the University of Leicester beckoned with a course in Mining geology, which led to nothing pertinent, but a wealth of experience in standing in the rain in remote parts of Britain, including an epic field trip to a quarry that turned out to be filled in.

After many years of working and living in Milton Keynes and Northampton. After the joys of late night shopping on a Thursday, I returned to live to a village near Aberystwyth in 2008.

I have had many roles in my life, working for a bank and in Telecomms, a rehab clinic, in solar energy, then finally a steam railway. I am now semi retired. It gives me so much more time to think!

Owain Thomas' tale continues in two future books. My previous novels are:

Railway Novels

- *By the Banks of the Rheidol* (Y Lolfa) ISBN 9781784615598 -
- *The Long Way Home* (Aberesto) ISBN 9781838135805

Estonian Novels

- *Forest Brothers* (Circaidy Gregory press), ISBN 9781906451691 -
- *Finnish Boys* (Aberesto) To follow in 2021, as well as the final part of the trilogy.